CRAFTY ALIBIS

CRAFTY ALIBIS

A BEE'S KNEES MYSTERY

JOAN RAYMOND

RED KNOT PRESS

ALSO BY JOAN RAYMOND

For Adults

Bee's Knees Mystery Series

Crafty Alibis (Book One) 2021

Crafty Motives (Book Two) - coming in 2022

Women's Fiction

Guardian of the Gifts 2019

For Children

Metamorphosis Series

Fly on the Wall (Book One) 2020

Spaghetti and Meatball (Book Two) - coming in 2022

Crafty Alibis: A Bee's Kees Mystery

Print ISBN: 978-1-7337915-4-0

Cover Design by Cathy Walker of Cathy's Covers

Red Knot Press
PO Box 41745
Bakersfield, CA 93384

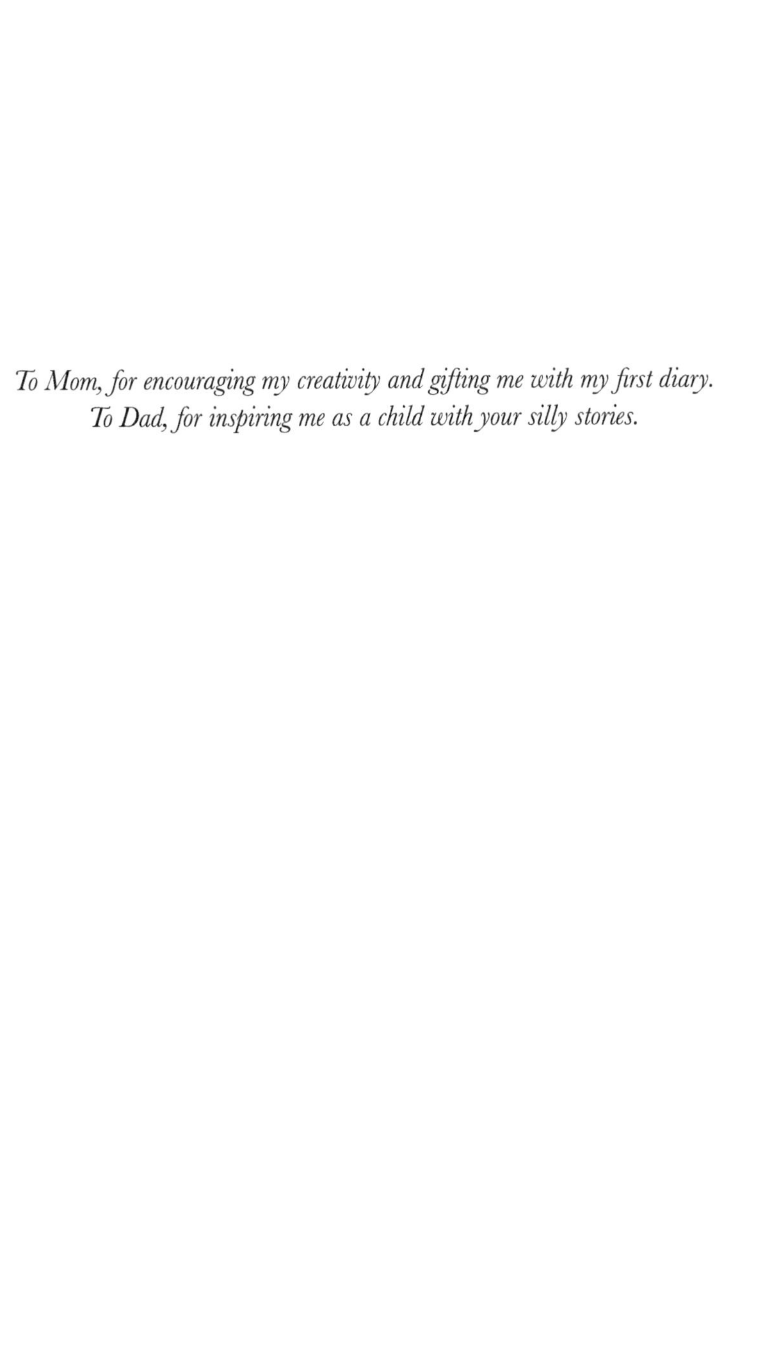

To Mom, for encouraging my creativity and gifting me with my first diary.
To Dad, for inspiring me as a child with your silly stories.

CHAPTER ONE

Shelby Heaton gripped the steering wheel of her jeep and took a quick peek in the rearview mirror. The CHP cruiser was still behind her, following since the last on-ramp. Was it her out-of-state plates? Or had she been speeding? After all, she wasn't in Texas, where the posted speed limit was more of a suggestion. After traveling halfway across the country, the last thing she needed was a ticket. Loosening her grip, she downshifted. Just in case. A few miles later, the cruiser zipped past, tailing a small red car darting in and out of traffic. *Whew.*

Continuing west on California state Route 58, Shelby bristled as the quiet of the road brought back the past. Eighteen months ago, Mac had landed her dream job with Strickland Oil in Houston. Moving with Mackenzie seemed like the only choice. Shelby didn't want to let down her partner, however she couldn't tell Mac the truth. She avoided confrontation at any cost. Even if it meant surrendering to common sense. In Houston, they bought the perfect home. Planned their perfect family. And settled in. After several unsuccessful in-vitro attempts, Shelby's positive pregnancy test thrilled them. Life seemed perfect in every way.

Six weeks later, Shelby lost the baby. Not what she had planned for her thirty-fifth birthday. The doctor reassured them. "Things like this happen. You should try again." After several miscarriages in ten months, Shelby lost hope. Mac lost patience. Their conversations turned cruel as Mac's words dug deeper with each loss. 'It's your fault.' 'Why don't you lose weight?' 'You should try harder.' Shelby's only response was to hide under her comforter, surrounded by pillows.

WITH MAC'S EVERY REPRIMAND, Shelby felt like she was sixteen again, terrified of her father's temper. Anything could set him off. Why didn't she date? Why did she eat so many cookies? Why didn't she eat her mother's dinners? Shelby couldn't tell him she didn't like boys, that cookies made her happy, and her mother's liver and onion dinners tasted horrible. His questions spun into anger, then rage. Shelby would run to her room. Lock her door. Hide under her pillows. Listening to his heavy shoes coming down the hall, she would hold her breath when he twisted the doorknob and swore. Moments later he'd give up and leave, forcing his way into her brother's room. Then came the swearing. The shouting. The slapping. The crying. Shelby hated herself. For not protecting her brother. For not standing up to her father.

TWO DAYS EARLIER, the air was uncomfortably warm. Rare for a November morning in Houston. Shelby sat in front of a slow-moving fan, wiping trickles of sweat from the back of her neck with a balled-up paper towel. Finally, she gathered what little courage she had and confronted Mac. "Can't *you* at least try to get pregnant?"

Mac's response was the same. "I'm not doing anything to jeopardize my career. Besides, you agreed to have our baby."

Shelby hated Mac's condescending voice. She hated herself for not standing up to Mac. She couldn't sleep. She couldn't stop eating. She trembled anytime her partner was in the same room. Frightened and fed up, Shelby packed her clothes. Her laptop and design journals. Her bolts of fabric. A hideous green and yellow pineapple lamp along with a few days of snacks, water, and cat food. With Mr. Butterfingers in his cat carrier, Shelby walked out the front door of their imperfect house and didn't look back.

"Hey Siri, call Ella." Several rings later, the call connected. "Mornin' El. Hope I'm not calling too early."

"Always good to hear from you, Shel. Just getting up. How's it going?"

Shelby clenched her jaw. "You have room for overnight guests?"

"You know you and Mac are always welcome. When do you plan on visiting?"

Shelby checked her mirrors and slowed for a speeding car. "Thirty minutes?"

Ella's voice tensed. "Shel, where are you?"

"Just passed through Mojave." She braced for the inevitable question.

"Just you, hon?"

"And Mr. Butterfingers."

"Everything okay?"

Shelby's throat tightened. The silence between them drowned out the road noise. Though she owed Ella the truth, it would have to wait.

"I'll put on some coffee," said Ella. "We can talk once you get settled."

Ella Denning glanced out the window. Dark clouds hovered over the mountains. Last night it had snowed, covering everything in white. She picked out a gray and blue cable-knit sweater to match her black jeans and dressed. Oatmeal lay on the bed, snoring. "Come on, dog. We've got company coming." In the kitchen, she started a pot of hazelnut-flavored coffee and let the dog out. He obliged without his usual 10 minute sniff-and-pee routine. Ella's constant companion since her husband's death, the fluffy white dog came in when called, wagging his tail.

Buck Wilson killed Ella's husband Doug on Halloween night two years ago. Buck had been drinking and swore he never noticed Doug jaywalking across a dark street a few blocks from downtown. Charged with a misdemeanor, Buck only served a few days in jail. Afterward, Ella couldn't cope with anything. Panic attacks kept her awake. She stopped eating. Not only had she lost her husband, but she also had to close The Steamed Bean, their coffee house off East Pheasant Valley Boulevard.

Ella's only peace came from crafting wreaths from the funeral flowers. Following months of therapy to work through grief and anger, her therapist suggested she put her talents to use. "You're only fifty. Too young to give up and become a recluse." Ella used part of the death benefit and opened The Bee's Knees. Within several months, she had rented most of the seventy crafter's booths to local artisans and out-of-towners. She wished Shelby could have been there to help. But her best friend had already moved away.

Once Oatmeal finished eating, he scratched at the back door. Outside, the breeze had picked up. Shivering, Ella hugged herself. Thankfully, Oatmeal pooped right away. Heading back inside, she tensed. Buck Wilson was outside again.

Being neighbors never mattered before Doug's murder, but afterwards Ella couldn't stand the sight or sound of him. Woodworking in that confounded eyesore of a shed. Whistling when he chopped wood. Was it her imagination? It seemed Buck went outside every time she did. He even had the gall to talk to her. At least his wife Hope had the decency to leave her alone. Ella wished Buck had died that night instead of Doug. She knew freak accidents happened, and if something were to happen to Buck, it wouldn't bother her in the least.

Oatmeal headed to the fence that ran the length of their shared property line. Ella slapped her hand on her thigh. "No walk today, boy. Tomorrow, I promise." Moments later, a mud-splattered jeep pulled into the driveway. With her dog following close behind, Ella hurried over to greet her best friend.

CHAPTER TWO

Shelby's jeep lurched to a stop on the long, snow-covered driveway. She got out, stretched, and gazed at the Dennings' two story home. Weathered maples and massive oaks encircled the ranch house like hugs from loving grandparents. When Doug and Ella moved up from the Valley years earlier, they bought it for a fraction of the asking price. The house backed up to the Old Pheasant Valley Cemetery, but no one knew if that had anything to do with it. The idea of old ghost stories creeped Shelby out, though Ella never minded. Deciduous trees blocked the headstones throughout the summer and the evergreens during the winter. Besides, she wasn't one to spend time in the backyard when the weather turned icy.

It had been years since Ella and Shelby were together in person. Phone calls and video chats had helped ease the separation, but only left them missing each other more. Their warm embrace was comfortable and lasted several minutes. Shelby grasped Ella's hand and stepped back, taking in her friend's features. Ella's steel gray-hair and clear blue eyes matched her sweater. "El, it's so good to see you again. I've missed you."

Ella's eyes sparkled. "You always know how to brighten my day." She pointed down to a mop of quivering white fur. "Meet Oatmeal."

"Hello there, dog. You're much better-looking in person." Shelby released Ella's hand and took in a lungful of clean, frosty air. Her breath hung in front of them before drifting away.

Ella crouched down and peered into the vehicle. "Mr. Butterfingers. Bet you're ready to explore with Oatmeal. Shel, how about I carry him inside while you get your things?"

"Thanks." Shelby walked to the back of her jeep. Her bright pink sneakers crunched on a thin layer of ice and snow. A moving shadow caught her eye. She stopped. Should she say anything? Curiosity won out. "What was that?"

Ella grasped the handle on the cat carrier and clenched her jaw. "More of a who than a what. Probably Buck wanting to talk."

Shelby hugged two oversized pillows. Buck Wilson had been creepy even before he'd killed Doug. She shuddered when his hulking shadow disappeared behind a fiery-red, full-grown maple hedge. A ragged breath escaped and she refocused on the white and teal home. Her creative getaway when Mac left on job-related business for weeks or months at a time. Shelby stepped up onto the wrap-around front porch where she and Ella had enjoyed their favorite seasonal beverages. Fresh-squeezed, frosty lemonade in the summer. Hot chocolate (with or without chocolate liqueur and whipped cream vodka) in the winter. She nodded to the sitting area protected from the elements. "You still have the rocking chairs."

Ella opened the wooden screen door and held it with her hip. "Oatmeal and I come out occasionally, though not as much when you were here. Or when Doug was alive—" Ella moved over, letting the door snap against the frame once everyone was inside. She waited for the satisfying click, confirming it had latched. Then, she closed the heavy oak door and locked the deadbolt. Oatmeal sniffed the cat carrier and bounded into the kitchen ahead of the two women.

Shelby inhaled the scent of liquid caffeine and inched a computer bag off her shoulder onto a wooden chair. "Can't you stop Buck from talking to you?"

"I called the sheriff's department several times and complained. Sergeant Nolan suggested a civil harassment restraining order. I filled out the paperwork, but never went through with it." Ella couldn't bring herself to tell Shelby she didn't have the courage to face Buck in court, which was the real reason she gave up her chance at privacy.

Shelby walked into the mudroom and placed the litter box on the floor, pushing it against the wall with the toe of her shoe. She popped her head around the corner. "Sergeant Nolan… That wouldn't be Dawn Nolan, would it?"

"One and the same. Made sergeant a while back and still works out of the local substation here." Ella set the carrier on the hardwood floor, undid the latch, and propped open the wire door. Mr. Butterfingers sniffed the dog's nose and crawled out. Soon the orange tabby sprawled on the floor with Oatmeal right beside him. Ella smiled. "Looks like somebody's made themself at home."

Sidestepping around the cat's tail, Shelby moved to the kitchen table and pulled out a chair. She rested her chin on her hand and thought back to when Dawn had a crush on her. The feelings weren't mutual. Shelby should have told Dawn she wasn't interested, but it was easier to ignore it than cause any conflict.

Ella set two steaming mugs filled with coffee on the table. "How about some eggs? Won't take but a few minutes." She grabbed a carton out of the refrigerator and turned on the gas burner.

Shelby picked up the red and white striped cup and added sugar. "Dawn ever settle down with someone?" She held the warm liquid to her lips and inhaled. Hazelnut. Her favorite.

"Haven't heard or read anything that suggested otherwise." Ella handed Shelby a plate of perfectly scrambled eggs with a toasted bagel. After pouring skim milk into her blue mug, she sat and stirred the coffee until it resembled melted caramel.

"Read about it?" Shelby spread strawberry jam on the thick, doughy bagel. "You referring to that gossip column in the local newspaper? What was that called again?"

"The 'Rumor Roost.' Whoever writes those anonymous articles sure knows what's going on around here." Ella laughed. "Nothing gets past them."

"Just like the Hollywood tabloids." Shelby added more sugar to her cup and licked the back of the spoon.

"Gossip sells more papers..." Ella remembered the questions posed about Doug's death in the weekly column. Why weren't there more witnesses? Why had he been jaywalking downtown on a dark road? The same lingering questions gnawed at her. Unfortunately, many of the small town's residents didn't hesitate to discuss their theories within earshot of Ella.

Shelby sipped her coffee. "You mentioned Dawn made sergeant. Must have struck a nerve with her brother. Didn't they have a sibling rivalry thing?"

"Funny story." Ella blotted coffee from the tablecloth. "About the same time Dawn promoted with the sheriff's department, Alton promoted to sergeant with the Pheasant Valley Police Department."

Shelby laughed. "So, nobody got bragging rights?"

"Not that time. Oh, before I forget, Dawn dropped by the

shop a few months ago looking for a birthday gift for Alton. She asked about you."

"Well, if she asks why I'm here, tell her I'm visiting." Shelby had too much on her mind to deal with Dawn. Especially if she wanted to rekindle their friendship. Shelby sighed and stared into her half-empty cup. She needed to talk to Ella. Explain how she was figuring out her life. Time wasted with Mac. Time wasted leaving Pheasant Valley. Emotions. Feelings. Things that finally made sense.

Ella gazed over the rim of her cup. "Something you want to talk about?"

Shelby looked up. "Maybe later." She knew Ella wouldn't press the issue. At some point she'd have to tell her the truth. That she wanted to stay. She needed to stay.

"Shel, how long were you on the road?"

"I left Sunday and drove about twelve hours each day. Planned to be in last night, but when I got to Barstow, I couldn't stay awake. Pulled over in a Wal Mart parking lot to take a quick nap. When I checked my phone, it was five o'clock in the morning." She covered a yawn and smiled. "And… here I am."

"So glad you stopped to rest. No telling what could have happened if you'd fallen asleep at the wheel." Ella glanced up at the burnished copper kitchen clock. "The shop opens soon. I'll help you get settled upstairs, then I've got to head out. We'll chat when I come home."

Shelby followed her friend up the narrow wooden staircase. They stopped on a small landing admiring the framed pictures hanging on the walls. Many of them were of Ella and Doug—wedding, honeymoon, vacations. Others were of her and Ella. Shelby ran her finger over their images in front of The Steamed Bean. "Seems like so long ago."

"I hated losing that place. I just couldn't go on—"

Shelby squeezed Ella's shoulder and leaned in close until

their hips touched. Staring and pointing at the pictures, they reminisced. Time stood still.

Ella patted Shelby's arm and led her into the next room. "You okay staying in here?"

"My old pink room." Shelby swept her hand along the edge of the thick, quilted bedspread covering the canopy bed. She sighed. "The wingback chairs."

"In your chenille rose pattern."

She fingered the lace curtains that covered double-hung windows. "We decorated this place together."

"Your old sewing machine." Ella pointed at the ancient Singer.

"You tried to entice me to move up to Pheasant Valley." Shelby stared at a dusty spool of cobalt-blue thread balanced atop the machine, then turned. "It almost worked—"

"Until Mac transferred to Houston."

"And I left with her."

Ella walked over and hugged Shelby. "You can't beat yourself up forever."

"I never wanted to leave. It was less than six months after Doug's death."

"We're not going over that again." She motioned toward an adjoining bathroom. "There's a new claw-foot tub in there. Filled with hot water, it's guaranteed to soothe and calm tired muscles. And don't be shy about raiding the fridge. I'll bring dinner home from the Corner Café after six." She walked to the door, then stopped. "No matter what's happened or what you need to talk about, I'm happy you're here. You were my bright spot when life spun out of control. Now, it's my turn to be yours."

CHAPTER THREE

Ella pumped the gas pedal of her small, late model car and turned the ignition key. She waited until the inside warmed and the windshield defrosted. Heading into town, the sun pushed through lingering clouds, melting the snow on the roadside. Driving this familiar route, she usually let her mind wander as she meandered along. This morning was different. Unable to shake the image of Buck's shadow beyond her property line, Ella shuddered and glanced down at her aching hands. Her knuckles were white from gripping the steering wheel. She flexed her fingers, hoping the movement would help shake Buck's image from her brain.

Ella's mood lifted as the brick facade of The Bee's Knees came into view. More than a dozen cars were in the parking lot, a good sign they'd be busy. She walked through the front door. A calming scent enveloped her. Lavender. When she first opened the shop, Ella asked her other neighbor, Laura Vega, to be her first vendor. Along with being the co-editor of the town's weekly newspaper, *The Pheasant Valley Roost*, Laura grew several varieties of lavender and sold her products online. Laura's booth was closest to the front door and filled with many handcrafted lavender products including soaps, scrubs, essential oils, and potpourri. It was an instant success with all the customers and other vendors.

Ella glanced around the room. She marveled at all the creativity and how far she'd come in just eighteen months. Her shop was full of unique items made by a variety of artisans. Handcrafted pieces from simple pine cars to exotic wooden tables. Cross-stitched dishtowels to crocheted scarves. Plus, seasonal items including homegrown herbs, honey, and homemade apple butter. Much bigger and more profitable than she'd ever expected.

Grabbing a cotton cloth, Ella walked over to her own booth and dusted the top display. She picked at the tiny pink rosebuds nestled in several grapevine wreaths, then spread them apart to make the booth appear fuller. With a dwindling inventory and the upcoming holidays, she'd need to get busy and make more seasonal items. Taking mental notes about colors of ribbons and flowers needed, she looked up and noticed Paige Melton stocking her booth. A server at the Corner Café, Paige enjoyed crafting and selling her teddy bears to make a little extra money. Paige caught Ella's attention, and they waved to each other.

Before Paige rented a booth, Ella had only seen her a few times, though Paige wasn't hard to miss. Her red lipstick and bottle-blonde hair caught everyone's attention. Plus, she flirted with all the customers. No one seemed to mind until she got a little too cozy with Buck Wilson. His wife Hope strolled in one time just as Paige started rubbing Buck's shoulders. Hope grabbed Buck by the ear and dragged him out of the Café. Everyone knew the details after reading about it in the "Rumor Roost" column. At first Ella assumed the writer embellished the story, but apparently not. Whoever wrote it knew all the sordid details, which unsettled her. She wondered what else the unknown writer saw and would write about next.

Ella walked up to the booth. Paige's flowery perfume hung in the air and burned Ella's nostrils. She muffled a cough and watched Paige brush the fur of a large, hand-sewn teddy bear with big, brown eyes. Satisfied, Paige stopped, pulled a pair of curved embroidery scissors out of her bag, and clipped several threads hanging from the bear's paw. After giving it the once over, she set it on the top shelf. Paige turned and smacked her gum. "Hey, Ella. How's life?"

"I'm good. And you?"

"Same ol' same ol'." Paige grabbed a few smaller bears from a box on the floor—just the perfect size for a child's hug. She set them on the middle shelf, then placed a softball-sized bear between them, flashing her red, glittery fingernails. Fiddling with the display for a while, she stood back admiring her handiwork. "Just fillin' the booth before me and a friend meet up."

"Looks great. I've always loved teddy bears." Ella walked away to prevent her eyes from watering. Plus, she wanted to avoid *the* conversation. The one where Paige asked her to forgive Buck for Doug's death. They'd been over it before, and Ella didn't care to hear it again. She never could figure out why Paige stuck up for that murderer.

Ella stood behind the cash register and watched Paige. Oblivious to her own powerful scent, she waved goodbye to no one in particular. Her green dangly earrings swayed and her metal bracelets clinked together when she left the store. Mesmerized by her skin-tight, lime green outfit, Ella watched Paige saunter down the sidewalk. Her heart rate increased when she noticed her nemesis, Buck. Unmistakable with his scraggly beard and tatted up neck just above his denim jacket collar. And, that dirty ball cap. Ella swore he never took the thing off. She tried to look away, but they drew her gaze when they stopped to talk. Ella couldn't hear them, but it was obvious the unlikely couple was getting cozy-close as they exchanged pleasantries.

Ella drew back from the front window and walked around the side of the shop to get a better look. She knew she was spying. She didn't care. If Buck was cheating on his wife, Ella felt somebody needed to be a witness to it. As she watched the two interact, Buck moved in closer. Paige didn't back away. They laughed, and she caressed his arm.

Ella thought about turning away, but she couldn't help herself. Her hate ran too deep. Getting dirt on Buck would satisfy her to no end. She saw them turn and head in the opposite direction of the Café. A moment before they were out of sight, Buck reached over and squeezed Paige's butt cheek. And not just a tiny pinch. Buck's meaty hand squeezed her backside like it was a warm loaf of bread.

Minutes later, Buck's wife, rushed into the shop. "Where is she?" Hope marched over to Paige's booth, flared her nostrils, then looked up and down each aisle. "I know she was in here. I smelled that cheap gardenia perfume outside."

Ella cleared her throat. "I think you just missed her." Hope was muscular from stacking wood and hand-washing their laundry. Ella didn't want to give her any reason to start busting things up, which she knew Hope to do on occasion. Wide-eyed, Ella stared as she stomped to the bathrooms. Ella pitied the poor person who might be having a quiet 'sit' in a stall.

Hope marched up to the front, passing several customers. She threw her head back, flipping her shoulder-length dirty-blonde hair from her face. She pointed out the window. "That's his Ford across the street. She ain't at the Café. Something's up between them two." Hope snorted and pushed open the front door. "Lord, help me. If I ever catch them together, I'll kill that cheating sack of manure."

CHAPTER FOUR

Just after dark, Shelby came downstairs and turned on the porch light knowing Ella would be home soon with dinner. Oatmeal yipped and scratched at the door when Ella's car come up the gravel driveway. Mr. Butterfingers yawned, jumped off the couch, and made his way to a spot next to Oatmeal. Shelby opened the door. "Can I help you carry something in?"

"Perfect timing." Ella nodded to a dessert box balanced atop two carry-out bags. "You all waiting on me?"

Shelby's hazel eyes danced. She placed the back of her hand on her forehead. "We're all starving and I didn't have the strength to cook anything."

Ella walked into the kitchen followed by her best friend and parade of pets. She opened the refrigerator, then looked at Shelby. "Oh, and I suppose you never touched the leftover roast in the fridge?"

Shelby shrugged and stifled a laugh. "Well, it's been such a long time since lunch. And even though it's only six, it's like eight Houston time. So, technically I'm double starving."

"You poor thing." Ella tore open the carry-out bags, revealing their contents. "This should help."

Shelby slipped her hand around Ella's waist and gave her a lingering side hug. "Fried chicken. Curly fries. Macaroni and cheese and coleslaw. Wow, it looks and smells amazing." She helped set the table and waited for Ella to join her.

"If you eat all your dinner, there's apple pie for dessert." Ella pointed to the square box. She shook off her jacket and massaged her left shoulder. "Give me a minute to hang this up and change out of these wet shoes." She disappeared into the mudroom and came back wearing mismatched knitted socks. Sliding her feet across the kitchen floor Ella joined Shelby at the table. "You must have slept well to build up such an appetite."

"I did…" Shelby laid a crispy chicken breast on her plate, followed by a few fries. "…until early afternoon when your neighbors decided to have a big fight."

Ella placed a small spoonful of macaroni and cheese on her plate and then arched a brow. "What happened?" She picked though the chicken, choosing a drumstick.

"That Buck guy and his wife. Boy, they were whooping and hollering for what seemed like hours." Pulling the skin off her chicken breast Shelby bit off a small piece.

"You mean Buck and Hope?"

Shelby nodded, her ponytail bobbing.

"Their place is a few hundred feet away, how did you hear?"

"You know how voices carry over the snow? Well, I heard yelling. Naturally, I cracked open the bedroom window—"

"Naturally." Ella took another bite of chicken.

"Seems Hope was upset about Buck doing something with some chick. I couldn't make out her name. Hope told Buck she'd raise all kinds of heck, not to mention how she'd use his backside for a target." Shelby paused to take a drink of water.

"She went on about some guy, Glenn—or something like that, and told Buck she didn't want the guy hanging around anymore. She kept yelling and marched inside the house. Next thing I knew, armfuls of clothes were flying out the window."

Ella scooped coleslaw from the container and plopped it onto her plate. "Hope's a spitfire when she's upset. I think the guy she referred to was Ben. Ben Brixley. He's that ex-con who befriended Buck after Doug's murder. They both do odd jobs fixing things for the locals." Ella took a bite of coleslaw, then wiped her mouth on a napkin. "Here I thought you'd missed out on the excitement at the shop. Guess you got part two."

"Part two? What are you talking about?"

"Earlier today, Paige Melton came in to restock her booth. After she left, I saw her and Buck carrying on. A few minutes later Hope marched into the shop searching for her wayward husband. Promised to do him in if she caught him, ahem, doing Paige."

Shelby thought for a moment and then her eyes widened. "Paige. Must have been who Hope was yelling about. Makes more sense now." She finished her fries and served herself a second helping. "This food is amazing. How you're still so thin baffles me."

Ella couldn't eat when she was upset. Or sad. Or angry. She placed her fork on her plate and pushed it away. "Nervous energy?"

"I'm always nervous and still the same size." Shelby couldn't stop eating when she was upset. Or sad. Or angry. She pointed to herself. "These thighs don't lie. I love pie, and everything else."

Ella took her plate to the sink and brought back two small plates, a pie server, and two clean forks.

"Seriously?" Shelby licked her fork and placed it on the tablecloth. "No reason to dirty any more plates."

"You and your one utensil. How you can eat dinner and

dessert with the same fork…" Ella stifled a laugh and ran her fingers through her short hair. The stress from Doug's death aged her, but Ella didn't feel old. Especially around Shelby. Though there was a fifteen year age difference between them, Shelby made her feel young again.

Shelby pointed her fork at Ella and winked. "Did I mention how gorgeous that color is on you?"

Ella tucked a strand behind her ear and cut the pie into several slices. "Everyone wants to be gray. And they're paying big bucks for it. Now, I'm in style and it didn't cost me a dime. One of these days you'll get tired of keeping up that Auburn Number Six."

As Ella served them pie, Shelby pointed to her messy ponytail. "It's Butterscotch Blonde. And it brings out the green in my hazel eyes." She took a bite. The apples melted in her mouth and the crust was perfect and flaky. "Nothing better than fresh apple pie."

Ella nodded. Using the tines of her fork, she pushed a rogue apple slice around on her plate. "Hope tossed Buck's clothes out the window?"

"Then told him to 'git out, or else'."

"What did Buck do?"

"He yelled at her and said a whole lotta things I shouldn't repeat. Then he got in his truck and roared off, throwing dirt and gravel everywhere. When Hope started bawling, I shut the window."

"While I don't care about Buck, I feel for Hope," said Ella. "She's put up with his drinking and philandering for too long. Plus, she lost all her privacy with Ben living there. Buck invited him to stay about a year ago after Ben was released from the state prison. Rumor had it that it was only temporary. But Ben never left. Guess she reached her limit on all Buck's friendships." Ella placed her fork on the plate. "I just hope Buck doesn't get plastered and kill someone else."

CHAPTER FIVE

Buck Wilson stomped up onto the dark wooden porch. He caught the tip of his boot on a broken step and stumbled, scraping his hand on the rough, unpainted doorway. Dagnabbit, still hadn't fixed that light. He rubbed the heel of his fist and pounded on the wooden door. "Hurry up, woman. Freezing my arse off out here." A coyote howled in the distance. Buck shivered and pounded on the door again.

Paige pushed it open, hands on hips. "You finally leave her?"

"Darlin', I'm here, ain't I?" Buck gave her a peck on the cheek and staggered into the living room holding a tangle of clothes. "That not good enough for you?" The lingering odor of breakfast, burned toast and overcooked bacon, wafted through the room.

"Guess that's a 'no'." She turned and walked into another room.

He dropped his pile of possessions on a stack of tabloid magazines laying on a threadbare couch. "Where you headed, darlin'?"

Paige appeared in the doorway, beer in hand. "Want one?"

"You know I can't. Almost two years sober."

"Aww, one little sip won't kill you." She sauntered over and waved the open bottle under his nose. Placing the tip of the bottle against his lips, she smirked. "Just… one… little… sip..."

Buck's swatted at her hand. "Knock it off, woman."

Paige backed away, then put the amber bottle to her lips. She tipped her head catching the last drop. "If you didn't leave her, why you showing up at my place with those stanky clothes?"

He swept a pile of her unfolded laundry out of the way and plopped down on the creaky couch. "It's complicated."

Paige sat next to him. Her bathrobe gapped open, exposing a small black rose tattoo on her bosom. "Only 'cause you still put up with her." She tucked her long legs underneath her body and looked up at him. "Sooner you leave her, sooner we don't have to hide no more." Tracing his jawline with her long red fingernail, she licked her lips and grinned. "Life would be much better."

Buck pulled back staring at the rose. "You gonna harp on me all night or let me be?" He loosened a boot with his other foot and let it drop to the floor.

"Time you stood up to her."

"You didn't complain earlier today. What's gnawin' at you now?"

Pulling the edges of her robe together, Paige sighed. "Tired of being number two."

He leaned in close and whispered. "You're always my number one when we're together."

Paige sat back and glared at him. Times like this she had no idea why she was attracted to the man. He couldn't hold a job. He hardly ever bathed. And though the court didn't find him guilty of murder, he had killed someone. So much baggage.

Kicking off his other boot, Buck wiggled his toes. The

pinky toe, resembling a tiny, rotten potato, poked out of a small hole in his sock. Cracking his neck, he rolled his shoulders, "Darlin', got a knot on my back. If I could lay down and you could just..." He unbuttoned his flannel shirt and got up.

She pointed to the couch. "My room's off limits 'til you figure out who's number one."

"Aww baby. That's not fair. What about a good night kiss?"

Springing off the couch, Paige turned away. She hoisted up her bathrobe, backed up to him and exposed a bare cheek. "You can kiss this."

Buck reached out and swatted her. He liked her. Maybe even loved her. After all, anything was better than that horrid wife of his.

Paige yelped and turned around, scowling. She knotted the ties of her robe, and without saying a word, she yanked a chain hanging from a crooked lamp balanced on a rickety end table and stomped up the stairs, leaving Buck alone in the dark.

CHAPTER SIX

The smell of fresh-brewed hazelnut coffee woke Ella just after sunrise. With the recent 'Fall Back' time change, it didn't bother her to get up early. After a quick shower, she dressed and applied a smidge of blush on her cheeks and forehead. She walked down the short hall and into the kitchen, almost stepping on Mr. Butterfingers, who lay on his back near the glowing embers in the hearth. Still on Houston time, Shelby sat at the table with a plateful of fried eggs, thick bacon, and several pieces of well-buttered toast.

Ella grabbed a cup and filled half with coffee, the rest with skim milk. Pulling out a chair, she joined Shelby and waited for the caffeine to kick in. Oatmeal rested against her leg and wagged his tail. "Hopefully, you'll sync up with California time soon. Then maybe you'll sleep in like the old Shel I remember."

"Always the last one up—"

"And never on time." Ella hated being late and arrived early for every appointment. She opened the shop early. Sent her Christmas cards out the day after Thanksgiving. She couldn't understand how Shelby never set an alarm. Or how Christmas cards from her arrived after Valentine's Day.

Shelby smiled, her warm hazel eyes twinkling in the early morning light. "Can I make you something to eat?"

Ella waved her off. "Thanks, but no. I have an early appointment in town and wanted to give myself plenty of time in case the roads were still icy." Her phone beeped, reminding her of the upcoming meeting. "Oh. Gotta go." She finished her coffee and placed the cup in the dishwasher. After giving Shelby a quick hug, she nodded to the pets. "See you later."

Taking her time driving into town, Ella still arrived twenty minutes early. After signing in, she glanced around the waiting room. Though a half-dozen therapists worked out of the office, the waiting room was still empty. Now she wouldn't have to make small talk with someone sitting next to her—another reason she preferred to arrive early. A small plastic pumpkin filled with leftover Halloween candy sat on one end of the counter. A hand-painted wooden turkey holding a "Give Thanks" sign sat on the other end. Cinnamon spice filled the room from a candle burning on a desk behind the counter. Little white lights twinkled on a Ficus tree in the corner of the waiting room.

"Ella?" Jasmine Green, a slender African American woman in her forties, stood near the hall door. Her dainty blue earrings matched her jacket, and looked beautiful against her mahogany skin. From her clothing, to her jewelry, to her make-up, Jasmine radiated confidence and professionalism.

Ella stood and followed Jasmine back to her office. She'd been seeing Jasmine since Doug's death, though the sessions never seemed to help. Why she kept coming was anyone's guess.

"Good morning, Ella. Enjoying the fall weather?" Jasmine poured two coffees. After adding creamer to hers, she placed the bright green mugs on the short, wooden table between them.

Ella held a mug, warming her hands. "It was nice to get some snow, though I'm not sure I'm ready for the holidays." She took a sip, focusing on Jasmine's deep brown eyes, and waited for the next question.

Jasmine sat back in an upholstered chair covered with an indigo diamond pattern, then picked up her notebook and pen. "How are you doing?"

Ella shrugged. "I'm here." She took another sip of coffee. "Seems pointless, though."

"Ella, you've made a lot of progress since Doug's accident—"

"Murder."

Jasmine tucked a strand of coarse, tight curls behind her ear. "You might not see progress, but I do. Let's talk about that for a bit."

Ella was just as angry as the night of her husband's death when the police and coroner woke her up and told her the horrible news. The only positive was that the nightmares of Doug's twisted body had ended. She stared at Jasmine's framed certificates hanging on the wall and bit the inside of her cheek, willing herself not to cry. Ella gathered her thoughts and eyed her therapist, forcing a smile. "I received a pleasant surprise yesterday."

Jasmine sat forward. Her eyes wide. "And what would that be?"

"Shelby came back from Houston. She might be back for good."

"How does that make you feel?"

"I'm delighted she's back. I've missed her much more than I realized." Ella stared at her mug. "She showed up without Mac. Things were strained between them for a while. Every time I asked Shelby how things were going, she changed the subject." Ella watched Jasmine write in her notebook and waited before continuing. "Something big must have happened. I don't know any details. I'm sure we'll talk once she gets settled."

Jasmine finished making notes, then peered over her glasses. "If you think it will help, you can always encourage her to talk to me."

Ella suppressed a smile. "You already talk to half the town. Seems like you know all our secrets."

Jasmine winked. "And I pride myself on keeping all of those secrets too."

Ella understood people in their small town would know if a therapist wasn't keeping their client's privacy. She watched Jasmine get up and refill her mug, then motion to the coffee pot. "More?"

"No, thanks. I'm good."

Jasmine sat and set her mug on the coffee table, then picked up her notebook again. "Other than Shelby coming back, anything else been on your mind?"

She gazed into her empty mug. "Is it normal to lose things? I mean, does stress cause memory loss?"

Jasmine looked up from her notebook. "Studies have shown stress and anxiety to be one cause of memory loss. It can also heighten memory. Can you be more specific?"

"I seem to lose, or maybe just misplace, things."

"That doesn't sound like you. What kinds of things are you referring to?"

Ella knew it wasn't like herself to misplace things. That's why she asked. "Personal things. Like a glove. And my knitted scarf." She shrugged her shoulders and gazed at her therapist. "Weird, huh?"

"Where were you when you noticed them missing?" Jasmine held her pen, ready to make notes.

"At the shop."

"Both times?"

"I always put my personal items behind the counter. At first, I thought my glove had fallen when I got out of the car and blamed myself for losing it. But when I discovered my scarf missing too, I checked with Gladys, Laura, Paige, and Vivian. Those were the vendors who had volunteered that day. None of them had a clue."

Jasmine gazed at Ella and frowned. "Who else has access to that area?"

Ella thought for a moment. Basically anyone who put in hours each week. It was where everyone left their belongings—purses, cell phones, and other things while tending to the store. "Everyone, I guess."

"Tell me more about the glove and scarf? Do they mean something to you?"

"Doug gave them to me." Ella bit her lip. "Birthday gifts, the year he was murdered."

Jasmine made notes. "Anything else bothering you?" She looked Ella in the eye. "Has Buck tried to contact you again?"

"No, not really. I mean, he stays on his property. Yesterday I saw him cavorting with someone other than Hope. And when I came home, Shelby told me all about their fight."

"And this concerns you, because?" Jasmine held her pen to her notebook, waiting.

Ella shrugged her shoulders. "I don't know. I hate him and feel happy when he's unhappy." She picked at a loose thread on her jeans." Does that make me evil?"

Jasmine's eyes softened. "No, Ella. It doesn't make you evil." She walked over to her desk and opened her laptop. Concentrating on the screen, she clicked her mouse several times. "Have you worked on those mental exercises I gave you?"

Ella looked out the window.

"Do you feel like they help?" Jasmine clicked again, and the printer whirred to life. Soon several pages slid into the tray.

"When I'm upset, I can't remember to stay in the moment. All I want to do is to be angry." She clenched her jaw. "And stay angry."

"It takes time. And practice. When you face a trigger, like seeing Buck, your first response is anger. We need to work on changing how you react." She retrieved the papers and handed them to Ella, then returned to her chair. "I printed out some new mental exercises. These will help you practice letting go and how to respond to a negative trigger. The past cannot be changed, but if you could reframe your focus and forget about what's going on in Buck's life, you could be much happier."

Ella turned the pages over in her hand. "This green color is different."

Jasmine smiled. "They were having a sale on copy paper at that big-box store in Bakersfield. You know, one of those "Buy One-Get Two Free" deals. I thought I grabbed three cases of white, but when I got home and opened the first box, it was mint green. Didn't think it was worth another trip down the hill and back to exchange it. I suppose it is easier on the eyes."

Ella nodded and glanced at the clock.

Jasmine followed Ella's gaze and tapped her pen on her notebook. "We still have a few minutes left. Would you be open to walking through one of those mindfulness exercises?"

"Maybe another time." Standing, Ella went to the door and left before Jasmine could respond. When she reached the car, she got in and threw Jasmine's "mindfulness" papers into the back seat. After closing and locking the door, Ella buried her face in her hands and cried. She hated herself for hating Buck. But she couldn't help it. And to be honest, she didn't want to stop.

CHAPTER SEVEN

Paige paced on the sidewalk, engaged in a heated conversation. "You promised you'd tell her last month. And the month before. But you ain't told her crap." She looked down at her phone and adjusted the volume. "Don't tell me to hush. I'll yell all I want. Just 'cause we ain't gabbin' in private don't mean I won't make a big stink in public." She walked over to the bus stop and sat on the edge of the hard, wooden bench.

"I thought you was through with her when she kicked you out yesterday. You had the nerve to show up at my place all sad and forlorn. And you didn't mind none when I let you stay the night." She nestled her phone under her chin and searched her handbag for some gum.

"You say you love me? Then prove it… How…? Go home and end it. Once and for good." Paige stopped and thought for a moment. "No... You end it to-day… Don't tell me you have to wait till the end of the month… Yeah, yeah, you need your disability check. Darlin', I need you. The whole town already knows somethin's going on between us with all them gossip column updates. It'd be a shame to disappoint people if we didn't get together..." She squeezed a piece of soft, pink gum between her fingers and popped in her mouth.

"Sweetie... No, you listen to me. I don't want no more excuses. You got till tomorrow night. Yeah, Friday night. If you ain't by my side by then, then we's through." Paige slammed her flip phone shut and tossed it in her purse. Stomping past a parked car outside her therapist's office, she caught the sound of someone blowing their nose. Strange. She wondered if they had been listening. As she turned, a display in the sporting goods store window caught her attention.

Paige walked over and stared at the poster of a shiny new hunting rifle. She'd grown up on a farm around guns. Her daddy and brother went deer and pheasant hunting each year. Though she never went with them, she was a crack shot in taking out foxes and coyotes threatening to eat the family's chickens. She thrust out her lower lip and pouted. She was tired of being just another one of Buck's lovers. Without caring who might see her, Paige raised her hand, pointed at the poster, and pulled an imaginary trigger. If Buck couldn't leave his wife, then he was gonna get what was coming to him.

CHAPTER EIGHT

Shelby pushed the floral curtain aside from the front room picture window. Though it was mid-morning, the sun was hidden from view. Dark clouds brooded, threatening snow. She remembered to turn off the coffeepot and leave a light on in the kitchen and a lamp on in the front room. The dog and cat were right on her heels, hoping for one last indulgence. Picking out a crunchy treat for each pet, Shelby handed them out with a reminder. First, she advised Oatmeal. "I don't want to come back and find something chewed." Then, Mr. Butterfingers. "Or shredded." She knew pets would be pets, but she wanted nothing damaged. If something were to happen, she'd have to face Ella. Shelby couldn't bear to disappoint her friend. Oatmeal followed her to the door, and Mr. Butterfingers settled on the back of the couch. "You guys be good."

Shelby pulled her sweater around her and shivered. Walking down the long driveway, her pink tennis shoes crunched on the gravel. White-dusted, silvery-gray junipers sprawled inside flowerbeds. She gazed up at the darkening sky and watched a hawk circle a pine tree and call out with a shrill screech. Shelby waited for its mate to answer back, but the air was silent. People say it's good to be alone, but it sucked. Shelby hoped life would be different in Pheasant Valley. Maybe she'd finally be able to be herself without so much emotional pain.

Speaking of pain, her tooth was aching again. Not a fan of the dentist, Shelby never dealt with it back in Houston. On the scale of one-to-ten, the pain was a nine—which on the Shelby-scale was up there with losing an arm or dying. Whatever it meant, eating breakfast reminded her of falling off a bike. On the pavement. In the summer. With shorts on. Everything hurt.

Yikes. It was stupid cold out. If only the car would warm up right quick. When Shelby was cold, her teeth chattered. Then her heart pounded. And then her anxiety kicked in because she was going into town to find a dentist. With the defroster running at full blast, she rubbed her hands together and waited until the frosty windshield was clear. While freezing weather was on Shelby's list of least favorite things, she much preferred it to Texas humidity. Big girls and humidity didn't get along. Between the painful thigh rub and the constant sweat dripping everywhere, Shelby avoided all unnecessary outside activities from May through October. Now, in a much colder climate, she could walk around without having to wring the moisture out of her ponytail every ten minutes.

Driving down the two-lane road into town, Shelby arrived at The Bee's Knees and parked out front by the curb. She scanned the parking lot for Ella's car, but didn't see it. Ella was probably at her appointment. Shelby didn't ask Ella why she left early. They always respected each other's privacy. Another reason they got along so well.

Shelby walked into the shop and took in the thick scent of lavender. Her stress evaporated in front of Laura's calming booth. It thrilled her to see the store filled with a variety of vendors and gingham-lined wicker baskets for shopping. Shelby grabbed a basket and started down the first aisle. Handcrafted scrunchies and hair barrettes. How awesome was that? She picked out a pink scrunchie with white polka dots and a fancy bowknot-shaped hair clip with pink rhinestones and dropped them in her basket. The next booth featured wooden lamps and cutting boards. So many choices for Christmas gifts. The next aisle offered painted primitive wood designs, cloth dolls, and needle-felted sheep. She marveled at the realistic animals made from sheared wool and a needle. Shelby couldn't resist a set of three tiny wool sheep and added them to her half-filled basket. This could be dangerous. Only two aisles in and she wanted just about everything. While standing in front of a booth filled with greeting cards and paper crafts, a familiar voice broke her concentration. She turned and smiled.

"Shelby, is that you?" Although the woman was in her late seventies, she appeared to be much younger. Gladys Purcell was unmistakable in her sensible walking shoes, crisp tan slacks, comfy hand-knit ivory-colored sweater, and the large-brimmed gardening hat she wore year-round, even indoors.

Pulling Shelby into a warm embrace, Gladys stepped back, holding her hand. "What are you doing back in our tiny mountain town?"

"Staying with Ella… temporarily."

"Hopefully longer—"

Shelby turned at the sound of Ella's voice behind her. A warm flush rose in her cheeks. "Well, yes. But, we hadn't discussed it."

Ella leaned in close, brushing a strand of hair behind Shelby's ear. "I'm sorry, didn't mean to blurt out your secret." Ella patted Shelby's shoulder, then turned. "Morning, Gladys. What did you bring in today?"

The spry older woman motioned for Ella and Shelby to follow her to a booth a few aisles over. "More apple butter and apple cider vinegar. Plus, a variety of dried fruit and jams, of course." Gladys and her husband, Ed, owned Purcell's

Orchards, a sprawling business outside town with acres and acres of trees, including apple, pear, persimmon, and pomegranate. One of Shelby's favorite memories was fall apple picking at their farm, alongside traditional and homeschooled children on field trips. Everyone in Kern County knew about the farm, and just about everyone showed up in the fall. The Purcell's apple cider, blackberry jams, and fifteen-degree drop in temperatures were worth the forty-five-minute trip up the hill from Bakersfield in mid-October when the valley could still swelter in triple-digit heat.

Gladys took Shelby's hand. "Nice to see you again, hon. Hope you'll be here for a while. Ed and I would love for you to come by for lunch."

Shelby smiled. "I'd like that. Nice to see you, too. Say 'Hi' to Ed for me."

Gladys nodded, then turned to Ella. "Before I go, would you mind checking the schedule? I think I'm supposed to be here tomorrow."

Ella walked to the front of the store and went behind the counter. She pulled out a clipboard, scanning it with her finger. "Yes, Friday between nine and noon. Does that still work for you, Gladys?"

"Yes. Thanks." She adjusted her hat, then rushed over to the door and held it open for a customer carrying bags in both hands.

Ella set the clipboard back under the counter and straightened a stack of holiday flyers. "What do you think of my little shop, Shel?"

Shelby set her basket on the counter and gave two thumbs up. "It looks great. You should be proud." She knew the shop was the only thing that kept Ella sane during the emotional upheaval after Doug's death. When they talked on the phone, Ella's entire demeanor had changed once she rented the building. While transforming it from a carpet store into a crafter's outlet, Ella told Shelby about every improvement, like it was a child reaching significant milestones.

Ella glanced at her. "Glad you stopped by."

"About that." Shelby reached up and touched the right side of her jaw. "Started hurting before I left Texas. It's nothing."

Ella leaned over the counter. "You should get it checked out." She took her cell from a pocket and scrolled through the contacts. "I recommend Doctor Harland Parke. Nice guy. Very professional. Office is right up the street."

"Thanks. I'll give them a—"

Too late. Ella had already found a number and swiped 'call' on her phone. She handed it to Shelby and stepped back.

"Thanks El, but…" Darn, someone answered. "Um, this is Shelby Heaton. Sore tooth… I guess I can come in. Now?" She stared at Ella. "Just north of Juneberry and West First. Yes, I know where that is… Goodbye." Shelby handed Ella the phone. "Thanks a lot."

Ella's blue eyes sparkled. "I know you too well. You'd put it off. Then complain. Then a week from now when you couldn't eat anything but oatmeal (the cereal, not my dog) you'd beg me to call a dentist." She patted Shelby's hand. "You can thank me later."

Now Shelby had to deal with her tooth. And a new dentist. She walked to the front door and turned back. "Wish me luck." She knew she'd need it. Once outside, she raised up on her tiptoes to check the outdoor thermometer. Fifty degrees, warm enough to walk without shivering. Plus, it would help calm her nerves. Thank goodness it was only a few blocks away. Reaching the corner, a familiar rumble vibrated under her feet. It was one of a dozen or more freight trains traveling through town each day, carrying loads to unknown destinations. Shelby watched the beast speed past. Two engines followed by boxcars, tankers, flat cars, a low one filled with gravel who's name she forgot, and two engines in the back. She let out a deep sigh. Like a missing period at the end of a sentence, the train didn't seem complete without the red caboose.

The train passed, but Shelby didn't move. She wouldn't let herself leave until she remembered the name of that one car. Between her fear of the dentist and her memory of her father's high-pitched voice, the train car's name eluded her. A kid growing up in the Valley, her family lived across the street from a large dirt lot divided by train tracks. During the day, Shelby and her brother would sneak through tall foxtail weeds to place their pennies on the tracks. After a train passed, they'd race to find their flattened coins. But in the evening, her father would make Shelby and her brother stand on the porch while he called out the names of each car. They were forced to repeat the names like they were prepping for a school test. If either hesitated or forgot, her father lashed out at whoever was closest. During the Christmas season, Shelby hated the N-Scale set that ran around their tree each year. She might have enjoyed the clickety-clack of the little train if her father wouldn't have been so obsessed with perfection. Just one more thing reminding Shelby of his sudden outbursts of anger.

Gondola. Shelby smiled, pleased she had remembered the name of the gravel-filled car. "Gondola," she whispered. With the small burst of confidence and the wind blowing around her face, Shelby didn't feel any jaw pain. Maybe she'd been cured. Maybe nothing was wrong. She had been grinding her teeth. Stress. That was it. Nothing to worry about. By the time she reached the office, she'd come up with several more reasons to cancel. After all, it was a last-minute cancellation that helped her get an appointment. Shelby would pay it forward. Someone else in worse pain could take her appointment.

Squaring her shoulders, Shelby opened the office door, mentally listing all the reasons for canceling. She waltzed up to the counter, overconfident and smug, about to explain why she didn't need to be there. A man in a bulky jacket bumped into her. Shelby turned to get a better look. His mouth drooped. Bits of white gauze stuck out of his half-closed lips. Though she hadn't seen him up-close in years, his face was all too familiar. Buck Wilson. Standing less than three feet away. Shelby froze when Buck's gaze caught her by surprise.

CHAPTER NINE

After Shelby bumped into Buck, her excuses for canceling evaporated. Averting his gaze, she rushed to the sign-in sheet. Without thinking, she added her name and contact information on the next empty line.

Shelby walked away, but the receptionist called her back to the counter. "Hon, wait a sec. I need you to fill out some paperwork." Louise, a friendly, dark-haired woman pointed to a pile of forms. "Make sure you sign, here… here... and here." She underlined each part with a yellow highlighter, then with a few sharp taps on the counter, straightened the papers. Louise handed them to Shelby, along with a clipboard and a bright blue pen with Dr. Parke, D.D.S. printed on it.

Shelby scanned the waiting area. A thirty-something mom and a pre-teen kid sat at the end of one row, both absorbed in their phones. On the other end, an older gentleman with a Santa Claus beard flipped through a gardening magazine. The chairs near the front window were empty. She eyed the middle seat, knowing it would provide elbow room on both armrests. Stepping between the padded, beige chairs and the low, wooden coffee table, Shelby stumbled over a grimy backpack shoved halfway under a seat in the middle of the row. She leaned over and picked it up, holding it away from her body. The stench reminded her of armpit odor and something else. Onions? Garlic? Whatever it was, she breathed through her mouth to avoid smelling it again. "Did someone lose a back—?"

Buck turned from the counter and stumbled toward her. "It's mine."

Louise rushed to help steady him. "Buck, let's wait for the nitrous to wear off."

He tottered over to Shelby. "Gimme my backpack." Buck swiped at it, catching only one of the shoulder straps. Several items spilled out of the top pocket. Muttering several choice words, he bent over and picked up a card and some coins with his thick fingers and shoved them in a small compartment. A handful of other items lay on the carpet, but he didn't take notice. Swinging his pack over his left shoulder, he patted his face. "Still can't feel nothin'."

"Buck, Doc said you'd be numb for several hours. We need to change your gauze again. How about you come back over on this side? The dental assistant will help you."

While the assistant dealt with Buck's gauze, Shelby glanced at the carpet. A bottle of small pills and an assortment of round, bronze tokens lay by her shoes. Her eye caught the word "nitroglycerine" on the pill bottle. Picking everything up, Shelby walked to the counter and handed them to the receptionist. "He dropped these."

"Thank you." Louise glanced at Shelby and turned to a woman in green scrubs. "Doris, please give these to Buck."

Before Shelby got back to her seat, Louise called out. "We're ready for you but need that paperwork before we can take you back."

Shelby hunched over the forms and scribbled in her information. She took a deep breath to compose herself and handed Louise the mess of papers. A few minutes later a bubbly, scrub-dressed woman called Shelby's name.

Shelby jumped up. She held her sweater against her face when she and Buck passed by each other. Between avoiding him and seeing the exam rooms, Shelby's brain went fuzzy. She tried to focus on a happy place to calm her nerves, but it didn't help. Shelby didn't even know if she had a happy place. At least, not yet.

A perky dental assistant waited. She pointed to pale yellow exam room. "Have a seat. I'll be back in a moment."

Navigating around the overhead dental light, Shelby sat in the narrow, padded chair. She reminded herself not to look at the shiny instruments. Lowering the armrests to support her elbows or grip for dear life, she let out a long, shaky sigh.

Ms. Perky stepped back into the room and attached Shelby's paper bib with metal clips. "What seems to be our problem today?"

"Well, our problem is a sore tooth." Shelby swallowed hard. "Probably from grinding my teeth. I do that when I'm stressed."

"How about we take some x-rays and let the doctor decide?"

Ms. Perky seemed a bit curt, but Shelby let it go. No need to upset someone about to shove plastic thingies in her sore mouth. She crossed her legs, then uncrossed them. She gripped the armrests and closed her eyes, trying to concentrate on an image of the ocean. And someone else… *Yikes.* Why did Dawn Nolan's face just pop into her head? Shaking off the mental picture, Shelby closed her eyes again. Another face materialized…

"Hello. I'm Doctor Parke. And how are we today?"

Shelby's eyes popped open and the image in her mind faded. "Um. Okay, I guess." She stared up at a man dressed in a dark blue button-up shirt and black slacks.

He reached out a warm hand and shook hers. "My, such cold hands."

"Only when I'm at the dentist." Licking her dry lips, Shelby attempted a smile and sized him up as he continued to introduce himself. Classic taper cut. Sandy brown hair. Just a few rogue strands above his brows. Green eyes. A square jaw with half-day's stubble and perfect teeth (of course). Shelby flinched when he walked around her chair.

"No need to be nervous." He stared at a computer monitor displaying enlarged images of her teeth. "Just looking at the x-rays."

Shelby scrutinized the screen, although she had no idea what she was looking at.

Dr. Parke rapped his knuckles on the counter area next to the sink a few times. Ms. Perky next to him stood ready with a clipboard and pen. He rattled off some alpha-numeric jargon.

"Looks like 3MOD, 5DO, 13MFD."

The assistant wrote everything down and left the room.

Shelby's heart pounded. "Is that bad?"

The doctor turned and smiled. "Cavities in three teeth. Two here." He pointed to two spots on her upper right. "One on the upper left side." He pointed to the third offending tooth.

"Guess that's why I've been in pain."

"Yep. If you take care of them at the same time, you'll feel better. Just a few shots. You won't feel a thing."

Shelby gripped the armrests until her fingers ached. Everything she hated was coming at her at once. Small places. Dentists. Needles. Her trifecta of fear. If only she'd brought a pillow to hug. "Shots? Like, how many?"

"Not too many. I can give you nitrous. Cheapest high you can get, plus it wears off quick." He rapped his knuckles on the counter again, then looked back at the computer screen. "What are we doing today?"

Shelby wanted to say she was leaving and never coming

back. But her jaw throbbed, and she knew she couldn't keep putting it off. "Are you sure nitrous is safe? I've never had it before."

The doctor chuckled. "You should be fine. Unless you have chronic pulmonary disease or have had a recent ear infection."

Well, that didn't help ease Shelby's fears. "I don't think I have anything like that." Or did she? Her brain was so fuzzy, she couldn't remember.

Dr. Parke walked around to Shelby's right side. He slipped on a pair of exam gloves and a mask. "Let me take a quick look inside, then I'll start the nitrous." He poked around her mouth, humming along with a country song piped into the room. "This will be over with before you know it."

CHAPTER TEN

Ella paced inside The Bee's Knees. A habit from when she was in college, the steady movement calmed her nerves. But in this case it was not an overdue paper or mid-term causing her distress. This time she was waiting for Shelby to return from the dentist's office. It had been over two hours since she left. Ella knew Shelby would be okay, but that didn't stop her from fretting. Ella stopped when the front door opened. She hoped it was her friend. Instead, it was her therapist.

"Good afternoon, Ella." Jasmine removed a pair of camel-colored cashmere gloves, folded them in half, and placed them inside her purse. She loosened her matching scarf and smiled. Her eggplant-colored wool skirt and cable-knit sweater looked stunning.

"So happy you stopped in." Ella walked up and offered her hand. "New necklace?"

Jasmine fingered the delicate crystal beads around her neck. "I needed something to go with this outfit and made it last night."

Ella stood back, admiring the jewelry. "Love how it pulls in the colors of your sweater and scarf."

Jasmine turned and gazed at the variety of crafter's booths. "Couple of months ago, you commented on how my handmade jewelry would be a good fit for the shop. Thought I'd check out the competition and chat about renting." She turned back and faced Ella. "That is, if you have any openings."

"Viv, would you watch the counter while I help Jasmine?" Ella motioned to a quiet, red-haired woman wearing a plain blue blouse, faded jeans, and cat-eye shaped glasses with yellow highlights on the black frames. In her late sixties, Vivian Conte always hummed while dusting the wall of shelves behind the cash register. Her ruddy cheeks reminded Ella of two perfectly polished apples. "Viv's a local resident who sells pen and ink and watercolor paintings, but today she's here for her volunteer hours."

Jasmine nodded to Vivian.

"Like Viv, I require each crafter to be here five to ten hours a month," said Ella. "It provides the help I need to run the shop, plus keeps costs down and my crafters earn more. A win-win for all of us."

Jasmine and Ella walked down an aisle, past a small wooden table and four chairs painted in primary colors. Further down, Gladys Purcell's fruit booth greeted them with the scent of orange potpourri. "We're almost full. Only a few spots left." Ella pointed to three empty booths side-by-side. "I reserved the middle one for Shelby's clothing line. Which side would you prefer?"

Jasmine strolled down the aisle and stood in front of each space. "Either is fine. No one nearby has jewelry?"

Ella shook her head. "We only have one other jewelry maker, and she uses seed beads and found stones. Nothing like your wire and crystal creations."

Jasmine took pictures of each booth with her phone, then flipped between images. "Just trying to get an idea of the space and layout." She backed up, taking in the surrounding booths. After a few minutes, she pointed to the space at the end of the aisle. "I'll take that one."

Ella gave a thumb's up. "Great choice. Let's go up front and you can fill out the paperwork."

On the way back, Jasmine stopped at Gladys' booth. Scrutinizing the shelves, she reached for a jar of apple butter and picked up a basket from a stack on the carpet. "You go ahead, Ella. I'll be there in a moment."

Ella continued to the front counter. She stepped behind it, picked up a floral file box, and pulled out two booth agreement packets. One for Jasmine. And a second packet for Shelby. While she was printing names on the top of each agreement, the front door opened. Shelby walked in, wide-eyed and flushed.

Dropping the paperwork, Ella rushed over to her friend. "You okay?"

"Still numb." She pointed to her droopy face. "But at least I survived."

Ella pulled Shelby close and hugged her. "Shel, I knew you could do it."

Shelby stepped back and gave Ella a half smile. "The shots made my heart race. But the nitrous eased my anxiety. When Doctor Parke placed that little thingie over my nose, my hands and feet went all tingly. After a while it got better." Tottering over to the sitting area, she plopped down. "Need to rest before driving to the house."

Jasmine came up carrying a basket full of jams, apple butter, and a wooden welcome sign. She pointed to her pile of intended purchases. "Figured I'd do some shopping while I'm here."

"Do you remember Shelby?" Ella pointed to her half-numb friend. "She just came from the dentist."

Jasmine winced. "One of my least favorite places."

Shelby leaned her head back against the wall. "Hey, El..." Her voice carried across the large room. "... you'll never guess who I ran into at the dentist."

Ella braced herself for the reveal. She didn't want the entire shop to hear Shelby, just in case the nitrous was still coursing through her system. She handed her therapist a vendor packet and reached under the counter. "Jasmine, I need to take this water to Shelby. Read though the agreement and let me know if you have questions."

Ella hurried over to Shelby and offered the water. "Shel, while you've got my curiosity up, how about we talk about this at home?"

Shelby grabbed Ella's hand and pulled her in close, speaking loud enough for everyone to hear. "That's fine, but first I gotta tell you... It's that guy you wished were dead."

CHAPTER ELEVEN

Ella's cheeks burned. She looked around The Bee's Knees to see who might have been eavesdropping. "Shel, what did you just say?" Viv, who was hard of hearing in one ear, was with a customer and didn't even look up. Jasmine turned when Ella looked her way. She shuddered, knowing what they'd discuss in their next session.

Shelby opened her eyes and stared at Ella. "I literally ran into that Buck Wilson dude at the dentist's office."

Ella's hands fidgeted. Nervous embarrassment radiated from her like a fever. "Did he recognize you?"

Shelby patted her jaw, checking the lack of sensation. "Don't think so. I kind of hid my face when I was near him. Except… when I handed him his backpack."

"Backpack?" Ella stood and paced. "Shel, what happened?"

Shelby winced. "Owie. I need to take some pain medicine before all the numbness wears off." She opened a small plastic container and popped a red pill in her mouth. Although she took her time, water dribbled down her chin onto her pink sweater. "Aw, crap."

"Hold on." Ella rushed back to the front counter, grabbed a handful of paper towels, and took them to her. "Here ya go."

Shelby blotted her shirt and gave Ella a half-smile. "Thanks."

Ella looked over towards the counter again and noticed Jasmine wave her over. "Shel, will you be okay for a while? I'm needed up at the front."

Shelby nodded and gingerly patted her jaw again.

Ella made her way back to Jasmine. Stepping around busy customers picking out wooden toys and furniture, she stopped for a moment and took in a deep breath. She tried to push Shelby's statement out of her mind, but it gnawed at her. Like wondering whatever became of her missing glove and scarf. She arrived at the counter and shook off the feelings of despair. "How's the paperwork coming?"

"All completed except for my volunteer hours." Jasmine pulled out her phone and swiped the screen. "Just checking my schedule."

Ella tapped her fingers on the counter. "If need be, you can break them up over the month." She looked over the paperwork and added her name and date next to Jasmine's. Ella made a copy and offered it to her therapist, then filed the original in a heavy cardboard box. "Any idea when you want to get started with us? I take mid-month contracts."

Jasmine looked up and laid her phone on the counter. "How about November fifteenth? A week from today. Then I won't have to wait until December." She dug through her purse and pulled out a checkbook and key chain and placed them next to her phone. "I need to pay you for today's purchases and first month rent. Do you prefer two different checks?"

"One check is fine. I just need to make a notation on the receipt." Ella turned when Shelby joined them at the counter.

Grabbing the second vendor packet, Ella handed it to her. "One for you, too."

"Awesome." Shelby pointed to the booth next to the register. "Love that lavender scent. I feel much better now." She brushed a few stray drops of water from the front of her sweater and smiled. "Now, if I could only take a drink without spilling all over myself."

As they talked, Jasmine's phone rang, vibrating the key chain on the counter. She answered and stepped back, speaking quietly into her phone. "Be back at the office in fifteen—"

"Oh, hey." Shelby pointed to a medallion on Jasmine's key ring. "That looks like the token that Buck dropped."

Jasmine whirled around. Her dark eyes wide. She glared at Shelby, then stared at the counter. Grabbing the keys with her free hand, she shoved them into her purse.

Shelby and Ella stared at each other. Ella wondered why calling attention to Jasmine's keyring would cause such a reaction.

CHAPTER TWELVE

After leaving The Bee's Knees, dusk turned into darkness. The wind howled and pushed against Shelby's jeep. By the time she reached Ella's, chilly gusts changed leafless branches into menacing, long-fingered creatures beckoning inside. Climbing out of her vehicle, Shelby dashed to the porch as a single coyote called out. She shivered and sprinted up the steps, keeping her guard up in case something, or someone, was watching.

Shelby opened the front door. She sensed her shoulders relax, relieved to be back in the safety of Ella's home. The feeling in her mouth had come back, but now her jaw ached and her gums were tender from multiple injections. Though Dr. Parke called in a prescription for high-strength ibuprofen, it wasn't ready before she left The Bee's Knees. Thank goodness Ella offered to stop by the pharmacy for her. One less thing to worry about.

Yips and meows greeted Shelby. "Aww. You guys miss me?" She reached down and rubbed Mr. Butterfingers' back. After the obligatory scratching behind Oatmeal's ear, Shelby spoke to him. "You need to go out, boy? I bet you do, don't you?"

The trio walked to the back door together. When Shelby came in from taking the dog out to relieve himself, Mr. Butterfingers sat just inside the doorway, swishing his tail. The meows and yips intensified again.

"Anyone hungry?" The impatient cat twisted between her legs, while Oatmeal circled around them. Shelby opened the refrigerator and grabbed a partially-full can of cat food and fed Mr. Butterfingers. Then she scooped dry food into Oatmeal's bowl. Once the animals were fed, she searched through the refrigerator again. Leftover chicken sounded good, but maybe she should choose something easier to chew. Scooting a glass dish to the side, Shelby spotted the perfect comfort food. A bowl of macaroni and cheese. She set it in the microwave and pushed REHEAT.

The humming appliance dinged about the same time the front door opened. Shelby peeked around the corner, comforted to see Ella walking in holding a thin, white paper sack. The animals scrambled up to her, yipping and meowing. Shelby retrieved her dinner and sat at the table as Ella walked into the kitchen. "Hey, El. Hope you don't mind." She pointed to her bowl.

"Not at all." Ella reached down and stroked Oatmeal's head. "Were you a good boy today?" She ran her hand along the cat's arched back. "And Mr. Butterfingers, I didn't forget you." Ella laid the bag on the table and gave Shelby a side hug. "Shel, here's your prescription. It was ready when I got there." Ella removed two containers from the refrigerator and fixed herself a plate of chicken and coleslaw. "Feeling any better?"

Shelby shrugged. "Eating should help. I never had lunch." She placed a spoonful of the gooey cheese and noodle mixture inside her mouth. "Oh man, even better the second night."

Ella set a glass of water near her plate. She sat and picked at her coleslaw. Memories of their earlier conversation played in her mind—*that guy you wished were dead.* Had she really voiced those morbid thoughts out loud? Yes, she wished Buck dead. But hearing them from Shelby made Ella feel vile. And violated. Words spoken in anger and in confidence, shared with the world. Or at least in her shop, which was her world. Ella shook off the anxiety rising in her chest. She wanted to talk about Shelby's encounter with Buck, but something else was just as pressing.

Ella wiped her mouth with a cloth napkin. "You notice how Jasmine reacted when you mentioned her key chain?"

Shelby had just taken another bite. She nodded and waved her spoon in the affirmative.

Ella picked off a piece of chicken and fed it to Oatmeal. "I'd seen the key chain before and never thought about it. Jasmine never seemed to care. But when you pointed it out…"

Shelby looked down at her food. "Today was just… weird. From bumping into Buck at the dentist to Jasmine and her key chain. I guess he was dealing with the aftereffects of nitrous, though I have no idea why I upset her."

"I thought nitrous wore off almost immediately."

"From what Doctor Parke mentioned, it's supposed to. I'm not sure why Buck was stumbling around. Anyway, he grabbed his backpack and a bunch of coin-like tokens fell out, along with some nitro pills." Mr. Butterfingers placed his paw on Shelby's lap, looking for a handout. "Look what you started." She laughed and nodded toward Ella. "She has the chicken."

"Nitroglycerin? Isn't that what heart patients take in an emergency?" Ella passed a few pieces to the waiting feline.

"Yes. My mother always kept a bottle with her. When I saw everything on the floor, I took it up to the receptionist." Shelby used her spoon to scrape up the last of the cheese sauce, then licked it clean. "One less piece of silverware to wash tonight."

Ella rolled her eyes. "Did you ever figure out what the tokens were? Maybe from an amusement park?"

"Don't think so. Much too big to fit into a video game slot.

Like Jasmine's, they were about the size of a silver dollar, except they weren't money. His were bronze and had numbers and letters on them."

Ella got up and placed her plate in the sink, then opened the refrigerator and brought out the apple pie. She went over to the cabinet and pulled out two plates. "Want a piece?"

Shelby nodded. "I don't mind using the same bowl and spoon."

Ella stopped and stared at her friend. "You are so odd." She cut two slices of pie and after serving them, picked off a small piece of crust and slipped it to Oatmeal. He licked her fingers, getting every last bit.

Shelby thought for a moment. "You ever notice Doctor Parke's hands when he worked on you?"

Ella placed her fork on her plate. "I'm not sure I understand the question."

"His hands weren't steady. Like he was nervous."

Ella looked at Shelby. "Nervous?"

Running her spoon through the thick apple filling in her bowl, Shelby nodded. "They trembled. And not like he was nervous-nervous, but like he couldn't control the shaking. It was weird."

"Can't say I'd ever had that happen to me." Ella took a bite of pie and gazed at Shelby.

"Well, maybe he wasn't feeling well or something. I mean, I'm sure he's filled a zillion teeth. And he did a wonderful job on my fillings today—"

"Except for his shaky hands." Had Ella noticed his hands before? Not really, but dentists didn't bother her as much as Shelby. Being hypersensitive, maybe Shelby picked up on something Ella had missed.

Shelby finished her pie and washed out her bowl and spoon.

"Just leave them on the counter," said Ella. "I'll put everything in the dishwasher."

"Okay. Thanks." Shelby remembered Ella was meticulous. Each bowl, plate, and cup had to be perfectly stacked so everything would have equal coverage during the wash and rinse cycles. While Shelby wasn't fussy about dish placement, she was more inclined to fret over intangible things like how people made her feel or being able to sense others' feelings. Like right before her father got angry. Or before her mom became sick. Even though she wasn't living with them, Shelby sensed something was very wrong. Ella understood Shelby's premonitions and empathetic feelings. Things the two women accepted about each other and didn't need to talk about. Shelby smiled and walked out of the kitchen into the front room.

"Shel," Ella said. "You notice what kind of dental procedure Buck had done?"

"Not really. His face seemed numb, and I heard the nurses mention something about changing gauze before he left. Why?"

"Just curious," said Ella. "Sorry about your experience with Doctor Parke. I've never known him to be anything but professional."

"No biggie. Guess everyone's entitled to a rough day. I'm supposed to go back next week to get the other tooth filled. Hopefully, he'll be feeling better by then."

Ella straightened and placed the dishes in the dishwasher. "Don't forget your pain pills. I'm sure you'll need them in a few hours."

"Oh, thanks." Shelby went back into the kitchen. As she picked up the bag, Ella wiped off her hands and came over to where Shelby was standing. Ella's clear blue eyes sparkled as she pulled Shelby into a close, comforting hug. Tingles shot through Shelby's body as her afternoon daydream returned in her mind.

Ella pulled back and whispered. "Hope you feel better soon."

Shelby's heart quickened as she pulled away. "Thanks. See you in the morning." She called to her cat. "Come on, Mr. Butterfingers. Your momma had a rough afternoon."

Ella rested her hand on the back of a chair, "You can sleep in a bit tomorrow. Get back on California time. Especially if you're going to be here a while."

Shelby turned toward the stairs, smiling. Mr. Butterfingers meowed and ran ahead as she trudged up to her bedroom. Maybe Shelby would finally get a good night's sleep.

CHAPTER THIRTEEN

The icy air hit Shelby when she entered her bedroom. *Oops.* Cracking the windows before she left that morning, wasn't such a smart move. A habit from her days living in the Valley, Shelby relished sleeping in a cold room. Novembers in Bakersfield were still in the mid-50s, and the fresh air felt great. But at four-thousand feet, the frosty mountain air was too chilly.

Walking to the window, Shelby glanced at Buck's house. The lights were on. The curtains were open. Smoke from the chimney disappeared with the wind. Buck must have made it home after his procedure. Someone had parked the truck catawampus in the driveway.

Buck, Hope, and Ben stood a few feet from each other waving their hands and pointing. Shelby wondered if they were fighting. She crouched down to get a better look, then stood. What was she doing? What if they noticed her? Shelby told herself to let it go, she had her own problems to deal with without getting involved in theirs. A coyote howled in the distance. Another one answered. Shivering, Shelby locked the windows. To avoid temptation (and being seen), she let down the blinds and pulled the lace curtains together.

Tossing her jeans and sweater next to her suitcase on the clothes-strewn rug, Shelby changed into a sleep shirt and flannel pants. She should hang up her clothes. That's something her father would have required. Though the anxiety of disappointing him was just under the surface, Shelby knew he couldn't hurt her. After she moved out of her parents' house, she tried to be true to herself. Except for her design business, which was organized and tidy, the rest of her life was messy. And she didn't mind. Except for her relationship with Mac. Shelby thought they were good together. But after being apart for the last month, Shelby knew where she should be. She just hoped Ella felt the same way.

Too sore to brush, she rinsed her mouth with warm salt water. Good enough for tonight. Mr. Butterfingers lay curled up in the middle of the bed, snoring. Shelby pulled back the fluffy, quilted bedspread and sheets, then crawled inside. She turned off the bedside light and lay on her left side cocooned between a fortress of pillows. Two under her head. Three up against her tummy and one behind her back. Some people might think it was quirky. Shelby preferred to think she was safe. Snuggling under her covers at night not only kept her insulated from her own demons, but it also provided a barrier around her, keeping others at a safe distance. Closing her eyes, Shelby drifted off to sleep while high-pitched howls faded in the distance.

SHELBY JERKED awake and reached for her phone. The display showed a few minutes after midnight. She heard the dog barking downstairs and turned to switch on the bedside lamp.

Something hit the window. Mr. Butterfingers must have heard it, too. He sat up, staring at the curtains.

"Probably nothing. Right?"

The cat looked at Shelby and blinked.

"You're no help at all."

There it was again. A low rumbling and hundreds of little pings bouncing off the windowpanes. Her breathing increased when a flash lit up the room. A loud crash rattled the windows. A thunderstorm. Right over the house. Flash. Crash. Rumble. Rumble. Rumble. Mr. Butterfingers skittered off the bed and ran underneath. Shelby sat up, gathered her pillows, and held them against her body. While she was used to thunderstorms—and the ones in Texas were real window-rattlers—she didn't enjoy being on the top floor, right under the action. She had heard stories of how lightning traveled through windows, zapping people in their beds. Wondering if she should seek lower ground, Shelby swung her legs over the side of the bed and grabbed her phone. Ready to bolt, she heard a knock on her partly-closed door.

"Shel, you okay?"

A familiar voice. Thank goodness. "Yeah," said Shelby. "Just a little dazed."

Ella stood in the doorway holding two battery-operated lanterns. She handed one to Shelby. "Just in case you need it." Mr. Butterfingers meowed and came out of hiding, winding himself around Ella's legs.

Shelby jumped when another crash thundered overhead. Oatmeal barked and ran over to the window. Sitting back on the bed, Shelby grimaced. "Not afraid. Just startled."

"Power's out. Probably will be out for a while—" Another flash.

Shelby silently counted in her head. One Mississippi. Two Mississippi. Three Mississippi. Four… The thunder rumbled low and slow. "Almost a mile away. That's good."

"Sounds like it's headed east toward Mojave." Ella walked over to the window and lifted the blinds. "I heard we were in for a few days of thunderstorms and hail—" A small yip interrupted her. She turned and looked down at the dog. "Do you have something to add, Oatmeal?"

He bounded over to the bed, pawed at the comforter, and wagged his tail.

"This is not a slumber party. I just came upstairs to bring Shel some light." Ella put her hands on her hips. "Time to go back to bed—"

Another flash, followed by an ear-splitting crash. Shelby pulled her pillows closer. "Wow. It's still over us."

Ella turned. "I can bring chamomile tea up. With honey and milk."

Shelby reached over the side of the bed and scratched Oatmeal's ears. "Tea is a wonderful idea. Don't you think so, dog?" He wagged his tail and yipped again.

Ella laughed. "Partners in crime, eh? I'll be back soon."

Shelby watched the light of Ella's lantern disappear and placed hers on the nightstand. She patted the top of the bed and whispered. "Come, Oatmeal." He jumped up on the bed, then walked across the comforter and nuzzled Shelby's face. Next up was Mr. Butterfingers. He settled on his corner of the bed and licked a front paw.

A few minutes later, a light reappeared in the hall. Placing a steaming cup of hot tea next to Shelby's lantern, Ella motioned to the animals. "What do we have here?"

Shelby picked up her cup and stirred the creamy tea. "Apparently we're having a midnight tea party." She motioned toward the bed. "You know I adore the four-legged company. But some human company would be nice, too." Shelby propped a few pillows against the other side of the headboard as her friend walked around the bed. Ella set her teacup on the nightstand next to her, then sat and leaned back against the fluffy pillows. Letting out a long sigh, Ella smiled. "I always loved this bed. It just seems to hug you."

Shelby nodded and pulled a small, round, corduroy pillow up to her chest. "Since we have nothing better to do, tell me about that Ben guy."

Ella turned with a start. "What prompted that question?"

Shelby motioned toward the window with her head. "Well, just before I shut my windows."

Ella clicked her tongue. "Hard to break that old habit of sleeping in a cold room."

"What can I say?" Shelby sipped her tea.

"I don't mind the cold," said Ella. "Especially when it stays outside."

Shelby rested the teacup on her leg. "I noticed your neighbors having, what looked like, a heated conversation. I shut the window because I didn't want anyone to see me."

"Did you hear anything?"

Shelby shook her head. "Their windows were closed. Probably better. Those people creep me out."

Ella took another sip of tea. "Back to your question about Ben. I only know what I've heard around town.

Shelby laughed. "Which means the rumors are only half true?"

Ella nodded. "About three years ago, Hope and a few other ladies in town signed up for Christmas Cards to Inmates. Figuring they'd get paired up with someone incarcerated on the other side of the country, they all thought it would be a friendly gesture to reach out during the holidays. Turned out Hope's card went to Ben at the prison just outside town." Ella stopped and plumped the pillow behind her, then continued. "At first it was no big deal. But then rumor had it she enjoyed writing to Ben to make Buck jealous. Buck got curious about Ben and Hope's relationship and went to see Ben on visiting days. Oddly enough, they ended up becoming friends. When

Ben was released, he contacted Buck, asking for cash until he could find a place to stay and start work."

"Kinda strange, don't you think?" Shelby patted Oatmeal's furry belly. He snorted and rolled over.

"It got even stranger," said Ella. "Hope insisted they invite Ben to live with them until he was back on his feet."

"And Ben's still there?"

Ella leaned in close and whispered. "For more than a year now. Gossip around town says Ben and Hope are involved. But, you know small towns."

"And small-town rumors." Shelby slurped the last of her tea and set the cup on the nightstand. "They all seemed pretty upset a few hours ago."

"Who knows what goes on in that house." Ella clenched her teeth. "Just so they stay away from me. And you."

Shelby nodded. "I agree with you on that."

Ella yawned and checked her watch. "It's almost one. I need to get some sleep before work tomorrow." She leaned over and rubbed Shelby's back as she gave her a soothing hug.

A blush rose in Shelby's cheeks. She closed her eyes and slowly breathed in the scent of Ella's coconut shampoo.

Ella stood and smiled. "You get some sleep, okay?"

Shelby nodded. Oatmeal jumped off the bed and followed Ella out of the room. Shelby leaned back on her pillow, pondering how to talk about her feelings. For Ella.

CHAPTER FOURTEEN

The storm raged, then moved on as fast as it arrived. Nothing like a steady rain to help one fall asleep. Sleep. Something Ella had struggled with since Doug's murder. But the last few nights she'd gotten a full eight hours and woke up refreshed. Perhaps it was because another person was in the house. Perhaps it was because Shelby was there. Ella hoped this time she'd stay for good.

Even though Ella went to bed late, she was up before sunrise. Last night, as she and Shelby rode out the storm, Ella sensed feelings from Shelby that kept her tossing and turning. It seemed Shelby wanted to discuss something. Knowing her for such a long time, their friendship transcended words. They could finish each other's sentences and read each other's thoughts. And feelings.

Ella realized the power was back on when she noticed the glow of her nightlight. The alarm clock blinked two-fifteen. Her phone showed five-fifteen. As she stirred, Oatmeal padded over and licked her face. "You need to go out?" He yipped as Ella put on her robe and slippers. Once they were outdoors,

Oatmeal dashed to a plot of dry grass. "Hurry," Ella called. "It's freezing out."

Gazing out into the pre-dawn yard, Ella patted her thigh. "Come on, Oatmeal." No response. She didn't want to raise her voice, but she was shivering. "Oatmeal?" Ella walked down the wooden steps and out into the yard. Though she couldn't see him, she heard yips coming from a short distance away. Ella called out again. Finally he came running, but instead of going up the steps, the dog barked and turned around.

"I know you think it's a fine time to take a walk over to the cemetery, but not now, you weird dog." She pointed to her pajamas. "Not only is it barely light out here, but it's also freezing." Oatmeal yipped and started for the back of the property. Ella called to him again. "Oatmeal. Come." The dog hesitated, but eventually trotted back.

"I promise we'll go for that walk after breakfast. Besides, Shelby and I need to talk. Maybe getting away from the house will help her open up." Ella looked down. Oatmeal turned his head to the side, listening. "And yes, I'm talking to you. Just don't go telling everyone what I just said." Oatmeal hopped back up the stairs and waited for Ella at the door, tail wagging.

After he took quick drink from his water bowl, they went back to her bedroom just down the hall from the kitchen. She hung up her robe and placed her slippers next to the bed, then reset the clock to the correct time and crawled under the thick, warm covers. The electric blanket came in handy on wintery mornings such as this one. Oatmeal curled up in the small of Ella's back and they drifted to sleep.

Ella woke when Oatmeal jumped off the bed and dashed out down the hall. The sun peeked through the curtains. Her alarm clock on the nightstand showed seven twenty-two. The extra hours of sleep helped, but she still felt groggy. Ella lifted her head from the pillow, sniffed the air, and smiled. Hazelnut coffee. She took a quick shower and towel-dried her hair, wanting to make sure there was enough time to take Oatmeal for his walk and chat with Shelby before leaving for the shop.

Staring in the mirror, Ella wondered what had happened to the fun-loving woman who used to look back at her every morning. While she knew the woman was still there, Ella barely remembered her. Consumed with grief, then hatred, she had forgotten her own needs. What it felt like to be held. And loved. And how not to shoulder every burden herself.

As Ella fluffed her hair with the blow dryer and rounded brush, Shelby's face came to mind. Ella thought about her friend's giving spirit and unconditional love. Her heart swelled thinking of how much Shelby cared about her. The kind words and comforting hugs she offered. She wondered, did they have more than just a close friendship?

Ella placed the brush on the counter and stared at her reflection. Did she want Shelby to stay because she missed her being around? Or was it because there was something more between them? A special connection. A genuine love for each other?

While dabbing moisturizer on her face, Ella shivered, but not from the cold. She looked down at her trembling hands. Her thoughts went back to college when she had experimented. Jessica had told Ella she loved her. Ella had cared for Jessica, too. But, after Ella met Doug, she figured that relationship was a onetime thing. Now, with Shelby back, old emotions had resurfaced. Ella wondered if she truly had feelings for Shelby even though she had been happily married to Doug.

Ella walked back into her room and finished getting dressed. What was that gnawing in her tummy? Excitement? Fear? Ella grabbed her phone and swiped the internet icon.

She typed in "Am I bisexual?" Her hands trembled so, it to hold the phone. The first article that came up asked "Bi-Sexual or Bi-Curious?" It said the person should experiment. Good Lord, thought Ella. She experimented in college. Ella dropped the phone on the bed and closed her eyes. Even if her feelings were true, she knew she couldn't say anything. Not while Shelby was still sorting out her feelings for Mac.

Ella sat on the bed. She took in a deep breath and let it out. She repeated the controlled breathing until she calmed down. Ella got up, pinched her cheeks to add color and forced a smile. She walked down the short hall from her bedroom into the kitchen, trying to pretend nothing was different. But the second Ella saw Shelby sitting at the table, her stomach lurched. Darn.

"Coffee?" Shelby smiled and flipped her head to the side.

"Thanks." Ella's mouth felt like cotton.

Shelby jumped up and poured Ella a cup, then returned to an overflowing bowl of cereal.

Ella dropped two English muffin halves in the toaster and waited.

"Oatmeal seemed riled up this morning." Shelby pointed to the dog between bites. "He kept scratching at the door."

After joining Shelby at the table, Ella smeared her muffin with several dollops of the Purcell's apple butter. "When I took him out earlier this morning, he wanted to take a walk. Probably making sure I don't forget." Ella took a bite, relishing the sweet and savory spread.

Shelby picked up piece of cereal off the table and stared at Ella with wide eyes. "I don't mind taking him. That is, if you don't have the time."

Ella glanced at the kitchen clock. She couldn't let the chance go by without at least trying to chat. "How about I call Viv?" said Ella. "She has an extra key and can open this morning. Then we can both take him on a walk."

"That would be great." Shelby picked up her dishes and

placed them in the sink. "Give me a minute to brush my teeth."

Ella nodded and picked up her cell. "Hi, Viv. It's Ella… You mind opening the shop this morning? Laura and Gladys are supposed to be there by nine… No, everything's fine. I'll just be a few hours late… Thanks, hon. Bye." Ella placed her phone next to her half-eaten breakfast and thought about the internet search she'd done earlier. She hoped going for a walk with Shelby would give them a chance to talk.

CHAPTER FIFTEEN

Shelby stood in her bathroom. She brushed her teeth twice, then went back into her room. She grabbed her gloves and scarf and stared in the mirror. Maybe the pink would look better with her sweater? Shelby dug through her suitcase, tossing everything else on the rug. Then she stopped, wondering what was she doing. Her hands trembled. It was just a walk, she reminded herself. She draped a pink, fuzzy scarf around her shoulders and stared at her reflection again. Her hair. Should she tie it up, or leave it down? What about make-up? How much was too much just taking a walk? Shelby stepped away from her reflection, forcing herself to go downstairs. Her heart raced. Tiny beads of sweat formed on her upper lip.

Ella stood by the door with Oatmeal. Her hair was perfect. She smelled of coconut and wore an ecru cable-knit sweater over her blue cotton pants.

Shelby wanted to give her a hug, but hesitated. "Ready when you are."

Ella nodded to a retractable dog leash in her gloved hand.

"Out by the road I like to keep him close, but once we get to the fields around the cemetery, he gets free reign." Oatmeal yipped and strained on his leash. "As you can see, he loves his walks."

Once outside, Shelby glanced up at the cerulean sky. Wisps of clouds drifted along in the wind. "It's just beautiful here." A crow cawed and bobbed its head in a nearby pine tree. Another answered as they flew to the top of a taller tree.

"One reason I never moved," said Ella. "Despite the terrible memories, it's my home…" Her voice trailed off as their shoes crunched on the gravel driveway. With his long lead, Oatmeal bolted toward the back of her property. Shelby followed Ella and Oatmeal as they walked along the back side of the dead lawn near a chain-link fence. Once they passed Ella's pine trees and reached the paved road, she shortened his lead. The friends fell in step with each other, side-by-side.

Ella turned to Shelby. "Feeling better this morning?"

Shelby patted her jaw. "Almost as good as new." Shoving her hands into her jeans pockets, she knew it was time to start the conversation. But how? Blurt it out? Start with the weather and segue into her feelings? She knew she had been stalling and now, an awkward silence stood between them. Shelby smiled and took a deep breath. "I've been wanting to talk to you. About why I'm here. I suppose you figured out Mac and I broke up. We tried. But…" Shelby's voice cracked. "I don't think we were meant to be. I mean, I thought we were supposed to be together. But there were problems. We didn't agree on anything. And I missed… um, being here…" She swallowed a hard lump forming in her throat.

Ella stopped. "I'm so sorry, Shel." Streams of sunlight extended through the thin clouds, like illuminated fingers reaching down from heaven, they pointed to patches of snow melting on the road.

"I was losing who I was. Trying to get pregnant. Being the best partner. I stopped doing everything that made me happy just to keep us together. In the end, neither of us were happy."

Oatmeal sniffed the ground and pulled at the leash. Ella relaxed the lead and looked up at the sky. "Everyone deserves to be happy. And to be true to themselves."

Shelby followed Ella's gaze but noticed nothing. "I'm glad you believe that."

Ella turned and clutched Shelby's hand. "I was honored you trusted me enough to come out to me at work. You were tired of hiding your true self."

"El, you were the only one who knew, until I made the mistake of telling my parents."

"You were twenty-five, not that it mattered. I never understood why they kicked you out and refused to acknowledge you."

"As long as I've known you, El, you've never judged me. That means more than you know." Shelby kicked at the road with the toe of her tennis shoe. If only Ella had known what had really happened. Her father's horrified look. Her mother's uncontrolled weeping. Instead of rebuking her, her father got up out of his leather easy chair, opened the front door and told her she was no longer welcome in their house. He threw the keys to her pink VW bug out on the lawn, then waited for her to leave and closed the door. The only time she spoke to him after that was when he called to say her mother had died. Shelby never even had the chance to say goodbye.

Oatmeal barked and pulled at the leash. Ella tightened her grip and walked toward the cemetery. "Looks like he spotted his friends."

"El, I came back here because I felt safe and welcome. And because I needed to talk to you about some—"

Rounding the corner, Oatmeal's barks rose in pitch. He ran

back around Ella, tangling her in his leash. "Oatmeal. Sit." He barked and pulled. "Wonder what's gotten into him?"

Shelby followed them to the west end of the cemetery where the fence was broken in several areas, giving easy access to the grounds.

Ella brought Oatmeal up close and unhooked the leash from his collar. "Okay. Go play." He stopped, then sniffed the ground and bounded about a hundred feet away, stopping at a clump of dry grass near several tall, granite headstones. "Sorry about that," said Ella. "Now that he's off playing I won't be distracted." Ella looked at Shelby and smiled. "You were saying you needed to talk about something?"

"Ella. I'm not sure how you feel about—"

"I'm good with it."

"You're not upset?"

"Not at all. Why should I be?" Ella reached up and rubbed Shelby's shoulder, then started walking toward the grave markers. "It's perfectly okay if you want to move back in. You can stay as long you want. My home is your home."

Shelby felt a blush rise in her cheeks. "Thank you. But I kinda had something else I really wanted to tell you. It's not just about staying in my old room. It's more about—"

Ella stopped and pointed.

Shelby turned and stared at Oatmeal. He was digging at something.

"Is that a boot?" asked Ella.

As they inched closer, Shelby realized it wasn't just a boot. There was a whole person attached to it. "Oh goodness."

Ella held up her hand. "Wait here."

Shelby stood up on her toes and tried to get a better look as Ella walked a wide circle around the body. "Who is it?"

Ella motioned for Shelby to come closer.

She took her time walking over to where Ella stood. About

ten feet away, a man lay on his stomach, his body face down on the cemetery grounds. Oatmeal growled and pawed at his filthy jeans jacket. Shelby whispered. "Is he…?"

Ella looked at Shelby and nodded.

CHAPTER SIXTEEN

Ella stood in the cemetery. "He's finally dead."

Shelby gasped and studied her friend's face. "What did you just say?"

"I… I mean, I can't believe he's dead. I don't know what I'm saying." Though Ella was in shock, her words were intentional. Coming from deep within after years of loathing and secretly hoping a terrible fate would befall her adversary. Instead of a blunder, her words were uttered in wretched relief. Ella walked closer to the body straddling the property line of the old cemetery. She shivered and pulled her sweater closer. The dog sniffed around, then looked up and whined. She patted her thigh. "Oatmeal. Come here."

Shelby stepped closer. "Maybe he's still alive."

Ella shook her head. "You ever seen a dead body?"

"No." The closest Shelby had come to something dead was a deceased lizard found on the driveway. That was bad enough.

Ella stared at Buck's body. "I've seen a few. My aunt. My mom. There's a sense of emptiness. Do you want to come closer?"

"I'd rather not."

"His face is gray, almost ashen. I guarantee you he's dead."

Shelby turned and stared at the mountains in the distance. "What do you think happened?" A pair of shimmering hummingbirds chased after each other, clicking and swooping in and out of a hedge of dead lantanas, oblivious to the drama unfolding below them. They hovered over the dog, inched closer to the two women, then disappeared in a blur over the fence.

"No idea." Ella peered down at the body. "His head's near a broken monument. Maybe he got drunk and fell?" She walked around to the other side to get a better look. "Oh, no. There's a huge gash along the back of his head."

"Is there blood?" Shelby's voice rose in pitch. "I don't like blood. I never liked blood."

"Stay there." Feeling queasy, Ella's mind raced.

"I need to sit." Shelby leaned on a nearby tree. "My head's all fuzzy."

Ella walked back to Shelby and grabbed her trembling arm. "Hon, it's going to be okay. There's not that much blood. Focus on my voice and come with me." Ella led her friend to a rickety wooden bench and they sat. Oatmeal followed and stood by Ella's shoes. She reached down and stroked his ears. "Now we know why you were all riled up. Don't we, boy?"

Shelby looked up, her face pale. "My chest hurts and it's hard to breathe."

"Shel, just take a few deep breaths. It's probably a panic attack."

Shelby gulped for air. "How are you not freaking out right now? There's a dead body ten feet from us."

Ella shrugged. "I've always been calm in a crisis. But when we go back home I'll fall apart. Then you'll need to hold my hand and talk me through my panic attack."

Shelby let out a long, shaky sigh. "How long do you think he's been out here?"

Ella thought back to that morning. "Oatmeal was upset when I took him out."

"You hear anything?"

"No, but I stayed near the house… at the house." Ella tried to recall all the details of the morning, but her mind was not cooperating. She remembered the dog had been unusually persistent in wanting to take his walk. She also remembered she was cold and wanted to get back into her warm bed. Her head spun. She needed to pace, but couldn't leave her distraught friend.

"Who would do such a thing? Wait… you don't think this happened after the argument I saw last night?"

"Who knows?" She reached down and rubbed Oatmeal's ear. "No matter how it happened, I'm concerned."

"Why do you say that?"

"This has always been a friendly town. You can leave your doors open day and night." Ella stood and stared back at the lifeless body. "But now, to see this so close to my house…" It was troubling. And, if it had anybody else but Buck, it would have been downright unnerving.

"But we're safe, aren't we?" Shelby turned to Ella. "I mean, what if you'd taken the dog for a walk and stumbled upon this all by yourself?"

Oatmeal whined and pawed the ground. The wind carried the faint blaring horn from an early morning train passing through town. "I'm just glad I didn't take him to the cemetery this morning," said Ella. "Someone might have thought I had something to do with this."

"Why would you think that?"

Ella jumped up and pointed at the body. "Because the man who killed my husband ends up dead… practically in my backyard."

"But we were in the house all night," said Shelby.

"Until I took Oatmeal out. What if it happened then? What if I get blamed for Buck's murder?"

"El, why are you letting your mind go there? We both know you're not guilty. If we get our stories straight before we call the sheriff, no one will doubt your whereabouts."

Ella groaned. "I have a terrible feeling about this."

Shelby glanced back at the body and grimaced. "Can't we just say we found him? I mean, that's the truth, isn't it?"

The longer they talked, the more Ella concluded she would end up being the prime suspect. Her voice shook. "Shel, promise you'll vouch for me. Tell them you went outside when I did. No, that will sound worse. Tell them… the storm… there was a leak in your room. The rain made a puddle… you spent the night in my room. Oh man, now I'm pulling you into this too."

Shelby patted the bench. "Come sit next to me."

The wood creaked when Ella sat on the edge. She bounced her leg. Warm tears rolled down her cheeks. "Sure, I hated the guy. But…"

Shelby stroked Ella's soft cheek. "El, it will be okay. I'll say whatever you want me to say." She pulled her trembling friend close and caressed her shoulder. "You know I'd do anything for you."

Ella's body relaxed. She managed a smile. "Thanks."

Shelby rested her hand on Ella's thigh and watched Oatmeal run after a twitchy-nosed cottontail. She closed her eyes for a moment, hoping to clear her thoughts. If only she had her pillows. If only she could go back to bed and forget this morning ever happened. They were just supposed to go on a walk together and talk.

Ella cleared her throat. "One of us should probably call the sheriff—"

"Or…" Shelby opened her eyes and squared her shoulders,

"We could go back to the house and pretend we didn't see any of this."

The two women looked at each other and nodded.

Ella snapped her fingers. "Oatmeal, come." The dog looked up and barked at her. "Now." Ella stood and patted her leg as she and Shelby headed back toward the house.

"Just to get our stories straight," said Shelby. "We were never here."

"Sounds good to—" Tires on gravel stopped her. Ella turned and motioned toward the road. She lowered her voice. "We might need to rethink that last part. Looks like someone has already called the sheriff."

CHAPTER SEVENTEEN

Shelby turned and stared as a white patrol car with gradient-green "SHERIFF" letters emblazoned on the door parked just outside the cemetery entrance. Although she'd done nothing wrong, her heart rate quickened. "Now what?"

Ella grabbed her friend's hand. "We say we found the body but didn't have our phones and were headed back to the house to call someone because we didn't want to stay and disturb the crime scene plus we wanted to take Oatmeal back so he wouldn't get in the way…"

"El." Shelby caught Ella's eye. "Take a breath. You're making yourself sound guilty."

They stood and watched as a sheriff's officer exited a patrol car. Shelby rolled her eyes and shoved her balled-up fists in her pockets, trying to ignore the dead body to the left of them and the woman approaching in front of them. Oatmeal strained at the end of his leash, barking. Dawn Nolan hadn't changed since Shelby had last seen her. Blonde hair pulled back in a tight braid. Broad shoulders. Tanned face that reminded Shelby of a ski instructor whose glasses had blocked the sun, leaving her with racoon eyes.

"Morning, Ella. Shelby. We had reports of a barking dog since about…" Dawn pulled out a notepad and referred to it, "Five o'clock this morning." She talked to Shelby and Ella, but didn't take her eyes off Shelby. "Caller thought it was unusual and thought the dog might have been lost or unattended."

Ella shifted her feet. "We, um, came out here for the same reason. I mean, the dog. He kept barking. It was unusual. I mean—" A pair of hummingbirds buzzed over them, then skirting along the top of several broken headstones. Oatmeal watched them flit and hover over his head again.

Dawn gazed at Ella, then back at Shelby. "Something wrong?"

Shelby nodded. Ella pointed. "We think he's… dead." Dawn turned and rushed over to Buck's body.

Though they were only fifteen feet away, Shelby couldn't see what Dawn was doing. Probably a good thing. She imagined Dawn checking his pulse or something just as disgusting. She shuddered at the thought of touching something dead, especially a human being.

Ella tugged on Shelby's sleeve. "I'm going to see what she's doing. You want to come?"

"Are you kidding? I don't like cemeteries. Or dead bodies. And I really don't like cemeteries with dead bodies on top of the ground. I need to sit again."

Ella helped Shelby back over to the rickety bench, then made her way over to where Dawn was crouching.

Dawn looked up at Ella and nodded. She reached up to her collar and pushed the button on her radio mic. "Possible homicide at the Old Pheasant Valley Cemetery. Requesting a coroner and Pheasant Valley PD to the scene."

"Homicide? And the police, too?" asked Ella.

"We have a bit of conundrum."

Shelby's eyes widened. She leaned forward, trying to catch their conversation. Before long, curiosity beat out anxiety. She got up and stood behind Ella. "What do you mean by conundrum?" Shelby asked.

Dawn stood and wrote in her notebook. She checked the time, then added something to it. Before she answered Shelby's "conundrum" question, a black SUV pulled up. It had white doors and roof, and "Pheasant Valley" in bold gold script outlined in blue and "POLICE" in dark blue block letters ran the length of both doors. Radio chatter came from inside the vehicle.

"Copy that." An officer spoke into a microphone as he stepped out of his vehicle. He pulled a dark blue long-sleeved jacket over a short-sleeved blue shirt, then glanced in the side mirror and picked something out of his teeth. Standing at just over six feet with a beefy chest and muscular arms, buzzed chestnut brown hair and dark eyes, Alton Nolan looked nothing like his sister.

Dawn clenched her jaw. "About time."

Alton approached, glaring at Dawn. "I was downtown filling out paperwork on a burglary when dispatch called. Someone broke into the dentist's office on Juneberry sometime last night or early this morning."

"Oh no." Ella caught Alton's eye. "Hope no one was hurt."

Alton folded his arms across his chest. "No victim with a burglary. Only stolen property. You're thinking of a robbery."

"That's good to know. Did they get anything or break into any other businesses?" asked Ella. "My shop is right around the corner from there."

Alton cleared his throat. "Just the one. Someone called it in after they saw a broken window. Probably some kids looking for a cheap high."

"I don't understand," said Ella.

"Only thing missing was a cylinder of nitrous from Parke's office. Second time this year. But enough about that." He walked around Ella and glanced at Shelby. "Heard you were back in town."

Shelby dug her hands deeper into her pockets with such force, they made deep bulges in the knitted sides. Why couldn't this little reunion of sorts have taken place somewhere less intimidating, she wondered. Couldn't anyone see the dead body just feet away from them?

Alton turned his attention to the scene. "What do we have, Sis?"

Dawn tapped a pen on her notebook. "Could you be serious for once?"

"Pardon me, Sarg. What do we have here, Sarg?"

Dawn rolled her eyes and flipped through her notes. "Buck Wilson. Apparent homicide. Blunt force trauma to the back of the head. Note the skin coloring. Been here a few hours at least. Won't know until the coroner arrives and conducts a prelim."

"Have you checked the body?" asked Alton.

"Normally, I would have. But until we figure out jurisdiction, we can't begin the investigation." Dawn pointed to Buck. "Victim is right on the city/county line."

Alton walked over and scanned the area. "Eyeballing it, I'd say more of him is inside the cemetery. County's your jurisdiction."

Dawn marched over to the lifeless body. "His legs are longer than his torso, locating him more on the outside. City's your jurisdiction."

Counting off steps, Alton walked the length of the body inside the cemetery. "One, two, three…"

Dawn groaned. "Are you serious? Where's your measuring tape?"

Alton stopped and glared at her. "I'll bet my accuracy in steps against your flimsy tape measure any day of the week.

Remember when we competed in archery? I was never more than an inch off when I measured in steps."

Dawn tapped her foot. "This is not archery. It's a dead body and a crime scene. One of us needs to begin an investigation before evidence is destroyed. Plus, his wife needs to be notified before we draw a crowd or someone from the newspaper. And neither of us can do until we determine whose—"

"Jurisdiction. Yes, everyone heard you loud and clear." Alton walked around and counted off the steps outside the cemetery. "Body's more inside. I'd bet my ski vacation in Vail this year."

"We'll see about that." Stomping back to her cruiser, Dawn threw open the driver's side door and leaned in. After rummaging around, she emerged, holding up a silver metal tape measure. She slammed the door, then stomped back and glared at Alton again. "Pompous arse. Why must you make everything a competition?"

He folded his arms across his chest and smirked. "Not making this a competition. Just stating a fact. Body is more inside… by at least three inches. If you'd stop being stubborn and agree, we could start questioning witnesses." Alton glanced back at Shelby and Ella. "And suspects."

Pompous arse is right, thought Shelby. She cleared her throat and pointed back to Ella's house. "Too much coffee this morning. Do I need to stick around for this?"

"Yes." Dawn and Alton answered together. Dawn eyed Alton, then Shelby. "We need to question both of you."

Ella poked Shelby in the arm. "Can't you wait a few more minutes? I'm curious to who's right."

"Fine. But after that…"

Dawn handed Alton the end of the tape measure. "Hold it over the top of his back."

Alton winked at Shelby while addressing his sister. "Sure thing, Sarg."

Dawn walked over and measured the distance between the middle of Buck's back to the top of his head. Then she did the same for the distance from his mid-back to his boots. "Humph. The difference was only two inches."

Alton motioned to her. "Who's going to Vail?"

Dawn shoved the tape measure in her pocket and mumbled.

"What's that, Sarg? Didn't catch what you said."

"You are." Dawn said something else under her breath that only her brother could hear. He let out a chuckle and grinned. Shelby could only imagine the smug reaction. Of course, Dawn was no better. There always had to be a winner and a loser with those two. Male versus female. His humor against her seriousness. Or was it the other way around? No matter. One always ended up gloating over the other. Until the next competition.

Shelby held up her hand. "Now that it's settled, I need to visit the ladies' room. Promise I'll be right back." She started toward Ella's house as a white SUV pulled up outside the cemetery. A small white placard adhered to the windshield below the driver's side read "CORONER/TRANSPORT."

Alton held up his hand. "Tell you what, Sarg. Since I'm such a good sport, how about I walk our two eye-witnesses back to the house? That way you can chat with the coroner while I ask questions."

Dawn shook her head. "Since you won the bet, you need to stay here. Once the coroner's done, you can head over to Buck's house with the coroner and notify his wife."

Alton groaned and placed his hands on his hips. "Thanks for giving me the sucky job. I just figured you wouldn't want them to corroborate their stories before you have time to question them."

Shelby clenched her teeth. "What makes you think we'd do that?"

"Everyone in town knows Ella had motive." Alton held his hands up in front of him. "Not saying she did this. But..."

Dawn stopped writing and pointed a finger at her brother. "Alton, that was inappropriate. Ella is not a suspect. Even more reason for me to question her instead of you."

Ella's eyes widened. "Yes, I hated Buck. But not enough to kill him. Besides, there're others who—"

Shelby grabbed Ella's arm. "Maybe you shouldn't say anything else right now."

Ella looked at Shelby, then Alton. "Am I under arrest?"

He looked down at the ground, then at Ella. "No."

Ella turned to Dawn. "Am I under arrest?"

"No, but... I will need to interview you and Shelby."

"Then find us at my home." Ella glared at Alton. "It's too cold out here. And I'm not talking about the weather." She pointed to the group of houses behind the cemetery. "Green and white two-story on Peacock Trail Court. Dawn, you know my car. It will be in the driveway." Ella tugged at Oatmeal's leash and marched away.

Shelby followed, struggling to keep up through the tall brush with a full bladder.

CHAPTER EIGHTEEN

Ella paced around the front room of her home, waiting for the inevitable knock at the door. She probably shouldn't have left the cemetery in such a huff, but after what Alton said, she couldn't even look at him. His words burned in her mind. "Everyone in town knows Ella had motive." Yet, she couldn't deny how much she'd wished Buck dead since he killed her husband. Ella shuddered, remembering the image of Buck's body. Had he been attacked? Did he drink too much and pass out?

Shelby walked into the front room with two steaming cups of chamomile tea. She placed them on the coffee table, then walked with Ella until she stopped pacing. "It's going to be okay," Shelby whispered. "We'll get through this together."

"What if… "

"El. You're going to make yourself crazy with your what-if questions. Let's wait until Dawn gets here." Shelby stroked her friend's back and led her over to the comfy sofa. "Dawn's only going to ask questions. We were eye-witnesses. She needs our statements."

Oatmeal jumped up and snuggled in Ella's lap. She picked up a cup of tea and forced a smile. "Thanks."

Shelby sat on the sofa. "We should both tell Dawn what we know." Telling the truth was the best choice, though in the past it seemed to make everything worse. Images of her parents' flashed through her mind. She understood Ella's fear, but she also knew not telling the truth would only make things much more complicated. Though Shelby trusted Ella, something in the back of her mind nagged at her. How long had Ella really been outside that morning? Did she stay at the house the whole time? Shelby shook off the unanswered questions and took a sip of tea, hoping to hide her fears.

"But… " Ella's voice quivered.

"El, I understand your fear. But, lying won't do either of us any good. The truth is we were together until early this morning, then you went to bed. But don't forget I saw Buck, Hope, and Ben arguing last night." She reached down and stroked Mr. Butterfingers as he rubbed up against her leg. "Something bad must have happened after that."

Ella stared at Shelby, her eyes wide and watery.

Shelby held her friend's trembling hand. "While you might have had a strong motive, they need to prove means and opportunity."

Ella cocked her head. "How do you know all these fancy terms?"

Shelby chuckled. "I've read my fair share of who-dun-its. In fact, years before we met, I was so caught up in a mystery series set in Hawaii, I'd stay up all night trying to figure out who did it before the detective. Seems silly now when I think about it."

"Not silly at all." Ella smiled. "With your amateur expertise, maybe we can figure out what really happened to Buck."

"Expertise? From a bunch of library books I read eons ago.

I highly doubt I can be much help." Shelby walked over to the window and peeked out the curtain. "You notice Buck's truck this morning?"

Ella straightened. "What are you talking about?"

"Remember how I told you it was parked all wonky last night? Well, now it's parallel with the driveway. You hear anyone leave?"

Ella shook her head. "You're the one who loves to spy on our neighbors."

"I'd have sworn it was at an angle before—" Shelby let loose of the curtain, rushed over to the sofa, and plopped on a cushion. Oatmeal stood on the arm of the sofa and barked. Seconds later, several sharp raps came from behind the door.

"Ella? Shelby? It's Dawn Nolan."

"Oatmeal, quiet." Ella placed her cup on the coffee table, then went to the door and opened it. "Good morning, Dawn. Or would you prefer I call you Sergeant, since this is 'official business'." Ella used finger quotes to emphasize her disdain.

"Whatever you prefer. I've known you a long time, Ella. While I am conducting a formal investigation, this is an informal interview. I'm just gathering information." She walked in and glanced at Shelby. "It's really is good to see you, Shel. After the dust settles, we need to get together for coffee and catch up."

Shelby didn't respond.

"What's the next step?" asked Ella.

The petite sheriff glanced around, silently observing the room. An unlit fireplace, though there was a stack of firewood on the hearth and ashes below the grate. Were the brass and iron fireplace tools missing a piece? Spade, tongs, brush… The poker, perhaps? Dawn held her breath and quickly scanned the area. She noticed a fine layer of dust on the tops of the other tools. Half-burned candles of assorted sizes and shapes decorated a stained wooden shelf above the hearth. She made a mental note to ask about the poker and turned toward the women. "Since we're just doing an interview, I'll talk with both of you at the same time. Maybe something one of you says will spark the memory of the other. Then we can get through this and I can get out of here."

Ella motioned to the beige wingback chair next to the sofa. Mr. Butterfingers had already settled in Ella's spot. She could either push him off the cushion or scoot in next to Shelby. Ella opted for the second choice, knowing Shel's comforting touch would help get her through the ordeal. Ella looked at Dawn. "Tea?"

"Maybe later." Dawn removed her jacket. After she sat, she laid the jacket across her lap. She pulled out a pen and small, spiral notebook from her shirt pocket and opened it to a clean page. After clicking the pen a few times, she looked at Ella and Shelby, then made notes. "First, I want to establish a few ground rules. When I ask questions, I want each of you to answer as truthfully as possible. No guessing. I want to know what you remember, not what you think you remember. Got it?"

The two women on the couch looked at each other, then nodded.

"Also, if I address one of you, I'd like the other to wait before interrupting or adding anything." She tucked a strand of hair behind her ear, then tore two pieces of paper from the notebook and handed one to Shelby, then the other to Ella. Digging in her pocket, she retrieved two small pencils, like the ones used to keep score during miniature golf. "If you think of something, write it down so you don't forget. Then we can get back to it later." She locked eyes with Ella. "Shall we get started?"

Ella let out a ragged breath. It was already ten o'clock. She wanted this over with as soon as possible and was relieved Vivian had agreed to open the shop.

"Let's start with the body," said Dawn. "Who found him?"

Ella placed her hand over Shelby's. "I did. We were walking Oatmeal in the cemetery."

"What time was this?"

Ella thought for a moment, mentally calculating the time frame from when she woke up until they left for the walk. "Maybe eight?"

"I need you to be sure. Was it seven forty-five, eight, eight-fifteen?"

Ella looked at Shelby. "Eight-fifteen?"

Shelby nodded.

"Ella," said Dawn. "Describe what Buck looked like when you found him."

Ella gave Dawn the best description of Buck as she could remember, even down to the mottled bluish-purple skin and gray fingernails.

Dawn made several notes, then turned to Shelby. "Did you notice anything different? Hear anything?"

"No." Shelby cleared her throat. "Didn't get close enough to get a real good look at the body. Me and dead bodies…" She shuddered.

Dawn smiled. "Got it. But, just in case. Think about it for a minute. From where you were, did you notice anything else?"

After a few seconds, Shelby snapped her finger. "His head. It was resting near a headstone. Maybe he fell."

"Are you speculating or know for sure? Do you understand the difference?"

"Sorry." Shelby averted her eyes. "Guess that was speculating."

"Did either of you notice anything around the body?"

Ella looked up, closed one eye, and thought for a moment. "Only what I've already mentioned."

Dawn watched Ella's facial reactions and waited. "I'd like both of you to close your eyes and revisit the scene. Do you see anything around the body? Anything out of place? Footprints?"

"No footprints. The grass was mostly dead. Hold on… I remember something…" Shelby kept her eyes closed and moved her hands in front of her, like she was fashioning the abstract into more concrete images in her mind. "It wasn't near the body. It was under the bench I sat on. At first I didn't give it a second thought, but…"

As they waited, Ella focused on how Mr. Butterfinger's soft snoring contrasted with the harsh ticking of the clock counting off the seconds. She stared at Shelby, willing her to remember.

Shelby's eyes popped open. "A long-necked, empty bottle in a paper bag. The label was torn… it was black or red. Beer? Maybe something else. It was under the bench."

Dawn scribbled as Shelby talked. "What made it stand out?"

Shelby chewed on her bottom lip. "Everything else was covered with dust and raindrops. But the bag… it was wrinkled. No water drops. Like someone had just finished it and tossed it under the bench after the rain stopped."

"Speculation?" asked Dawn.

"Kinda, but not really. When I got up from the bench, my pants were damp and dusty. Yet, the bag wasn't wet or dusty." Shelby smiled. "Do you think it's important?"

"Everything that can help us determine what might have happened is important. Give me a moment. I need to call a deputy to recover the evidence and have it dusted for prints." Dawn pushed the button on her lapel microphone and made the request. She turned back and smiled. "Good job, Shelby. Now, let's refocus for a minute." Dawn watched Ella. "When was the last time you used your fireplace?"

Ella put her hand to her mouth. "I don't know. This past spring? Maybe even longer. Birds made a nest in the chimney. I didn't have the money to have someone come out and clean it. So it hasn't been lit it in a while. Why do you ask?"

Dawn waited.

Ella struggled to take in a deep breath. "I do still light the candles in the evenings, sometimes. The glow helps me relax. But this shouldn't have anything to do with Buck's murder. Should it?"

Dawn stood and went over to the fireplace. "What happened to the other tool?" She turned and stared at Ella.

Ella crossed her legs, then uncrossed them. She stuttered, then regained her composure. "Other tool? What are you talking about? I bought the set at a yard sale years ago. It only came with what you see there."

Dawn tapped her fingernails on the polished wooden shelf. She moved one candle to the side and noticed a fine layer of dust around it. She smiled, then went back to her chair and sat down. "Let's talk motive. Can either of you think of anyone who might hate Buck enough to kill him?"

Ella rubbed her eyes and whispered to Shelby. "This might take a while."

CHAPTER NINETEEN

Shelby shifted on the couch. Her mind raced. A lot of people hated Buck besides Ella. But enough to kill him? "How much time do you have?"

Dawn frowned. "I'm sorry?"

Ella placed her hand on Shelby's arm. "I think she means there were more than a few people who were upset at Buck."

Dawn tapped her pen against the spiral notebook. "I only need names and why you thought of them. That will give me a list of suspects to interview."

Ella bristled. "You mean like what you're doing now?"

The tension in Ella's voice caused Shelby's stomach to flinch. She wondered why Dawn hadn't brought up Alton's accusation. Was she waiting to catch them off guard?

As Dawn flipped to a new page, her stomach growled. She rubbed her hand across her shirt. Her eyes focused on Shelby's hands knotting and unknotting a piece of loose yarn dangling from her pink sweater.

Shelby noticed. The room closed in. There wasn't enough air. She jumped up, startling the animals. "You sure I can't get us some snacks? Breakfast was hours ago. Maybe crackers? Or fruit?"

Ella caught Shelby's eye. "I could go for a muffin with the Purcell's apple butter. What about you, Dawn?"

She smiled and attached the pen to her notebook cover. "That would be great. Tea too, if you don't mind."

"No problem. Be right back." Thank goodness, thought Shelby rushing into the kitchen. She needed a break. Even though it was only minutes, it seemed like they'd been talking for hours. And, most likely, still had a way to go. Filling the kettle with water, she tried to listen as Dawn and Ella chatted, but couldn't make out what they were saying.

AFTER EVERYTHING that had happened with Mac, seeing Dawn again confused Shelby. Dawn looked great and while Shelby wasn't looking for anything with her, she still had a thing for dimples and blue eyes. Memories, and regrets, of a clandestine encounter flooded back.

With Mac taking extra shifts for months, Shelby had driven up to Pheasant Valley to stay with Ella and enjoy the cooler summer weather while working on her clothing line designs. One afternoon, Dawn stopped by after work to show off her new patrol car.

"I'm off-duty," she said. "Wanna ride?"

"I've never been in a sheriff's car before. Why not?" Shelby sat in the front seat and asked about the fancy gadgets as Dawn drove them a few miles west of town to Ladybug Lake. After answering all of Shelby's questions, they stood on the shore watching the sunset. Caught up in the moment, Dawn kissed Shelby. Once. Twice. Shelby returned the affection, then regretted it, demanding Dawn take her back to Ella's. Afterward, Shelby pretended it never happened. Deep down, she knew things weren't right between her and Mac and wondered why it wasn't clearer until after they'd moved away?

Dawn stood, placing her notebook on her jacket. She stretched her arms over her head and cracked her neck. Walking over to the front window, she pulled the curtain aside and stared outside. Turning back, she smiled. "Delightful house, Ella. Don't think I've ever been inside."

"Thank you. No, probably not."

Dawn walked across the length of the front room and stopped next to the stairs. She looked up. "Three bedrooms? Or, four?"

"Three. One down, two upstairs." Ella cleared her throat. "Shel… You need any help?"

Shelby appeared at the doorway from the kitchen. "No, just waiting for the water to boil. Be there in a sec."

Ella squared her shoulders. "Shelby should tell you about the argument from last night."

Dawn went back to the couch and sat. "What argument?"

"Let's wait for her to tell you the details." Ella stroked her dog's ears, willing herself to stay calm.

Shelby entered the front room carrying a tray of muffins, apple butter, a variety of tea bags, spoons, and napkins. "Let me get the teapot and we can get started again." She wiped perspiration from her upper lip and shook off the memories of her and Dawn. Had Dawn thought about their kisses? Was she thinking about them now? It didn't matter. Shelby needed to be strong for Ella and put the past behind her. She forced a smile, came back, and sat.

"Thanks, Shel." Dawn poured herself a cup and dunked a cranberry tea bag in it several times. "Appreciate the hospitality." She took a napkin and a muffin, then set them on the jacket draped over her lap. "Ella was just telling me about an argument you witnessed last night."

Shelby glanced at Ella, then spoke. "It appeared to be an argument. I mean, I couldn't hear anything, but…"

"Tell me what, and who, you saw." Dawn picked up her pen again and waited.

Shelby explained her observation of Buck, Hope, and Ben's animated conversation. "There was lots of arm waving and finger-pointing." She took a sip of tea, then spread a spoonful of the cinnamon-apple spread on her muffin.

"And what did you hear?" Dawn asked between bites.

"Nothing. And to be honest, I only watched them for a few minutes. I was afraid someone might see me. Plus, my jaw was still sore."

Dawn looked up from her notebook. "Your jaw? I'm not sure I understand."

Shelby patted her cheek. "I'd been to the dentist… fillings. And so had Buck."

"What was that last part?"

Shelby sipped her tea. "I ran into Buck at Doctor Parke's office yesterday. I mean, I literally ran into him. He was all woozy after a dental procedure and bumped into me when I walked into the office." She stopped and licked a blob of apple spread off her finger. "He'd had nitrous and dropped his backpack. I gave it back to him."

"Do you think he recognized you," asked Dawn.

"He was stumbling around. The nurse had to help him because he could barely walk. I have no idea how he even drove home in that condition."

"What happened to Buck later?" Dawn finished the last of her muffin, waiting on Shelby's response.

"Dunno. They took me back for my appointment. When I finished, I just wanted to get out of there. Guess he got home somehow."

Dawn looked up from her notebook. "We're crossing over that speculation line again, aren't we?"

Shelby nodded.

Dawn underlined, or crossed out something, then made notes as she finished the muffin. "So, to recap. Buck was at the dentist. Had a procedure and was unsteady. Then the next time you saw him he was arguing with his wife, Hope. And friend, Ben?"

Shelby wiped her mouth with a napkin. "That was the last time I saw him. Until this morning."

"Ella, anything to add?"

She turned toward Dawn. "Not about Buck. But I remembered something about Paige and Hope."

"Okay, let me finish up these notes."

Shelby grabbed another muffin and covered it in apple butter, then poured enough water to fill her cup. She dropped an orange-spice tea bag in and let it steep. She pointed to Ella's cup. "More tea?"

Ella nodded.

"Dawn?"

Dawn picked up her cup and held it closer to Shelby. "Yes. Please."

Shelby swallowed and stared at Dawn's cup while filling it with boiling water.

Dawn set the cup down, not taking her eyes off Shelby. "Let's talk about Paige… remind me of her last name?"

"Melton," said Ella. "She works at the Corner Café."

Dawn nodded. "Yes. Thanks. Okay, tell me what you saw."

Ella recounted the intimate scene between Buck and Paige on the sidewalk outside The Bee's Knees, then how Hope stormed in and made threatening remarks about what she would do if she caught them together.

Dawn looked up; her expression unchanged. "Anything else?"

"Yes," said Ella. "After my therapy appointment, I overheard Paige talking on her phone. She was real upset."

"Do you know who she was talking with?"

"Not exactly, but after she hung up, she threatened to 'make them pay' if they didn't leave their wife by Friday… Oh my gosh, that's today."

"What do you think that means?"

Ella held back a smile. Was Dawn asking her to speculate? Ella used her hand to make a gun, with a trigger finger to demonstrate. "She referred to a hunting poster at the sporting goods store and made that motion."

Dawn turned the page and continued writing. "Thank you." She looked up at both women, her face serious. She cracked her neck again before continuing, then focused on Ella. "As much as I'd like to ignore Alton's accusation…"

Shelby let out a small gasp. Oh no, here it comes.

"You said you hated Buck."

Ella shifted her position on the couch. Oatmeal jumped down and settled on the floor by her feet.

"Yes. After he killed Doug. I… But I'd never…" Her voice faltered. She paused and looked down at her hands.

"I'm sorry, Ella. You know I must question everything. I'll give you a moment." Dawn turned and gazed at Shelby. "Which reminds me. You and Buck had an altercation a few years ago, didn't you?"

Shelby nodded but said nothing.

Dawn eyed Ella. "Might as well get to tough questions. Ella, where were you this morning, between three and seven o'clock am?"

"Sleeping. But then I took the dog out. He… he wouldn't stop barking."

Dawn tapped her pen on the pad. "About what time was that?"

Ella glanced up at the clock on the wall. “Before six. It was still dark.”

“And then what did you do?” Dawn asked.

“I went back to bed.”

Dawn raised an eyebrow. Her piercing blue eyes focused on Shelby.

“I… I was sleeping,” said Shelby. “The whole time.”

Dawn made more notes. “Can either of you vouch for the other’s whereabouts?”

Ella and Shelby looked at each other and shook their heads.

Dawn let out a long sigh. “Darn.”

CHAPTER TWENTY

Ella closed the front door behind Dawn and rested her head against the smooth oak surface. "I need a nap. Or a drink, then a nap."

"You aren't kidding. That was intense."

"You think they've told Buck's wife by now?" asked Ella.

"Probably. Let's hope the coroner did all the talking. I'm sure she had more compassion than Alton. Geeze, what an idiot."

Ella walked over to the sofa, sat, and drew her knees up to her chest. "We should have vouched for each other. They think I'm a prime suspect."

Shelby sat and patted Ella's arm. "No more motive than any of the rest of us. Especially after that argument." She motioned toward the side window. "I still say that truck was in a different place than it was last night."

"I guess we won't know more until they have autopsy results."

Shelby leaned against the back of the couch. "You going into the shop today?"

"I should, but under the circumstances… I don't know." Ella rubbed her eyes. "Once Hope and Paige get wind of this, all heck is going to break loose. I don't want to be anywhere near them if they go blaming each other." She sat up and pulled out her cell. "I need to call Viv to make sure everything's okay."

Shelby stood and gathered the empty cups, crumpled napkins, and leftover muffins on the tray and took them into the kitchen. She made another trip for the teapot and silverware.

"Viv, how's it going down there? I'm thinking about staying home… Yes, we found the body… It's a terrible shame… How did you hear? Oh, I suppose word gets around fast."

Shelby came back and stood behind the wingback chair. "You want me to leave you alone?"

Ella cupped her hand over the mic. "No, you're fine." She resumed her call with Vivian. "Laura and Gladys make it in okay? That's good. What about this afternoon, will you have enough help?... The break in at the dentist's office?… Yes, I heard about it. On second thought, I should come in to make sure everything is secure… We'll close early. I'll bring Shelby if she's up to coming with…"

Shelby gave an exaggerated nod.

Ella glanced at the clock. "It's past eleven. Let's say close to noon. Can you stay that long?... What about Laura and Gladys? Sure, I'll hold on…" She held the phone away from her mouth and smiled at Shelby. "Sure you're okay coming into town with me? I just thought the company would be good for the both of us… Yes, Viv. I'm still here. They'll stay until one. That's great. Thanks so much… We'll see you shortly. Goodbye."

Shelby sat and shifted in the chair. "Why go in, especially if Paige will be in later?"

"Viv said Paige called and cancelled her shift. I need to boost morale. Not good for the owner to stay away during a crisis. And maybe… you can do some sleuthing while we're there. You know, nose around a bit. See if anyone heard about Parke's break in."

"Moi?" Shelby pointed to herself, then snorted.

"Yes, you." Ella chuckled. "Such a goofball." She got up and walked into the kitchen. "I need a quick snack, then we can go. You hungry?"

"After all those muffins? I need to go upstairs and change into my stretchy pants. Be right back."

Shelby ambled up the stairs as Ella cracked a boiled egg, sprinkled a dash of salt and pepper on it, and took a bite. She turned around to four eyes staring at her. "Yes, you both can have some too." She pinched off a tiny piece of egg white and fed it to Oatmeal. Then did the same for Mr. Butterfingers. After popping the last bite in her mouth, she faced them with open hands. "All gone."

Shelby walked into the kitchen and laughed. "They begging again?"

"What else is new? We eat. They eat. It's the universal law of having pets." Ella walked over to the sink and washed her hands. "Probably should put on lipstick and blush. Be right back."

On the way to her room, Ella thought about the conversation they were to have before everything got crazy. Somehow it was easier talking about feelings while walking the dog. Now, she wasn't so sure. After using the bathroom, she checked her face in the mirror. Not as bad as expected, although a bit pale. Who wouldn't be after finding a dead body? Then being accused? She shook her head. Don't go there, Ella. She sniffed her underarms. Still fresh. Gargled. Egg breath was the worst. Ran a brush through her hair. Lookin' good. Then turned and walked down the short hall into the kitchen.

Shelby and the animals waited at the back door. "No. This time y'all are staying home and I get to go bye-bye." They stared at her with sad, soulful eyes. "And don't go making me feel bad for leaving."

As the women walked down the driveway, Ella noticed a sheriff's car parked at Buck's house. After backing out, they drove past the south end of the cemetery. Yellow tape cordoned off the area around the entrance. Outside, a few county vehicles sat parked. "Unreal, isn't it?"

Shelby stared ahead. "I feel bad for Hope."

"At least she's got Ben there with her."

She glanced at Ella and gasped. "You said Ben and Hope might have had a thing going on. Do you think…?"

"I don't want to even hazard a guess."

"What did you say he'd been in prison for?" asked Shelby.

Ella slowed down and waited behind two cars at the four-way-stop. "Don't remember. But, it had to be something significant. They house the death row inmates there."

"So it could have been for a violent crime?"

Ella nodded. "But he served his time and got out. Never caused trouble."

"You know…" Shelby slapped her pant leg. "He had motive. And means. And opportunity."

Pulling into the parking lot, Ella parked and looked at Shelby. "Still speculating?"

Shelby rolled her eyes. "Now you sound like Dawn. Just going over new ideas. It helps me get into my sleuthing mode." She got out and closed the door, then shoved her hands into her pockets. "Wind really picked up."

Ella wrapped a scarf around her neck and shivered. "À propos for how everyone must feel today." Walking across the lot, she waved to a young woman pushing a child in a stroller along the sidewalk. Several crows flew low and landed in the middle of the street. They picked at something, then flew off again. As the women rounded the corner and prepared to open the front door, Ella turned to Shelby. "Let's hope coming in was a good idea. Don't think I can deal with any more surprises today."

CHAPTER TWENTY-ONE

The comforting familiarity of The Bee's Knees greeted Ella and Shelby when they walked into the shop. Gladys stopped stocking her booth and headed toward the women, her large-brimmed hat flopping like bird wings. She pulled them into a close hug. "Oh, goodness. So sorry about your terrible morning." Her thick, heady-scented perfume hung in the air. For a moment Shelby was back at her grandma's house. Granny Marie wore a similar scent. It always made Shelby's eyes water as Granny bear-hugged her when the family visited. She smiled, remembering how kind the older woman was, especially to Shelby when she came out to her family. Granny said, "I love you for being you." She only wished her parents had shown the same compassion.

"Thank you, Gladys." Shelby stepped back and wiped her eyes. Ella eased out of the tight embrace and nodded.

"Just making sure you ladies are okay. Don't know what I'd have done…" She patted their shoulders and returned to her booth.

Laura hurried over with sprigs of lavender in each hand. Her long, flowing shirt floated around her her a soft cloud. She waved the dried flowers over Ella's head. "This should ward off all the bad karma. Inhale, sweetie." Then she turned and did the same for Shelby.

Ella looked at Shelby, then Laura. "Thank—"

"No talking," Laura whispered. "Just concentrate on breathing." She fluttered the lavender around them. "In. Out. Again. Your auras are murky right now. Let's chase away those negative, fearful thoughts."

While Shelby didn't believe in the aura analysis, she felt better listening to Laura's calming voice. Plus the lavender helped take away the odor of Gladys' lingering perfume.

"Ah yes. Positive energy is returning…" Mumbling something about being grounded, she moved her hands above Ella's shoulders, then Shelby's and handed them sprigs of dried flowers. "Place a pinch of petals close to your heart, the rest in your pockets. Don't forget to leave some under your pillows. It will bring calming dreams." She smiled and hugged the women, then set off back to her booth. A few moments later she returned with a basket of lavender soaps, oils, and bath salts. "I'm taking this to Hope's home later this afternoon. I'm sure she could use the company and calming scents. Ella, would you like to come with?"

Ella put her hands up. "I don't know if I'm up to it today. Shelby?" She turned and stared at her with wide eyes. "Maybe you can go with Laura. I'm sure Hope would be happy to see you. And maybe… chat a bit?"

Laura placed her warm hands around Shelby's. "I've got a few more things to do before heading home. Let me know what you decide, sweetie." She turned and hurried away.

While Shelby cleared her throat and tried to come up with an excuse, Ella leaned in close. "You should go. It would give you time to, you know, s-l-e-u-t-h."

She frowned at Ella. "Why are you spelling it out?"

Ella shrugged. "I don't know. In case someone was listening?"

"Like who, El? That toddler in the stroller?"

Gladys came back, wiping her hands on her olive-green pants. She pulled a tissue from her bra and dabbed her nose. Then, tucking it back inside, she leaned close to the women. "Should we check around to make sure nothing's missing from the shop? From what I heard, those thieves took a few things from the dentist's office."

Ella squared her shoulders. "Like what? I thought it was just a bunch of kids that broke in for the nitrous."

"Police scanner said a cylinder and cash were missing. And they ransacked a file cabinet."

"Gladys, since when have you listened to a police scanner?" asked Shelby.

"Ed has always had one. It started as a hobby. But later when he couldn't sleep, he'd go in the den and listen. Keeps him out of my hair." She smiled. "I paid it no never mind, 'til now that is."

Ella folded her arms across her chest. "What do you mean?"

"Well," Gladys lowered her voice. "This morning Ed came into the bedroom as I was getting up. You know we get up early on the farm. Well, I'm heading to the little girl's room, and Ed knocks on the bathroom door telling me to hurry and come down to have a listen. Well, you know how it is. I can't do anything until I've, you know, tinkled. But, afterwards, I followed him down to the den and had a listen to all that chatter. Most of it was numbers and codes, but 'ol Ed, he has a deciphering book. Well, he'd written a few codes and showed me. Sure enough, a break-in at Doctor Parke's. Cash and N-O-2 taken… that's the nitrous." She smiled, proud as a peacock. "And they said cash, plus a file cabinet had been… well, I already told you that."

Shelby held the lavender sprigs up to her nose and stepped back from Gladys. "And what else did you hear?"

"Normal chatter. You know you can hear all kinds of stuff on those radios. Bakersfield PD, Pheasant Valley PD, CHP, Sheriff… But then…" She raised her voice and both women jumped. "A call came over the radio about the disturbance at the old cemetery. They didn't say it that way, but Ed translated the ten-codes to English."

Shelby looked at Ella. "Ten-codes?"

Ella shrugged.

"You know. Those police-talk codes. So us citizens can't figure out what's going on. But Ed said it was more than a disturbance. It was a dead body. And that's how we all knew that something bad had happened. I tried to call you, but you didn't answer."

"Oh, Gladys," said Ella. "I'd left my cell at the house when Shelby and I took Oatmeal for a walk. Sorry I gave you cause for concern."

Gladys patted Ella's hand. "Once you called and talked to Vivian, we all felt better."

Ella rubbed her eyes, the overpowering cologne getting to her. "This has been a long morning for everyone. Let's each walk a section of the shop to make sure everything is all right." She pointed to different areas and assigned tasks to Vivian, Laura, Gladys, and Shelby. "If we all work together, we can close up early and be out of here."

As they went to their designated areas, the front door to the shop opened, then closed again. Shelby continued looking around, though she wasn't sure what to look for. But, to ease Ella's (and Gladys') mind, she'd do everything possible to help.

Shelby stopped in front of her future booth of hand-designed clothing for big women. She glanced at the empty shelves. So much had happened since the last time she sketched out ideas. Losing the babies left her empty. The breakup with

Mac left her broken. She wanted to come back and start fresh, hoping the safe environment would spark creativity. But seeing Dawn brought back painful memories.

"Shelby?" Ella stood next to her. "You okay?"

She cleared her throat. "Just thinking about my booth."

"That reminds, me. I need to talk to you about something important. Maybe later this afternoon when you come back from Hope's house."

"Don't remind me." Shelby shuddered. "Why do I always get roped into these situations? I have no idea what to say."

"Listening is best." Ella smiled and took her hand. "You have a wonderful way with people."

"Yeah, between my listening and 's-l-e-u-t-h-i-n-g' abilities."

They walked back to the counter together. While waiting for the others, Shelby glanced at her phone. "Almost twelve-thirty. You said you wanted to close early, right?"

"I'd rather, considering what happened." When everyone came back to the front and reported nothing unusual, Ella thanked them for coming in. "I'll be in first thing in the morning," she said. "Hopefully, tomorrow will be much better."

Laura walked up to Shelby as they were leaving the shop. "If it's okay with you, hon, I'll come by in a few hours. Let's say two-ish."

Shelby gave a thumbs-up to Laura while everyone walked out the door and Ella locked up. Making their way across the parking lot to Ella's car, she unlocked the passenger side door for Shelby. She got in but stared at a long, white envelope with ELLA hand-written in block letters laying on the dash.

"What's that?" asked Ella.

"Someone must have slipped it through the top of the window." She handed it to her friend.

Ella opened it and removed a piece of green copy paper. After reading the typed note to herself, she looked at Shelby.

"What?"

"It says, 'It's not what you think. He was never the one'." Ella looked at Shelby, then at the paper. "What the heck is that supposed to mean?"

CHAPTER TWENTY-TWO

Ella sat in the car and buckled her seatbelt. "Who was 'never the one'?" She handed the letter to Shelby. "Can you make any sense of it?"

She turned it over and shook her head. "Someone might want to tell you something. But who? And why?"

A crow cawing overheard made Ella turn. Her eyes caught sight of the paperwork from Jasmine in the back seat.

Shelby followed Ella's gaze. "Where did that come from?"

"My therapist. She gave them to me a few days ago." Ella jumped out of the car and retrieved the papers from the back and got back in.

Shelby held Ella's letter beside the green papers. "Same copy paper," she said. "But wouldn't that be too obvious? Why would someone leave a cryptic note on paper that could be traced back to them?" She rubbed both papers between her thumb and fingers. "Is Jasmine the only one using green copy paper?"

"She said she bought three cases."

Shelby examined the paperwork from Ella's therapist

alongside the strange message. "If we could find out who else has this paper, then we might narrow down a list of people who could have left this in your car." She paused for a moment. "Though, we can't go around town and take a poll of what color copy paper they prefer to use."

"I agree," said Ella. "Didn't you say you had to go back to the dentist for another filling?"

She winced. "Yes. I suppose."

"You can use that time to do some snooping, I mean sleuthing." She laughed. "I need to see Jasmine again next week. I'll tell her I need green paper… for the shop."

"Might be a long shot, but at this point we have to start somewhere." Shelby reached into her pocket and pulled out her sprig of lavender. "Do you think we should tell anyone else about this? Like Dawn."

"Good heavens, no." Ella started the car and rested her hand on the shifter. "I'd prefer to keep this to ourselves. Speaking of Dawn…" She backed out and pulled onto the street. "You should take her up on that offer to go out for coffee. You could ask about the investigation. Or how Buck died."

Shelby sighed. "I'll think about it."

Ella slowed and stopped at the four-way crossing. "If we're going to fish around for clues, we need to cast our lines out for all possibilities of information."

Shelby chuckled. "Look at you and your fishing analogies."

"Thank you. My college English professor would be proud." Ella smiled as she accelerated through the intersection. "Back to Dawn. Being her friend might prove useful."

"Suppose you're right. I just hate using her like that."

"She invited you for coffee," said Ella. "You'll have to talk about something. Why not her big case?"

Shelby stared out the window. Why Dawn? She was the last

person Shelby wanted to confront, besides Mac. She turned. "Other than Dawn, who else should we talk with?"

"For starters, Hope and Ben. They were probably the last ones to see Buck alive."

"Got that covered this afternoon, thanks to you."

Ella snapped her fingers. "And Gladys. And Ed. She said they wanted you to come by for lunch or something. I bet Ed would love to show you all his radios and tell you about those infamous ten-codes."

"That might be fun. We could both go and gather clues."

"Don't forget Paige," said Ella. "Someone should talk to her."

Shelby patted Ella's arm. "I might have a hankering for some of that macaroni and cheese."

"Don't forget the pie."

Shelby laughed. "Of course."

The car followed the curve in the road and they came to the corner of the old cemetery. Though all the city and county cars were gone, the yellow tape reminded Ella of that morning's findings. She turned into the cul-de-sac and pulled up into her gravel driveway. Getting out, Ella glanced at Buck's house. No sheriff's car there either. She grabbed the green papers, then locked the car door and shivered. The wind whipped around the women. The pine trees swayed, dropping needles as gusts raced through.

Shelby pulled her sweater closer. "That wind goes right though you."

Ella pointed at the sky. "Another storm coming in. By the looks of those clouds and the feel of the air, it might snow." Tromping up the wooden steps, they heard yips and scratches coming from behind the door.

"Looks like someone's glad we're home," said Shelby.

Ella unlocked the door. Oatmeal ran out to greet them,

yipping and whining. Mr. Butterfingers meowed and stretched his front leg forward as if to wave and say 'hello.'

Shelby walked inside and crouched down so she was eye-to-eye with their pets. "Oh, you poor neglected babies." Steadying herself against the couch, she scratched the cat behind his ear. The white mop of a dog nudged in closer and got a back rub. "Bet you're both starving."

Satisfied with his back rub, Oatmeal ran around Ella, barking. "Just a poor puppy dog, aren't you?" She patted him on the head. "Better get treats before you're too weak to beg." She dropped the paperwork and keys on the kitchen table, then walked into the mudroom and hung up her coat and scarf. "What time is Laura coming over?"

Shelby glanced at the clock. "About an hour." She pulled the lavender sprigs from her sweater pocket and laid them next to the papers. "Suppose I should eat something."

"I've just the thing." Ella walked over to the refrigerator and opened the door. "What sounds good? Turkey? Pastrami? Roast? What about some cheese? Swiss, Provolone, or cheddar?"

"Yes." She took the food from Ella and placed it on the counter. "And mustard. Mayo. Oh, and those little pickles."

Ella handed Shelby the condiments and grabbed a head of lettuce. "I think that's about it. Oh, and the French bread."

Shelby looked back with a sheepish grin. "Found that the other day. Nothing better than a thick toasted slice slathered with butter." She retrieved the bread and a few knives, along with plates and glassware.

They made sandwiches and concentrated on eating, though both focused on their own thoughts. Shelby wondered what she'd say to Hope. Ella wondered about the mysterious message. Every so often the women would stir from their thoughts when a small paw would touch them. One or both animals would be there, staring up with wide, hopeful eyes.

Being soft-hearted pet-moms, they'd drop tiny pieces of meat or bread.

Ella looked up and noticed Shelby's faraway look. "You doing okay?"

"Thinking about Hope. And practicing my listening skills." She popped the last of her sandwich in her mouth.

Ella glanced around the kitchen, then settled on the ticking clock. One-thirty. She wanted to chat with Shelby and hated to put it off. Would a half-hour be enough time? She walked over and gripped the counter for support, then turned and faced her friend.

"You know…" said Shelby.

"Shel…" blurted Ella.

Talking together, they stopped and laughed.

They pointed to each other. "You go first." More nervous laughter. Ella walked over to the table and sat.

Shelby's eyes sparkled. She pointed to Ella. "You go first. Mine can wait."

Ella's voice caught. The clock ticked. The cat snored. She glanced away for a moment. When she looked back, her eyes caught Shelby's. "I know things have been tough." She paused again to remember the words she planned to say earlier. They sounded perfect in her head. I care about you. And feel you care about me. Why was it so hard for her to say them out loud? Ella picked up a piece of bread crust and squished it between her fingers.

"Ella. I—," said Shelby.

Ella held up her hand. "Let me keep going or I'll never get this out." She squared her shoulders. "Doug's been gone for two years. I've been so lonely." She bit her lip. "Since you've come back… I'm… better. I don't know a lot right now. But I know I don't want you to leave."

Shelby opened her mouth but said nothing.

Ella stood and paced. Somehow all the words she had

practiced before disappeared. Her brain grasped at phrases, but everything seemed jumbled and out of place. My feelings for you are strong… I care for you… Though she knew what to say, she could only manage, "You're a special friend."

"I care about you too."

Ella smiled, then continued to pace. Her thoughts raced. What if she told Shelby she might be… could be interested…? But if Shelby felt differently… Ella couldn't handle Shelby leaving again.

"El." Shelby's soft voice made Ella stop. "Something else you wanted to say?"

"This was much easier this morning."

"What was easier?"

"Talking. Outside on the walk." She sighed while her brain spiraled again. Ella, you're an old lady with stupid feelings. Stop kidding yourself. She stood behind her chair and gripped the back rails. A tear rolled down her cheek, but she didn't bother to brush it away. She felt it plop on her sweater.

"It's okay, El," whispered Shelby. "If it will help, we can go on another walk." She stood behind Ella and wrapped her warm hands around her friend's shoulders.

Ella exhaled as the tension left her body.

"El. I'm not leaving."

Ella turned. "I'm happy to hear—"

Oatmeal jumped up from under the table and ran into the front room. Several loud knocks came from behind the door. Ella looked up at the clock. "Must be Laura."

Shelby stepped back. "I need to grab something from upstairs. Please tell her I'll be down in a jiffy."

"Quiet, Oatmeal," said Ella. She went into the front room and opened the front door.

Laura stood on the porch. She held up a basket of lavender luxuries from the shop. "Shelby ready?"

Ella nodded and opened the screen door. Just as she was

about to close it, a car pulled into the driveway. A door slammed. Heavy footsteps crunched on the gravel.

Dawn Nolan walked up the steps and stared at Ella. She reached out and grabbed the frame. "Sorry to stop by without calling first. I have more questions."

CHAPTER TWENTY-THREE

Before heading downstairs, Shelby looked in the bedroom mirror. If they would just take it slow, everything would be okay. Right? She shook her head. Who was she kidding? She was never good at positive-self talk. Maybe encouraging other people, but never good at convincing herself. As far as she knew, everything with Ella could blow up in her face. But then what? She closed her eyes, willing herself to stop overthinking.

"Shel…?" Ella's voice came from downstairs. "Laura's waiting."

Shelby shook off the negative thoughts and tromped down the stairs. Ella, Laura, and Dawn stood in a corner of the front room talking in hushed tones.

Ella's wide eyes met Shelby's.

"Everything okay?" asked Shelby, though not sure she wanted to know the answer.

Laura turned, her long-tailed cotton blouse billowing around her. "I feel tension in this room." She moved closer to Ella. "Here… and here," she said, pointing to Dawn.

Dawn squared her shoulders. “I came by to chat with Ella. Official business. Where can we go for privacy?”

“Shelby and I were just leaving,” said Laura.

Shelby stared at Ella. “You need me to stay?”

Ella’s voice tensed, but she feigned a smile. “We’re good. You two go ahead.”

Dawn folded her arms across her chest as Shelby walked past.

Laura pointed to the basket. “Just taking a gift of calming to Hope. Poor dear. She must be beside herself.”

“Nice gesture,” said Dawn. “I’m sure she’ll appreciate the support.

Shelby felt Dawn’s eyes watching as she walked out the door. She pretended not to notice, but since her face felt flushed, she could only imagine what Dawn might be thinking.

As Laura and Shelby walked down the front porch steps, a small kit fox scampered across the lawn chasing something furry. Radio chatter came from Dawn’s patrol car, though Shelby couldn’t make out the words. A brisk wind tugged at her sweater. She shuddered at the thought of Ella facing Dawn by herself. Shelby clenched her fists, but determined herself to refocus.

Shelby followed Laura across Hope’s unkept lawn, watching her steps as they made their way over patches of dirt and dried, overgrown weeds. Gopher mounds and the inevitable gopher holes complicated their path. Making it to the front steps unscathed, Shelby noticed a broken terra cotta pot on the top step. Dead, leafless stems poked out of the dry soil along with faded cigarette butts. A sun-damaged wooden bench with a brick under one leg leaned against one corner. Patches of white paint peeled up along the edges of the exterior walls. A rusty nail held the oxidized wire of a washed-out, wooden welcome sign.

Shelby stomped her pink sneakers on a thin doormat as

Laura rang the doorbell. A faint ding-dong-ding came from behind the door. As they waited, she glanced at Laura and smiled. Laura smiled back, then rang the bell a second time.

Voices, male, and female, became louder. "Who's there?" The door opened about a foot and Hope stared out through a filthy screen door. "What do you want?"

Shelby's throat tightened. She glanced at Laura.

"Hope, dear. It's your neighbors. Laura Vega from the corner house, and Shelby, from next door. We brought you a condolence basket."

"A what basket?" Hope turned and blew her nose, then opened the screen door and scrutinized the women. "Give me a minute." She turned and whispered something to someone behind her. Footsteps faded, then Hope opened the creaky door and motioned for them to come in.

Laura stepped through the doorway first. "Hope, we've brought you homemade lavender soaps and other things to help bring calm."

Hope placed her hands on her hips. "House is a mess. I haven't had time to clean."

An icy chill hit Shelby as fish and onion odors assaulted her nostrils. Someone should open a window to get rid of the smell. She inhaled through her mouth, but still tasted the odors, making it worse. Water-stained boxes, piled on more boxes, lined the walls of the front room and hall. Everywhere Shelby turned she saw containers, many of them teetering on stacks taller than the top of her head. In one corner, what looked like ten years of stacked, yellowed newspapers reached up to the ceiling. A threadbare couch with pillows and a blanket rested against another wall. A football game played on an older TV set; the volume silenced. Beer bottles and a half-eaten sandwich (probably tuna) sat on a TV tray along with a remote, a pile of tawdry, romance paperbacks, a bag of pork rinds, and several amber prescription bottles.

"I'm so sorry, Hope," said Shelby. "We didn't mean to interrupt your lunch."

"I ain't hungry. That's Ben's."

Shelby counted the beer bottles, four, no five of them. Plus, one half-full. Another TV tray sat next to the first one with an open bottle and bag of off-brand BBQ chips.

"Come on into the kitchen. I'll find us some room to chat. Ever since Ben's been stayin' here, I had a tough time keepin' up with the housework. You know men. Make a mess, then 'xpect the woman to clean it up." Hope let out a small laugh, but Shelby didn't think she was joking. By the looks of things, it didn't appear anyone tried to clean anything in a long time. Stacked dishes crusted with moldy food covered the countertop and jutted out of the sink. A moldy stench came from the refrigerator. Shelby looked at Laura.

Hope walked over to the stove and grabbed the cracked handle of a tarnished kettle. "Where're my manners? Some tea? Something to drink. Beer?"

"No, hon." Laura rushed over to Hope. "You sit. We're fine, aren't we Shelby?"

She nodded and smiled.

Hope set the kettle back on the burner and turned, watching them through swollen eyes. She wiped a tear rolling down her cheek with the back of her hand. "I just don't know what to do…"

Laura embraced Hope as she broke down and sobbed while Shelby stared at the grimy table covered with mail, boxes of baggies, and magazines, not knowing what to do or say. The poor woman. Shelby couldn't imagine living in such a depressing house covered in filth, stacked ceiling-high with boxes, newspapers, and junk. The woman was distraught. She wondered if Hope had any friends to confide in.

"Can we fix you something to eat?" asked Laura. "Maybe a sandwich?"

Hope shook her head. "It's all my fault." More tears and sobbing followed.

Laura stroked her back and led her over to the table. Shelby jumped up, pulled out a wooden chair, and helped her sit. The two women took a seat on either side of Hope, each holding one of her cold, trembling hands. Shelby noticed napkins (clean ones) on the kitchen table and handed her a stack.

"What do you mean?" Laura used her calming voice. "What's your fault?"

"Last night," Hope cried. "We argued."

Laura and Shelby looked at each other but said nothing.

"Me 'n Buck hollered. Then Ben 'n Buck disagreed on somethin'. Buck was fumin'. He stormed out." She narrowed her eyes. "He took off in that truck of his to see her. Fool." Hope blotted her eyes with a napkin. "Told Ben to follow him. Didn't care to see neither of 'em last night. So I went to bed."

Laura rubbed Hope's hand. "You didn't know—"

"I know he darned well went to her house. Always ended up there when we argued. Then this morning… the sheriff showed up. Told me my cheatin' husband was dead."

The sound of food crunching and papers shuffling came from the front room. Out of the corner of her eye Shelby saw a big, burly man walk past the kitchen doorway. She guessed it was Ben, though she'd never met him face-to-face. He didn't seem willing to come meet them, which was best given Hope's state.

"Our last words was ugly ones," said Hope. "Now he's dead. Stupid son of a gun."

Hope bumped the front door with her hip. It closed with a satisfying thud. She locked the deadbolt and smiled. Two years in the Valley High drama club and yet she'd just given her best performance.

Ben ambled in from the hall and plopped on the couch. "Thought them gals would never leave."

"Glad you'd told me that trick 'bout keeping onions handy," said Hope. "Helped with the 'grieving widow' look."

Ben chuckled and finished his beer. "So sorry for your loss," he mimicked in a falsetto voice.

"Least you coulda come in and tried to act concerned."

"And listen to all your hen-talk. No thanks, woman. Best I stayed out of everyone's way. After all, I'm just the boarder." He pushed a frayed blanket to one side of the couch and pointed to the space next to him.

"Hold your horses," said Hope. "Don't need no one snoopin' in our business." She walked over to the window and pulled the thin green cotton drapes together. Dust motes, visible from the light coming from the television, floated through the air. She rubbed her hands and walked over to the couch. "You ever gonna fix that heater? If it gets much colder…"

"Come snuggle. I'll keep you warm." He twisted the cap on another beer, held it up to his lips, and revealed a toothless grin. "Just trying to comfort the widow."

She pushed him away. "Ben, we need to be careful. At least for a while. Folks already 'spected something was up. We don't need no more cops puttin' their noses up our business. Spurned wife with a lover. It don't look good."

"Yeah, it was mighty nice of your hubby to croak, wasn't it?" Ben let out a guttural laugh.

"I'm serious. You're just lucky someone else took care of him. With your past, last thing you need is a third conviction."

"Well, whoever he, or she, was…" he said, tipping his bottle in the air. "I salute them."

Hope pulled the frayed blanket over her knees and opened

a bag of chips. "By the way. You never said where you went last night."

"Errand for a friend."

"Ben, tell me the truth. Did you—?"

"Woman, you don't need to know none of my personal business."

Hope shivered and pulled the blanket closer. "If you'd done it, would you tell me?"

Ben winked. "You really want to know?"

She stared at the open bag of chips and shook her head.

Ben elbowed Hope in the ribs, then pointed at the football game on the television. "That was a foul. Wasn't that a foul, darlin'?"

Hope glanced at the television, then at Ben. She sighed. "Yeah. Somethin's foul all right."

CHAPTER TWENTY-FOUR

From the moment they walked into Hope's depressing house, Shelby wanted to leave. Being closed in and out of control had been a trigger since her childhood. Her mother kept their home spotless. Anything out of place brought a rebuke from her father. Seeing the staggering piles of newspapers and teetering boxes in Hope's front room took every bit of Shelby's strength to hold off a panic attack.

They walked out to the street and stopped in front of Ella's home. "Thanks for coming with," said Laura.

"I'm so sorry for Hope, but that house—" Shelby noticed Dawn's patrol car still parked in Ella's driveway. Her eye twitched. Her panic was returning.

Laura nodded. "That house is not happy. Not enough sage and lavender to calm the anger and hopelessness there. Although…" Laura stopped and watched a hawk circle overhead. "I felt something else…"

"Like what?" asked Shelby.

"Not sure. Some sort of darkness. I can't always explain what I'm feeling. I just know it made me very uneasy." Laura gave Shelby a quick hug. "Gotta run. Maybe doing something else will help me figure it out." She turned and headed across the lawn to her house.

Shelby didn't need more darkness in her life. Not now. Not ever. She steeled herself to seeing Dawn again and marched up the front steps. Opening Ella's door, she walked in and forced a smile. Oatmeal bounded over, wagging his tail. The sweet scent of coffee hung in the air. Mr. Butterfingers lay sprawled across the floor on his back. He opened one eye, then closed it again, twitching his tail. Apparently unhappy about being disturbed during his afternoon nap.

Dawn sat on the sofa with Ella, but stood when Shelby walked in. "Perfect timing." Dawn tucked her pen and notebook in her pocket and glanced at Shelby. "We were just finishing up."

"I'll let you know if I think of anything else," said Ella.

"Appreciate it," said Dawn. She walked up to Shelby. "We should talk soon, Shel. I have a few more questions for you, too." She pulled out her cell and scrolled. "Tomorrow around lunchtime, okay?"

"Tomorrow's Saturday," said Shelby. Perspiration beaded on her upper lip. "Ella needs me at the shop."

Ella hesitated. "I can spare you for a few hours."

"Good," said Dawn. "Say twelve-thirty. At the Café?"

Shelby nodded. "I guess that will work."

After Dawn left, Shelby put her hands on her hips. "Thanks a lot."

"Might not be so bad," said Ella. "You might learn something about the case. In the meantime…" She walked over to the sofa, sat, and patted the spot next to her. "I need to show you something."

Maneuvering around the cat, Shelby sat on the plush cushion and drew her legs up under her. "What's up?"

Ella scrolled through images on her phone, then held the screen up for Shelby.

"I've already seen your mysterious letter."

"This one's not mine," said Ella. "Deputies found a second letter while searching Buck's truck. Alton caught wind of it and hounded Dawn to come by and interview me again."

Shelby frowned and used two fingers to make the screen image larger. "It's not what you think. He was never the one." She turned and looked at Ella. "The same message. Did you tell her about the one we found?"

"Not yet. But I suppose I will, eventually. Otherwise, she'll say I was withholding evidence or something like that." Ella hurried into the kitchen and returned holding their first letter.

"They found the second one in Buck's truck?"

Ella nodded.

"Do you think there could be more?"

"Have no idea," said Ella. "But, since I don't have a solid alibi, Alton's pushing Dawn to bring me in for questioning. It's asinine to think I should have to prove I was alone."

Shelby rubbed the old note between her fingers. "I'm curious about these messages. Dawn have any clues?"

"No. I'm sure it's why she came back and wanted to talk in private. And why she wants to meet with you, too. Though, I'm not sure why Alton is hellbent on putting his nose into everything."

Shelby rested her chin on her knee. "I wish we weren't meeting for lunch. It would have been just as easy at the shop."

"Maybe she wants to see how you'll react when I'm not around. Shel, I know this is hard, but I need you to meet with Dawn. Someone is trying to pin Buck's death on me. And any information would help clear my name. Speaking of help, what happened at Hope's?"

Shelby told Ella about the deplorable, bitter-cold house and Hope's emotional response. "I felt bad for her. Not because her husband was dead, but because of her living conditions."

Oatmeal jumped up into Ella's lap. She stroked his ear. "You think something's going on with her and Ben?"

Shelby shrugged. "He stayed out of sight for most of the visit, but I knew he was listening. Hope seemed distraught, but… I don't know. Something didn't seem right."

"Such as?"

"The TV trays."

Ella arched her brow. "TV trays?"

"They were right next to each other, like they'd been cozy on the couch watching the football game."

"And…"

"Hope mentioned the argument the night before. And about sending Ben after Buck. But then said she went to bed. Ben was elusive. Don't you think he'd have backed her up?"

Ella shifted Oatmeal to her other leg. "Probably tired of talking. I'm sure Dawn was very thorough with her questions."

Shelby tucked a strand of hair behind her ear. "Maybe. I'll think about it for a while." She compared the paper note and phone image again. "Who do you think put these in Buck's truck and your car? Was it Buck's killer? Or someone trying to make you look guilty?"

"We're now assuming Buck was murdered?"

"With what you said about his head injury, we should discuss plausible suspects while Dawn waits on that autopsy report. Besides, do you feel comfortable knowing somebody slipped a note in your car? What if they—?"

"Let's not jump to conclusions." Ella patted Shelby's thigh. "Let's talk about what we know. Okay?"

Shelby sighed. "Fine. We know they had access to green paper. The same paper Jasmine had in her office."

"And Buck, Hope, and Ben argued last night. Buck left. Ben went after him." said Ella.

"Deliberately?"

Ella frowned. "I'm not sure I follow you."

Shelby straightened her legs under the coffee table. "Did they provoke a fight knowing Buck would leave? Did Ben really follow Buck to catch up with him? Or, to kill him?"

Ella held up her hand. "All good questions. But I think you're getting sidetracked again. Let's go back to the notes." She pointed to the paper and envelopes. "Same envelope. Same block letters. One left in my car. One found in Buck's truck. Did Buck or the killer have them? Was that one in Buck's truck left by accident or on purpose?"

Shelby stood and paced. "They knew you'd find the one in your car after leaving the shop. But Hope, Ben, Dawn, or Alton, could have found the one in Buck's truck." She sat on the sofa again. "What if Ben killed Buck and Hope left the notes to make someone else look guilty? Or, what if Buck made it to Paige's house. And then she killed Buck and left the notes to put the blame on Ben?"

Ella shook her head. "Hope was home talking with Dawn when we left for the shop. I don't think she had enough time to drive into town, leave a note in my car, then drive home again. Plus, from what you said, she would have been too upset to drive."

Shelby snapped her fingers. "They could have been working as a team. Maybe Hope was mad at you, but in love with Ben. They made sure Buck was dead, then Ben left the notes."

Ella shook her head. "It's all too far-fetched."

"Remember how I told Dawn about the bottle under the bench?"

Ella nodded.

"What if Buck was all distraught?" asked Shelby. "Then went into town and bought liquor. Then he went to see Paige, but she rejected him. He went to the cemetery, sat on the bench, and got drunk. When he left, he dropped the bottle, stumbled, hit his head on the grave marker and died. No one killed him. It was an accident. Thus the note, 'It's not what you think'."

Ella looked at Shelby. "And why would someone write a note exonerating a man who died from his own drunken stupidity?"

"Okay, that was a long shot. This sleuthing stuff isn't easy."

"But…" said Ella. "If they find prints on that bottle, it might narrow down suspects."

"Maybe someone followed Buck back to the cemetery and they argued. Buck hit his head, by accident or on purpose, and died. Then the killer drank themselves into a stupor because they were distraught. They left the bottle by mistake. Then left notes all over town trying to clear themselves and Buck."

Ella smiled. "You have quite a few interesting theories. I think we'll know more after you talk to Dawn tomorrow. Plus, if you get to the Café early, maybe you could find out if Buck made it to Paige's last night. That would help with a timeline of events."

Shelby snorted. "Look at you and your Nancy Drew lingo."

Ella rolled her eyes. "We need to find out more about that copy paper. Which I can't do until I meet with Jasmine."

"Since someone addressed them to you, El, maybe they think you know Buck's killer. And they're providing an alibi."

"But why me?" asked Ella. "Why not tell the police or sheriff? Should I even care whose fault it was?"

"I have no idea." Shelby's eyes widened. "Oh no. What if the actual killer's setting you up? What if you're next? Oh, Ella. I'm worried."

CHAPTER TWENTY-FIVE

Sitting on the couch together, Ella grasped Shelby's trembling hand. "Shel, you're letting your imagination get the best of you. Why would I be the killer's next target? We don't even know if anyone murdered Buck."

"But you had a powerful motive for wanting him out of your life. You told me. More than once."

"But, that wouldn't make me a target…" Ella stood and walked over to the window. She pointed. "Look, it's snowing."

Shelby went and stood next to her friend. "The flakes are so big. Everything will look beautiful covered in white. A fresh chance at a new beginning."

Ella brushed a stray hair from Shelby's cheek. "You referring to my front yard or something else?"

"Both, I guess." She looked at Ella and smiled. "Coming here, I hoped to put the past with Mac behind me. Start fresh…" She turned and stared out the window.

"And now?"

Shelby cleared her throat. "I think Dawn still has feelings for me."

"Did she say something?" Ella wrapped her sweater around herself.

"No. It's the way she looks at me. I don't think she ever got over—"

Ella caught Shelby's gaze. "I thought nothing happened between you two. Or was there more?"

Shelby hesitated, then sighed. "Nothing that meant anything to me."

"But it meant something to her." Ella hated going down that path with Shelby. She didn't want to know, but had to know before sharing her feelings.

Shelby nodded. "A kiss." She turned and stared out the window again. "I told her it was a mistake."

Ella leaned against the window frame. "Since she knows Mac is out of your life, do you feel like she might try to revisit those feelings?"

Shelby nodded again. "When I came back, I wasn't interested in seeing her again. I was interested in seeing if…" She hesitated, keeping her eyes focused outside the window.

Ella hesitated. "I think Oatmeal needs to go for a walk." Oatmeal yipped and danced around their feet.

Shelby smiled. "Looks like he agrees."

Oatmeal ran ahead as they walked into the kitchen. "Probably should use his leash just to keep him close by." After several attempts to calm the dancing dog, Ella attached Oatmeal's leash to his collar. She handed it to Shelby and slipped on her jacket, gloves, and scarf.

Opening the back door, they walked out on the porch and down the steps into the backyard. Shelby slipped her arm through Ella's as she stopped and gazed up at the light pewter clouds hanging low in the sky. Snow swirled around them, wrapping everything in quiet. Oatmeal ran ahead and lifted his leg near a small bush.

"You think we'll get a lot?" asked Shelby.

"Couple of inches, maybe. Enough for a fresh chance at a new beginning."

Shelby pulled back from Ella and smiled. "You referring to your yard. Or something else."

Ella caught her gaze. "Both."

Shoving gloved hands in her sweater pockets, Shelby walked forward. "You know, El. I care about you." She stopped and caught Ella's eye. "More than just a friend."

Ella continued without responding. Not knowing where the conversation would go, she wanted to be careful. Though she also felt something for Shelby, she didn't want to complicate things. Shelby was dealing with her breakup with Mac, plus the added confusion of Dawn's budding feelings. Ella watched a crow and its mate fly from a tall pine tree, glide across the yard, and land on a patch of dry grass. She turned. "I… care about you, too."

"More than a friend?" asked Shelby.

Ella paused for a moment to find the right words. "When I was in college, I had a relationship with another woman…"

"I don't remember you ever mentioning it."

"It was before I met Doug." Ella lowered her gaze. "Now… I'm still figuring stuff out."

Shelby leaned over and brushed a thick snowflake from Ella's scarf. "I don't want you to feel pressured or anything."

Ella nodded. She pulled at Oatmeal's leash as he barked at the crows. "You should take time to sort out your feelings… with Dawn."

Shelby watched as the large, black birds picked at something. "I told you I don't have feelings for her."

Ella followed Shelby's gaze and clenched her jaw. With Buck's sudden death, her emotions were raw. And as much as she wanted and needed Shelby's affection, their underlying feelings for each other had to wait. "I'd be more comfortable knowing you both agree it's all in the past."

"Don't want her get the wrong idea," said Shelby. "So what do we do?"

"Come on, Oatmeal." Ella patted her leg. "We go back to the house. Build a fire. Make an early dinner." Oatmeal led the way to the back porch steps.

"Maybe watch a movie?" Shelby stood on the porch, shaking snow off her sweater.

Ella opened the door into the mudroom. "Popcorn?"

After pulling off damp gloves, Shelby hung her scarf and sweater on peg. "Sounds like a good plan." She opened the refrigerator and stared inside. Her heart pounded. Did they just agree to pursue something? Reaching for a jar of spaghetti sauce and a thawed package of hamburger meat, she was thankful to busy herself with dinner. Her hands trembled as she filled a pot of water and set it on the stove to boil. She tried not to stare at Ella, but her heart was full of anticipation.

Meanwhile, a few feet away, Ella sliced a pile of mushrooms into tiny slivers. She chopped a shiny red pepper and one small yellow onion. She slid the vegetables into a pan coated with sizzling olive oil. Stirring the mixture, she wondered how long she'd be able to hold back her genuine feelings for Shelby. Feelings she'd kept secret since Doug had been murdered.

CHAPTER TWENTY-SIX

The morning sun peeked through Shelby's bedroom curtains. She stretched, got dressed, and bounded down the stairs followed by Mr. Butterfingers. Ella snored quietly on the couch, her fluffy, white dog curled around her legs. As Shelby passed by, Oatmeal lifted his head and watched her. A few moments later he stood at the back door, tail wagging. "Need to go out, boy? Hold on a sec."

After tossing a pile of eggshells in the trash, she washed her hands. Mr. Butterfingers looked up and meowed. "I'll feed you as soon as I take Oatmeal out." A quick leg lift and they were back inside. Shelby rubbed her hands together as both animals stared up at her. "Yes, I should have worn my gloves." They watched as she opened the refrigerator door and reached inside for their canned food. As Shelby closed the door, she saw Ella standing in the doorway.

"Awesome hair." Shelby giggled. Who's your stylist?"

Ella looked at her reflection in the toaster and attempted to pat down the stray hairs. She gave up and went to the table. "Good morning to you, too. Mighty chipper, aren't we?"

"One of us is. Coffee?"

Ella nodded and pulled out a chair.

"You didn't even make it to the end of the first movie." Shelby handed Ella a ceramic mug and placed the coffee carafe on the table, then returned to the stove. "Eggs?"

"Yes, thanks. I'm sorry. Last I remember was the gal… forgot her name… was running to catch up with her friend whose name also escapes me. Then I woke up on the couch covered with my fleece blanket."

Shelby added a dash of salt and pepper to the pan and stirred everything with a wooden spoon. "So much for my movie night idea."

Ella sipped her coffee and smiled. "I'm sure we'll have plenty of time for another one. Maybe I'll stay awake next time." She pushed her chair back from the table.

Shelby held up her hand. "Enjoy your coffee. I've got breakfast covered. She slipped on a thick, red mitt, opened the oven, and pulled out an oven rack. A smoky, apple scent filled the kitchen. Flipping several thick slices of bacon on a cookie sheet, she closed the oven door and set the timer. "About five more minutes."

"My, this is a treat. What's the occasion?"

Stirring the eggs, she turned the knob to off, then grabbed two plates from the cabinet. "Just my way of saying thanks for being here for me." Shelby divided the eggs between each plate and carried them over to the table as the timer went off. After placing the bacon on a paper towel, she took strawberry and apricot jam from the refrigerator and put everything on the table. She pointed to the bag of English muffins on the counter. "Toasted or untoasted?"

"Shel, I can toast my own muffin."

Shelby walked behind Ella, brushing her hand across her friend's shoulders. "It's no trouble. Eat your eggs before they get cold." After the muffins popped up, she placed them on a small saucer and sat. "Did I forget anything?"

Ella shook her head, then smiled.

A blush rose in Shelby's cheeks as she reached for the strawberry jam. Spooning a large dollop in the middle of a muffin, she felt Ella's eyes watching. Her tummy fluttered. She cleared her throat and poked at the steaming eggs on her plate with a fork. "Food okay?"

Ella nodded. "Been a while since someone else cooked. You might regret spoiling me."

While Shelby had agreed to talk to Dawn before she and Ella moved forward, it took all her self-control to not get up, take Ella into her arms…

"Shel, you okay?"

Shelby blinked a few times, realizing the jam had oozed off the muffin and onto the plate. "Sorry, did you say something?"

"I asked what you'd planned to say to Paige. If you get the chance."

Shelby stared at her muffin. "Not sure. Figured I'd see what happens." She shook thoughts of Ella out of her mind, picked up a slice of bacon, and took a bite.

"You could ask if Buck came by her house that night."

Shelby caught Ella's eye. "Great idea."

"Take it slow," said Ella. "Maybe ease into things little by little—"

Shelby jumped up. "More coffee?" After rushing over to the counter, she realized the carafe was still on the table.

"No thanks."

Shelby leaned against the counter. The cookie sheet had cooled. The bacon grease solidified. To hide her trembling hands, she scraped the excess grease in the trash and placed the cookie sheet and frying pan in the sink. After filling the sink with hot, soapy water, she fished around for the scrubber which had gone missing in the suds.

Concentrating on the iridescent bubbles, Shelby heard a chair scrape the wood floor. She watched Ella out of the corner of her eye as she spooned leftovers into Oatmeal's bowl and Mr. Butterfinger's dish. Shelby stared at the faucet as Ella stacked plates, silverware, and cups on the counter next to her. She held her breath and waited.

Ella walked behind Shelby and slid her hands around Shelby's waist. She pressed her warm body against Shelby's back. "Thanks for breakfast." Then she loaded her dishes into the dishwasher.

Shelby watched Ella's reflection in the window, yet Ella never looked over or caught her eye. After placing the forks in the silverware compartment, Ella closed the dishwasher door and walked out of the kitchen, followed by Oatmeal.

Not sure how to react, Shelby washed and rinsed the egg-crusted pan and set it on a towel to dry. She dried her hands and headed up to her room to get ready for the day.

CHAPTER TWENTY-SEVEN

After dressing for work, Ella came back into the kitchen and filled the pets' dishes with dry food, then checked their water. "Don't want you two to starve while we're gone, do we?"

"No matter how much food's in their dishes, they'll still make us think we have neglected them all day," said Shelby. "Pet's perspective, I suppose."

Ella's breath caught as she saw Shelby standing in the doorway wearing a pair of faded denim jeans and a long-sleeved ivory, pink, and blue high-collared, cotton shirt, a loose-knit fuchsia cardigan, and her signature hot-pink tennis shoes. "I see you're dressed up for your lunch later today with Dawn."

"I wasn't trying to impress *her*..."

To hide her smile, Ella turned and glanced at the clock. "We better go. It's almost nine." She reached for her jacket and purse. "My car or yours?"

Stepping on the porch, Shelby pointed to the row of junipers. "Snow's already melted. How about I drive us this morning?" She pulled a set of keys from her pocket and opened the jeep's doors.

Ella nodded toward Hope's house after she buckled her seat belt. "Much quieter today."

Shelby glanced over. "Hopefully, it'll stay that way."

As they backed out of the driveway, Ella noticed a few determined clumps of snow clinging to the tall, dead grass. Passing by the old cemetery, Ella shuddered and rubbed her hands together in front of the heater vents.

After a long silence, Shelby cleared her throat. "Your hug this morning… it was nice."

Ella smiled and gazed out the passenger window. "Appreciated breakfast…"

Shelby rested her hand near Ella's thigh.

Ella squeezed it and faced her friend. "Just reminding you of what you'd be missing in case Dawn's still pining for you."

Shelby giggled. Releasing Ella's hand, she downshifted. The jeep slowed and came to a stop at the four-way stop sign. "Remind me anytime you want."

As USUAL, Vivian had opened The Bee's Knees and stood chatting with a few customers as Shelby and Ella walked in. The lavender scent greeted them and Vivian waved as Ella stored her purse and scarf under the counter.

"Only a few people in today," said Shelby.

"It'll pick up in a few hours," said Ella. "Locals don't come in early on Saturday. And the folks from the Valley come in just before and after lunch. They drive up here, browse a bit, eat, then spend the afternoon antiquing and craft store shopping." She straightened a stack of flyers on the counter. "That reminds me, when are you going to set up your booth? With the holidays approaching, now's the best time for promoting yourself and making sales."

Shelby picked up a jar of lavender balm from Laura's booth, checked the price, and set it back on the shelf. "Soon. I hope. I don't have a lot of inventory right now."

Ella wiped down the front counter with a rag. "You brought those bolts of fabric. I seem to remember seeing rayon and plaid flannel. Infinity scarves are popular right now, and both fabrics would work. I don't mind helping cut out squares." Ella tucked the rag in a back pocket and pulled out her phone. After scrolling through several images, she held the screen up for Shelby. "These don't even need sewing and only take about an hour to make. By Monday, you could be open for business."

Shelby studied the images and nodded. "Thanks. I need a kick in the arse to get creating again. It's been way too long."

The door opened. A man, woman, and a red-haired toddler came inside. He nodded to Ella and Shelby. "Saw your place and the family couldn't resist coming in."

"Welcome," said Ella. "Let me know if I can help you find something."

The woman headed straight to Laura's booth. The man grabbed the pudgy hand of the little girl and they headed down an aisle.

The door opened again and two women in their mid-thirties entered. "Morning," said the taller one. They walked behind the counter and shoved their purses and jackets under it.

"Morning," said Ella. She reached for a clipboard and set it on the counter. "Shel, come meet two more of our vendors. These are Vivian's talented daughters, Vickie Parr and Lilibeth Morgan, better known as the Wooley Sisters.

"Wooley Sisters?" Shelby walked over to greet them. "What's the story behind that name?"

Ella laughed and motioned to the women. "Lilibeth's husband, John, runs Morgan Farms, the alpaca and sheep farm outside town. Vickie and Lilibeth use the different fibers to create beautiful needle-felted animals and clothing designs."

The tall, strawberry-blonde extended her hand. "I'm Vickie. Nice to meet you, Shelby. Ella's spoke of you often." She pointed to a colorful design on the front of her sweater. "I'm wearing one of our creations."

"Oh my goodness," said Shelby. "It's beautiful."

The shorter, dark-haired sister wearing oversized, emerald-green framed glasses stepped forward. "I'm Lilibeth. Good to put a face with a name. Let me take you back to our booth. I'll show you more of what we do. My father started raising sheep when I was…"

As the women walked away, a man's voice became louder. He walked up to the counter, the little girl staying close to his side. Her clear blue eyes matched the faded blue of her tiny tennis shoes. She hugged one of Paige's Teddy bears.

"Looks like you just found a special friend," said Ella.

Hiding behind her father's tall legs, she peeked at Ella and nodded. A few moments later the mother approached the counter, her wooden basket full of jams, lavender soaps, greeting cards, and a set of hand-turned wooden bowls. She placed everything on the counter and held up her finger. "One more thing—" She raced back down an aisle, then came back holding a walnut and pine stained game board and a muslin bag of game pieces. "I think that's it for now." She smiled and looked at the man. "Got all our Christmas shopping done."

The little girl held up the bear. "Look, Mama."

The woman bent down on one knee. "And what have you named him or her?"

The little girl stole a look at Ella, then ran over and whispered in her mother's ear.

"Harry is a wonderful name." The mother winked at Ella.

The girl nodded and hugged Harry tighter.

Ella rang up their purchases and wrapped the breakables in several layers of tissue paper. Their shopping done, the family left. Mother carrying the bags. Father holding the little girl's hand. Little girl cuddling Harry.

Shelby strolled past the front counter with Lilibeth. "I just love everything in your booth. You and your sister are so talented..." They continued to another area of the store, chatting about the differences of the tensile strength and odors between sheep and alpaca wool.

Ella grabbed the clipboard and checked the schedule. Vickie, Lilibeth, and their mother were there until one o'clock. Then, from one until five, she expected three volunteers: Lilibeth's mother-in-law, Eleanor Morgan, a chatty woman in her sixties who knitted and crocheted faster than she talked; Kent Lowe, a hipster woodworker/woodturner in his forties; and Susan Rivas a quiet, friendly woman in her late-forties who crafted wooden game boards and carved wooden game pieces and animals. So many gifted artisans who made up The Bee's Knees. They were the ones who brought the customers back in again and again.

After a busy morning, Ella glanced up at the rustic clock. Almost noon. Shelby had been helping customers and tidying up the shop. Everyone loved her friendly, outgoing style. Ella was finally seeing the gal she remembered so many years before. Even though Shelby had been back less than a week, Ella could tell she was settling in.

Ella opened a bottle of water and took a drink, glad for a few minutes of quiet. Vickie and Viv came and stood next to her. She offered them water, and the women took an impromptu break. "Looks like it might slow for a bit," said Ella. "You ladies mind if I go grab lunch? Oh, and Shelby will be leaving, too."

"Go on, hon," said Vivian. "The girls and I will be fine."

Vickie nodded. “Lilibeth and I can stay later if you need us. We don’t mind putting in extra hours.”

“Thanks, ladies. I appreciate it.” Ella draped a scarf around her neck, then grabbed a wallet from her purse. “I’ll be back soon.” She walked down a side aisle and found Shelby admiring a little wool sheep at the Wooley Sisters’ booth.

Shelby looked up as Ella came closer. “It’s amazing how they can make this with a ball of wool and a needle.”

“And a very sharp needle at that,” said Ella. “I tried my hand at needle felting a while back. Ended up with a punctured fingertip and a sad-looking ball of fuzz. Didn’t even come close to resembling the image I printed off the internet.” She glanced down at her phone. “You know it’s past noon, right?”

“Already?” Shelby watched as Ella fastened her scarf. “You headed out, too?”

Ella nodded. As they walked out the door together, Ella motioned to a six-sided building across the street. “Thought I’d run over to the Pizza Palace for the lunch special. Any slice plus a salad just five bucks.”

“Sounds great,” said Shelby. “Maybe we should get one for dinner tonight.”

“I thought you were picking up macaroni and cheese. And pie.”

Shelby grinned. “I was. But pizza would be good for dinner. Or tomorrow’s breakfast. And pie is good—”

“Anytime,” said Ella.

“Righto.”

The women walked to the end of the block and stopped at the corner. Ella turned to Shelby. “I hope it goes well with Dawn. And Paige.” She wanted to hug Shelby, but reached out and squeezed her arm instead. “Hurry back,” Ella shouted over the traffic.

Ella rushed across the street but paused and turned before she opened the door to the Pizza Palace. Shelby had crossed and was headed north to the Café. Ella's stomach twisted. Shelby was meeting with Dawn but if they were to have any type of future together, Ella would need to trust Shelby.

CHAPTER TWENTY-EIGHT

Shelby pulled on the cold metal handle of the heavy wooden door and entered the Corner Café. Her stomach growled taking in the scents of smoky bacon, fresh-brewed coffee, and sweet maple syrup. Customers in booths lunched on tasty-looking meals, while others at the counter read or talked. Servers in blue and white aprons bustled about taking orders and serving coffee. One looked her way. "Be right there."

Shelby looked around the small cozy restaurant, but didn't see Dawn. Or Paige.

"Table or counter, hon?" The olive-skinned server's black hair was pulled into a tight bun, though a few strands slipped out, framing her thin face. The woman nudged a stray hair behind her ear and grabbed a menu.

"There'll be two of us," said Shelby. "A table would be great when you have one ready."

The woman turned and scanned the small, noisy coffee shop. "Be about five minutes."

"Oh, and if possible, would you put us in Paige's area?"

"Would love to. But she called in sick again."

Shelby's shoulders drooped. "Any table would be fine then, I guess." Delivering a handful of napkins to a family of four sitting in a booth, she walked away and disappeared behind a set of double doors.

While waiting, Shelby studied a wall of photographs displaying images of the town and its residents. Children playing in the snow. Apple orchards in full bloom. Kit foxes. Roaming coyotes. Colorful butterflies. Fireworks, parades, and softball teams. Even one of the ribbon cutting from The Bee's Knees grand opening.

"Hon, table's ready."

Pulling herself away from the pictures, Shelby followed the server to the back of the Café. The harried woman placed two menus on the table and pulled an order pad and pen from her front pocket.

"Coffee?"

Shelby glanced at her name tag. "No thanks, Cammilla. Water is fine."

She smiled and leaned her hip against the edge of the table. "Take your time. I'll be back to check on you soon." Before Shelby could respond, Cammilla rushed to another table.

Shelby picked up her menu and opened the large, laminated pages. So many tempting choices made her stomach growl even louder. They served breakfast all day, along with hot or cold sandwiches, macaroni and cheese, fried chicken, and other mouthwatering options. It listed lunch specials along with the soup of the day. A typed note paper-clipped inside the menu noted baked potatoes were only available after four pm. Lost in all the choices, Shelby jumped when Dawn plopped down in a chair on the other side of the table.

"Hey. How's it going?" Wearing her light green, long-sleeved uniform shirt, the overhead lights reflected off her gold badge. Dawn looked around, then snapped her fingers at a nearby server.

A young man in blue slacks and a white shirt marched over. He cocked his head and stared at Dawn. "If you're ready, I'll get your waitress."

Dawn peered at his tag. "Not ready, Mark. Just something to drink. Diet soda, with caffeine. Light on the ice."

Mark let out an exaggerated sigh and walked away

Shelby winced. Good ol' Dawn. Not the most tactful person. She closed her menu and laid it on the table. "Been a while since I've been inside."

"Hasn't changed one bit. Has it?"

Shelby could say the same thing about Dawn, but she let it go. "I swear the menu is three times bigger. I needed both hands and half the table to navigate through it."

Dawn nodded and opened her mouth, but stopped when Cammilla placed a tall, bubbling glass of soda in front of her.

Holding her pen above the order pad, Cammilla turned to Shelby. "Ready?"

"I'll have the large macaroni and cheese."

"Anything to drink, hon?"

"Water's fine."

Cammilla looked at Dawn and tapped her pen on the pad.

"Give me the same, except a medium, plus a half roast beef sandwich on wheat. No mayo. Extra pickle." Dawn pointed to her soda and pointed. "And a straw."

The dark-haired waitress pulled a straw from a pocket on her apron and put it next to Dawn's glass. "Anything else, ladies?"

Shelby handed her the menu. "Maybe some pie. Later."

Cammilla brushed another strand of hair behind her ear, then grabbed both menus and took off again, a blur of blue and white rushing to a booth, then the counter.

Shelby took a sip of water. Looking up, she noticed Dawn gazing at her.

"Been a while, Shel. Glad you're back. To stay, I hope."

"Congrats on making sergeant. I know you always wanted that."

Dawn tore the paper off the straw, then rolled it into a ball between her fingers and pushed the straw in her glass. After taking a long sip, she smiled, revealing a tiny dimple.

Shelby shifted in her seat. "How's the investigation coming along?"

"It's coming. Got a few leads. Just takes time."

Looking around, then back at Dawn, Shelby drummed her fingers on the tabletop. "They said Paige hadn't been in for a few days. Hope she's doing okay."

"Spoke to her yesterday." Dawn lowered her voice. "Seemed distraught."

Shelby thought back to Hope's reaction when she and Laura had visited. "I imagine the news came as quite a shock to everyone."

Dawn sipped her soda, then while eyeing Shelby, she traced the top of the straw with her finger.

Her throat dry, Shelby took another drink of water. She stared at the napkin holder. The bowl overflowing with jelly packets. Why did she agree to come? Her shoulders tightened, but relaxed when Cammilla brought their food and placed it on the table.

"Two mac and cheese, one large, one medium. One half roast beef, wheat, no mayo, extra pickle."

Dawn stirred thick mounds of macaroni and cheese, watching little tendrils of steam escape. She paused, holding her fork mid-stir. "What's the story with you and Mac?"

Shelby didn't look up. "Not much to tell."

"It's over then?"

Shelby scooped a bite into her mouth. She chewed, then

swallowed. If she kept eating, she wouldn't have to make small talk.

Dawn bit into her sandwich, keeping her eyes on Shelby. "So… talking about Mac is off the table?"

"Rather not go there." Shelby caught Dawn's eye, but looked away.

Dawn scooped up the last of her macaroni. "Where would you rather go? I seem to remember a trip we took up to Ladybug Lake. In fact, it's all I've thought about since I saw you yesterday."

Shelby's face flushed. "We both agreed that was a mistake." To avoid saying anything regrettable, she finished her meal. Placing the spoon in the empty bowl, Shelby pushed it toward the middle of the table and forced a smile. "You mentioned having questions. I'd feel better if we got those out of the—"

Cammilla stopped by the table. "Ready for that dessert menu yet?"

Shelby nodded. "Oh, and a few more napkins, please?"

"Sure." She glanced at Dawn. "Anything for you?"

Dawn dismissed Cammilla with a wave, then reached into her pocket. She pulled out a notebook and pen and arranged them on the table.

Shelby wondered what notes Dawn had made and who she'd spoken with. If she'd just go use the restroom and leave it there so she could peek…

Cammilla broke her concentration. "Two dessert menus. And napkins. Just let me know when you're ready."

Opening her notebook, Dawn studied Shelby. "I hoped we'd catch up first." She clicked her pen. "But, if you'd rather get straight to it." She flipped to an empty page, then cleared her throat. "You said you were sleeping, alone, during the time of Buck's death?"

"Yes. I was alone." Shelby clenched her jaw and twisted a

napkin under the table. "Sounds like his death wasn't an accident."

Dawn leaned closer. "That's what it looks like."

Shelby sat back. "I thought it took weeks for autopsy results."

"It does." Dawn gave a half smile. "Though in this case, the victim suffered a large gash on the back of his head. That made me very suspicious. And, when we have suspects without legitimate alibis, my brother gets very suspicious."

Shelby's stomach lurched. "What are you implying?"

"Nothing." Sitting back, Dawn spooned a piece of ice from her soda glass. Popping it in her mouth, her eyes probed Shelby while licking the end of the spoon. "But, if you had information, I'd hope you'd share it with me. Before my brother, or I, figure it out."

Gritting her teeth, Shelby fought the urge to pound her fist on the table. She refused to let Dawn think she was getting to her. Shelby grabbed the dessert menu and glared at it as her mind played through several scenarios. Did Dawn and Alton only suspect Ella? Or did they suspect both friends had something to do with Buck's murder? Maybe they hoped Shelby would implicate Ella, then Dawn or Alton would make the arrest? With Ella out of the way, would Dawn take up where they had left off? Shelby looked up and caught the eye of their waitress.

Cammilla came over to the table and smiled. "Ready for dessert, ladies?"

"A whole strawberry pie," said Shelby. "To go. Dawn, did you want anything?"

She pushed her plate toward the table's edge and winked at Shelby. "No, thanks. I'm good."

Shelby handed Cammilla the menu, then took a sip of water. Why couldn't she just tell Dawn to back off? To leave her and Ella alone? Why was it so hard to stand up for herself?

Courage had never come easy. Not when she was younger. Not now.

Dawn wiped her mouth and dropped the crumpled napkin in the middle of her plate. "So, hon…" She leaned in and whispered. "You interested in taking another ride up to the lake? The fall colors are quite spectacular this time of year."

"I'll pass." Shelby tore off the corner of a napkin and twisted it between her fingers. "Yes, Mac and I have split… but there's someone else. I don't want to do anything to jeopardize it." Shelby sucked in her breath. She surprised herself by saying what she really felt. Though, now that her secret was out in the open, she was more vulnerable.

Dawn stared at Shelby with wide eyes, then laughed. "That didn't stop you last time. Besides, it could be our little secret like before. But suit yourself." Tapping the notebook with her pen, she inched her hand closer to Shelby's. "I'd love to share everything I know about the case with you… if we were in a more secluded location. You could help me clear up a few muddy details. And then I could persuade my zealous brother to focus on another suspect."

As Shelby thought about throwing her water in Dawn's smug face, Cammilla brought a pink pastry box tied with a white string and placed it on the table. She held up two slips. "Who gets the damages?"

Dawn reached up and snatched both checks from the woman's hand. "Today, lunch is my treat." After Cammilla walked away, Dawn scooted the chair back, grabbed her hat and jacket, then caught Shelby's eye. "Think about my offer, Shel. But don't take too long. Alton doesn't have as much patience as I do."

Shelby narrowed her eyes and nodded but didn't get up.

"Enjoy the pie." Dawn turned and walked toward the cashier.

After Dawn had paid and left the Café, Shelby got up from

the table. On her way out, she walked by a family eating lunch. She stopped and placed the bakery box on their table. "Hope y'all like strawberry pie."

Shelby marched past the cashier, shoved the wooden door open, and walked outside. An icy wind blew freezing rain on her face, hiding the hot tears streaming down her cheeks.

CHAPTER TWENTY-NINE

As the evening sun slid behind the mountains, Ella turned the shop's wooden sign from "OPEN" to "CLOSED." She locked the front door, walked to the counter, and waited for the volunteers to sign out.

Eleanor, the chatty crocheter, pointed to the clipboard. "After today, I've done my hours for the month. But if you need me, I don't mind coming in."

"Thanks," said Ella. "I appreciate your enthusiasm."

A few moments later, Kent and Susan walked up together, engrossed in conversation. "I prefer clear pine for my game boards and carved pieces," Susan said to Kent. "Though finding wood with little to no knots isn't easy."

Kent nodded and reached for his umbrella. "That's why I prefer the hardwoods. Walnut and maple for my furniture. Low sap content and more fire resistant. Though cherry steams easily for my curved designs…" They headed toward the door, followed by Eleanor. Ella trailed behind to let them out, then locked up again.

Shelby strolled up to the counter and straightened a stack of flyers. "Holiday tomorrow?"

"Yes, always closed on Veteran's Day. Or Remembrance Day, as Doug referred to it. His parents were from Canada and always sent us poppies to wear. I meant to put mine on this morning, but after yesterday's craziness, I totally forgot."

"You two were the only ones I knew who wore them. I'm sure his parents appreciated it."

"It was important," said Ella gathering her scarf and purse. "Doug and I believed it was a day to show respect, not shop. Somehow Veteran's Day got confused with sales instead of remembering… You still want pizza for dinner? If I call it in now, it'll be ready by the time we drive over."

Shelby fumbled with her scarf. "Thought you had a slice for lunch."

Ella laughed. "Didn't know there was a one-slice-a-day rule."

"Not one I've ever heard of," said Shelby.

Scrolling through her phone's contacts, Ella swiped the call icon. "Large to-go. Pepperoni, mushroom, and…" She looked at Shelby.

"Pineapple."

"And pineapple… Fifteen minutes? Perfect. Name's Ella." She ended the call and dropped the phone in her purse. They stepped outside, greeted by a brisk, icy wind. Before Ella locked the door, she peered back inside. "Didn't you bring a strawberry pie?"

"Decided against it." Shelby unlocked Ella's door, then walked around the jeep. After turning the ignition key, she flipped on the heater. "But we can stop by the Café on the way home, if you'd like."

"Chocolate pie or cake sounds good. What about you?"

Shelby shrugged. "Either is fine. You choose."

"How about we go by the Café first, then come back and get the pizza?"

Shelby nodded and drove north to the Corner Café and

parked on the street. Her eyes followed a sheriff's car as it passed and turned at the next corner. She pulled a twenty-dollar bill from her pocket. "You mind running in?"

Ella pushed the money away. "It's my treat." She came back a few minutes later carrying a pink pastry box. Trying the door handle, it wouldn't open. Ella knocked on the window. Shelby startled, then unlocked it. Ella set the box on the floorboard and climbed in. "Everything okay? It's not like you to lock your doors."

"Old Houston habit, I suppose. Sorry." Shelby made a U-turn and headed back to the Pizza Palace. She couldn't tell Ella about Dawn. Not yet. All she knew was she had to protect herself. Without her pillows to hide under, locking the doors offered a small level of comfort.

Ella went in and picked up their pizza. This time when she came back, her door was unlocked. She placed the hot pizza on her lap and buckled the seat belt. "One thing about fresh-cooked pizza. It keeps one warm on these frosty days."

Shelby smiled and pulled away from the curb.

"By the way," said Ella. "You missed Jasmine. She came by while you were at lunch and dropped off a few display racks for her jewelry. I scheduled an appointment with her at ten o'clock Monday morning. Hopefully, I can find out more about that green paper."

"That's great, El." Shelby kept her eyes focused on the road.

Ella wondered what had happened to the happy Shel she'd seen earlier. After returning from lunch Shelby had kept to herself all afternoon, only chatting with customers when they asked a question. Ella thought about asking but didn't want to pry.

As they drove farther away from town, Shelby's demeanor changed. By the time they pulled into the driveway, she had even smiled. "I'll carry in the pizza if you'll grab the dessert."

Inside, two animals feigned starvation. Shelby placed the pizza on the counter and crouched down eye-level with their beloved pets. "You poor things. El, I'll take care of our fur babies if you'll get everything ready for us humans." Shelby filled their bowls with dry food and checked their waters. "Two down, two to go."

She talked little during dinner, but looked up occasionally and smiled. Something wasn't right, but Ella brushed it off as a tough day. She managed half of her second slice of pizza, then pushed the plate away. "Need to save room for dessert." Ella got up and brought the pink box along with a knife and put it in front of Shelby.

Shelby cut the string, lifted one flap of the box, and peeked inside. "No matter how rotten the day, chocolate always makes it better." She opened the other flaps and slid the cake out onto the table.

"Apparently, chocolate therapy was just what you needed." Ella reached out and touched Shelby's hand. "You know you can talk to me about anything, right?"

"Yes. I need to process things first." Handing Ella the knife, Shelby licked her lips. "You do the honors."

Eyeing the thick chocolate frosting and double layers, Ella served Shelby the first piece. Then cut herself a slice.

Turning the plate around, Shelby eased her fork into a thick, frosted corner. Placing it in her mouth, she closed her eyes. "Amazing."

Mr. Butterfingers stood on his hind legs and put his big, furry paws on Shelby's thigh. She reached down and petted him. "Chocolate's not good for kitties…" She turned and looked at Oatmeal. "Or doggies."

Ella tried to eat, but her stomach twisted. As much as she tried to be patient, she couldn't stay silent any longer. "I'm sorry I pushed you to have lunch with Dawn."

"It's okay." Shelby looked up with kind, patient eyes. "We needed to talk."

Ella poked her cake with a fork.

Shelby got up and stood behind Ella, holding her shoulders. "El, I'm not upset at you."

Ella nodded. If only she could tell Shelby how much she cared. How she hated seeing her friend so distraught. How it broke her heart knowing she and Dawn were having lunch. Ella couldn't bear to let herself love someone again just to lose them. But she had to wait. No matter how long it took. "How about we do something productive?" said Ella. "You still want help with those scarves tonight?"

"Yes, thanks."

There was so much Ella wanted to say, but now was not the time. She took a bite of cake while Shelby rinsed her plate and fork and placed them in the dishwasher. For the first time, she didn't feel a need to check and make sure everything fit perfectly. Maybe, life could be a little messy and still be okay.

Shelby gave Oatmeal and Mr. Butterfingers their treats, then turned to Ella. "Want to work on the scarves down here? Or up in my room?"

"Everything's upstairs. No need to drag the fabric bolts down here."

"Great," said Shelby. "I'm going to change into something comfy. Come upstairs when you're ready. "Come on, Mr. Butterfingers." She patted her thigh then bounded up the stairs followed by her cat.

Ella eyed Oatmeal. "Yes, we're going up to Shelby's room. Maybe this time she'll want to talk."

CHAPTER THIRTY

The morning sun's glare reflected off the small electric toaster. Shelby had just finished a second cup of coffee when Ella strolled into the kitchen. Shelby glanced at the clock. "Nine? Apparently, you enjoy getting up late so I'll make breakfast."

Ella laughed, then sat down at the table. "Can't fool a sleuth like you."

Shelby snickered, then took the egg carton out of the refrigerator. She whipped several eggs in a bowl, then dipped thick pieces of bread into the mixture. Laying them on the skillet, they sizzled, filling the kitchen with scents of cinnamon and vanilla.

Pouring herself a cup of coffee from the carafe on the table, Ella looked up. "What's on the menu this morning?"

"French toast. You up for two pieces?"

"Sounds great."

Shelby flipped two perfect pieces of golden brown French toast onto a plate, added a heaping spoonful of sautéed bananas, then sprinkled powdered sugar on top. "Here ya go."

"Restaurant quality. I'm impressed."

"After helping me with all of those scarves last night, I wanted to show my appreciation."

Ella looked up and winked. "You know, you are spoiling me. Between this amazing breakfast and all your help at the shop."

Shelby turned off the burner and placed her plate of breakfast yum on the table. After sitting, she refilled her coffee cup. "Are we complaining?"

Ella squeezed Shelby's hand. "Not one bit."

They continued eating as the animals gathered near their feet, hoping for a dropped morsel or two. Shelby fed a piece of egg to Mr. Butterfingers, who showed his appreciation by purring. Ella fed bits of the soft eggy crust to Oatmeal as Shelby finished her coffee. Once satisfied, the animals went back to their favorite spots. Oatmeal under Ella's chair. Mr. Butterfingers on the back of the couch.

"Nice to just take it easy today, huh?" asked Shelby.

Ella nodded. "It has been a most interesting week."

Shelby dipped a forkful of thick, golden toast in the buttery bananas. When she looked up, Ella was gazing at her.

"It was nice just to enjoy a quiet, uneventful evening," said Ella. "Like the old days when we worked together."

"It sure helped me get out of my funky mood."

Ella smiled and nodded as her cell signaled an incoming call. She glanced down at the caller ID, then swiped an icon. "Hello, Gladys. Everything okay? Yes, a solemn Veteran's Day to you and Ed… Dinner? This Tuesday? Hold on while I check with Shelby." Ella pressed the mute button. "I'm sure you got the gist of that. After Gladys told Ed we were interested in that police scanner thing, he's been pestering her to invite us over for a 'look-see.' You up for a dinner with the Purcells'?"

Shelby checked her phone calendar. "I've got a return dentist appointment scheduled for that morning at eleven, but I should be fine by dinner. Unless you have other plans."

"Nothing I know of." Ella unmuted her phone. "Gladys, yes. Tuesday is fine… Six o'clock? That should work. I'll close the shop by five. What can we bring? Well, our manners won't let us show up empty handed… A salad? Or dessert?" Ella looked at Shelby and shrugged. "Okay. Will do. Yes, tell Ed we're looking forward to it. Goodbye."

"What are we taking?"

"Gladys said not to bother. But my mother would turn in her grave if we didn't take something."

"Darn. I was hoping for another excuse to go into the Café and chat with Paige."

"And pick up another chocolate cake?" Ella laughed. "If Gladys won't let us bring food, then I'll just have to pick up something else. Maybe a scented candle?"

"Great idea. But I'm still picking up dessert for us. It'll give me a reason to see if Paige is back at work."

"Glad that's settled." Ella smiled. "How many scarves did we make last night?"

"Ten. If you count all the ones we cut and finished. But, if I'm going to make the booth look full, I'll need twice as many."

Ella stood. "How about I clean up down here, then come upstairs and help you? Another dozen scarves shouldn't take but a few hours."

Shelby finished her coffee and stretched. "Sounds good to me. Though after that big breakfast I might need a nap first."

Ella stacked the dishes in the dishwasher, then turned. "I suppose we could start with a break, then work." She reached into the dog treat jar on the counter and handed Oatmeal a biscuit. Mr. Butterfingers jumped from the back of the couch and padded into the kitchen. He sniffed the floor, then looked up at Ella and meowed. She picked some cat treats from another jar and placed them near his paws. "And some for you, too."

"No matter how much they eat, they always have room for snacks."

Ella laughed and nodded at the pink pastry box. "I seem to remember being in that same spot last night after eating pizza."

Shelby giggled. "Me. Turn down cake? You've got to be kid —" Her cell rang. She glanced at the caller ID and winced. Swiping "END," she shoved the cell in her pocket. "I'll call back later," she said. "We have scarves to make." A moment later her phone beeped, signaling a voice mail.

"Might be important," said Ella.

Shelby rolled her eyes and retrieved the phone. Swiping the voice mail icon, she listened, then looked up at Ella. "It was Dawn. She wants me to call her back this minute. So much for a relaxing Sunday morning."

CHAPTER THIRTY-ONE

Ella signed in at the desk, glanced around, then took a seat near the window. The therapists' office seemed extra quiet for a Monday morning. Only one other patient in the pumpkin-scented reception area. After waiting a few minutes, Jasmine called her name. Ella followed down the hall listening to her therapist's leggings swish-swishing against a long-sleeved, jade-green, knit dress. Only a week since Ella had seen her, though it had felt like a year.

Jasmine closed the door. "Coffee?"

"No, thanks." Ella shrugged off her sweater and sat.

Jasmine added cream to her red mug, placed it on the small table in front of them, and took a seat. Tucking a coarse strand of hair behind her ear, she picked up a notepad and pen. "The last few days must have been tough. How are you doing?" She sipped her coffee and waited.

"I'm not even sure where to begin…"

"Let's do some deep breathing together," said Jasmine. "It will help you focus. Breathe in. Then hold it. Now out." They repeated the exercises several times. "Better?"

Ella nodded.

"How about we start with Friday? I heard you and Shelby found the body."

Ella's heart rate quickened. "Yes. It was a shock. And maybe… relief? Mostly a shock."

Jasmine made notes and then looked up. "Let's talk about those emotions. Start with the shock."

Ella focused on the fringe at the edge of her scarf. "I don't usually see dead bodies behind my house."

"Thank goodness."

"It was just strange. I mean, as much as I hated him, I also felt… sad. Does that make sense?"

Jasmine peered at Ella over her glasses. "When people hate someone, they sometimes feel lost when that person is not in their life anymore. They no longer have a reason to hate."

"I never hid the fact that I hated the guy. But, for someone to kill him. Then leave him out there all alone. It's just sad. And disturbing,"

"Do you believe in karma?"

Ella frowned. "What do you mean?"

Jasmine caught Ella's eye. "After what he did to your husband."

"Why does everyone think I killed him?"

Jasmine jotted down several notes, then looked up. "Why do you feel compelled to defend yourself?"

Ella rubbed her forehead. "I don't know. The police… Alton, at least. He's all but arrested and booked me even though I told everyone I was asleep."

Jasmine picked up her mug of coffee. "I believe you, Ella."

"Thank you." Ella glanced at the clock. "You mind if we change the subject for a moment? I wanted to ask you about something."

Jasmine set her cup down and fiddled with her necklace.

Ella sat forward in her chair. "Remember that information you printed for me last week? The mindfulness stuff."

"Yes, of course." Jasmine let loose of her necklace and smiled. "How is that working for you?"

"Fine. But it's not the exercises I wanted to ask about. It's the paper."

Jasmine raised an eyebrow. "The paper?"

"Yes. I wanted to know if you had any more. I mean, this might sound silly…" Ella hesitated. "With the holidays coming up. You'd mentioned three boxes. If you still had some, I'd like to purchase it from you. For the shop, that is. You know, to make flyers and things like that."

Jasmine chuckled. "I had so much paper I took it to the Chamber of Commerce meeting last week. Told everyone to grab some for their businesses. I didn't see you at the meeting."

Ella sighed. "I forgot all about it after Shelby arrived."

"You could have had all you wanted," said Jasmine.

"So anyone at that meeting could have taken some?"

"Yes," said Jasmine. "And they did. Went though an entire case."

"Out of curiosity, how many sheets are in a case?"

"Let's see." Jasmine tapped the pen on her notebook. "Five reams to a case. Five hundred sheets to a ream…"

Ella sighed. "Twenty-five hundred sheets…"

Her therapist nodded.

"That's a lot of people using green paper. Isn't it?"

Jasmine went over to her desk and opened a file drawer. "I still have several reams left. I guess mint green is a popular color."

"If you don't mind. At least for flyers—"

"And things like that." Jasmine pulled out a stack of the paper, straightened it on the top of her desk, then slid it into a manila folder. She went back to her seat and handed it to Ella. "Enjoy."

Ella laid the envelope across her lap. Two thousand, five

hundred sheets unaccounted for. Anyone could have typed up those notes.

"What else is on your mind, Ella?" Jasmine glanced at the clock. "We still have some time. Did Shelby ever open up and talk to you?"

Ella twisted the fringe on her scarf again. "We talked."

"You seem bothered about something."

"She said everything was over between her and Mac. And things were good between us. Yet, the other day she was distant. I'm sure it was nothing."

"What concerns you?"

Ella squared her shoulders. "Phone calls. I'm sure it's none of my business or she would have told me. She's been receiving calls, but not taking them when I'm around. Like she's hiding something."

"Do you share every call you get with her?"

"Well, no. I suppose I don't with things that don't concern her."

"Maybe she's doing the same thing. Is there a reason you're feeling extra sensitive?"

Ella ran her fingers through her hair. "I care for her."

Jasmine leaned forward. "As friends? Or is there more?"

"More."

Jasmine sat back and made notes. "Oh, I see. Go on."

"I trust her. She's kind. And open. And caring…"

"But…"

"But, since Saturday, I feel she's been hiding something. I don't know what it is."

"Have you asked her?"

"I didn't want to pry. We'd just gotten to a good place with each other. I don't want to mess things up."

"For a relationship to work, Ella, you need to have open communica—" Jasmine's phone rang. After checking it, she held up a finger. "Hold on a minute, Ella. I need to deal with this." Jasmine got up and walked out, closing the door behind her.

JASMINE STOMPED out into the hall and adjusted her earbuds. She hit redial. "Why did you call my cell? I have patients during the day… Yes, I know your call is important, but you should've left a message with the receptionist… To be honest, your call interrupted me and my patient. Who? None of your business… Why couldn't this wait?"

WELL, that was a first. Ella stood and paced around the small room, clenching, then relaxing her fists. Part of her was angry for revealing her feelings for Shelby. The other part was angry because Jasmine left in the middle of their appointment.

Ella walked over to the window. Dark gray clouds filled the sky. Pine trees across the street pitched as the wind picked up. She checked her phone. Five minutes gone. Pacing around the back of Jasmine's desk, Ella glanced at the picture frames next to the laptop. Jasmine and a woman at the ocean. Another picture of a group of women in front of palm trees with a cruise ship in the background. Ella's eyes glimpsed the laptop screen. Jasmine's client calendar. She turned away. But frustration turned to curiosity. It was left it open. Why not peek?

Ella saw her ten o'clock appointment, along with other familiar names. Paige had been there at nine. Vivian was scheduled for eleven-thirty. Hope and Buck, two o'clock—though his name was crossed out. Tomorrow morning, Laura, a man's name she didn't recognize, and Hope again. Then Eleanor, Gladys, and Harold Madrigal in the afternoon. Ella couldn't believe it. Just about everyone she was acquainted with were patients of Jasmine's. She really knew the secrets of half the town. Ella glanced back at the screen. Wait, a minute. When did Harold get back in town?

JASMINE SCROLLED through her phone's daily schedule. She paused. "I'm looking right now. You're putting me in an uncomfortable spot… Fine, I'll hold while you check your schedule…" She checked her phone. Ten minutes since walking out of the office. Thunder rumbled outside. She knew Ella was waiting. Her next patient would be there any time. "I can't meet today… I don't care. This has gone too far. I have a reputation to protect… I'll see you tomorrow." Jasmine yanked out the earbuds and shoved them in her pocket. Flushed, she ducked into the bathroom and splashed water on her face. Leaving a patient wasn't at all professional, but it couldn't be helped.

ELLA CHECKED HER PHONE AGAIN. Almost fifteen minutes. She tiptoed over to the door and placed her ear to it. She heard muffled sounds. Then silence. Ella rushed back to her chair and plopped down. A few moments later, the door opened.

Jasmine walked in and dropped the phone on her desk. "Patient emergency. Sorry it took so long." She nodded to the clock and cleared her throat. "Unfortunately, our time is up." She opened the office door. "Let's meet again next week. We can continue where we left off." After Ella walked into the hall, Jasmine closed the door. Her neck ached, but rubbing it didn't help. She went over to the window and watched fat raindrops splatter on the sidewalk.

Ella stood alone in the hallway, her mind reeling. Why did Jasmine leave during their session? Why would she argue with a patient? And how would she and Shelby find who wrote the cryptic notes with half the businesses in town using the same paper?

CHAPTER THIRTY-TWO

Thunder crashed overhead. Rain pounded the roof and smacked against the large glass windows of The Bee's Knees. The door swung open and an older couple rushed in. A man with a dripping umbrella nodded to Shelby as he set it by the door.

"Mornin'," said Shelby. "Quite a storm."

The gray-haired, sweater-clad woman smiled. "Just happy to be out of that weather." She took the man's hand. They disappeared down an aisle as another woman walked in, equally drenched.

While customers were great for business, every time the door opened Shelby's heart skipped a beat. She expected Ella to return at any time, hopefully with some usable information.

The door opened again and Laura Vega breezed in carrying an armful of plastic-covered papers. "This week's edition of *The Pheasant Valley Roost.*" She removed the plastic and placed a stack on the counter. She squeezed Shelby's hand. "Can't stay and chat. Off to deliver more news."

"Thanks, Laura. Be careful driving in that weather." Laura

waved and headed back out into the deluge. Shelby opened the top copy and scanned the front page. Last week's storm with pictures of kids playing in the snow. Bill McTavish's interview about how he lost a dozen chickens to a coyote. Photos of flags placed on the veteran's graves at the New Pheasant Valley Cemetery. She turned the page and read the headline. "Local Resident Found Murdered." Shelby straightened the paper for a better view. "Buck Wilson, 41, was found dead at the Old Pheasant Valley Cemetery Friday, November 9… Neighbors reported a dog barking and alerted the sheriff's department … Eyewitnesses said they saw someone, possibly a woman, in the area just after sunrise… (Please see page 4)." What witnesses? What woman? She turned to page four. "According to the coroner, the victim died from apparent blunt force trauma to the head. An autopsy has been scheduled to determine cause and time of death. While no arrests have been made, the sheriff's department and the PV Police are working together in this investigation. Anyone with information is urged to call the Kern County Sheriff's Department and ask for Sergeant Dawn Nolan at 661-…"

Shelby chewed her lip. She and Ella didn't find Buck's body until after eight. Who was at the cemetery hours earlier? Did they have something to do with the murder? And why was Dawn now working with Alton? Nothing made sense.

The door opened again and a tall woman with short cropped blonde hair walked in. Shelby's breath caught. *Mac?* Wondering why she might be in town, Shelby moved from the counter to get a better look.

The tall woman nodded. "Good morning."

Shelby forced a smile while staring at her features. The resemblance was uncanny, bringing back painful memories of her failed relationship. She forced herself to breathe deeply and interact with the woman. "Still raining outside?"

"Almost let up. Thank goodness." The woman picked up a cloth-lined basket and walked over to Laura's lavender booth.

After the woman went down another aisle, Shelby's heart stopped racing. She opened the paper again, this time to a page with ads. Country Market reminding customers to order their fresh turkeys early for Thanksgiving. Pumpkin pies available at the Corner Café. The Bee's Knees Fall Sale. An article below the fold caught her attention. "Early Morning Burglary Keeps 'Em Laughing.' About 3 a.m. Friday morning, an unidentified caller reported seeing a smashed window at Harland Parke's dental office on Juneberry Street. After a thorough investigation, police determined a cylinder of nitrous oxide (better known as laughing gas) was missing. "This was the third break-in this year," reported a very shaken Dr. Parke. He was also quoted as saying, "Punk kids. Don't they know that stuff can be deadly?" When asked why his office might be a target, Parke shrugged and declined comment. Anyone with information is asked to call the Pheasant Valley Police Department and ask for…"

The door opened again and Paige sauntered in. She was wearing a red spandex-type outfit and carrying a bulky cardboard box. Shelby closed the paper and shoved it under the counter. As much as she wanted to talk, Shelby didn't want to rush up and startle her. Paige's bright red lipstick caught Shelby's eye. "Morning."

Paige stopped for a moment, then headed toward her booth.

Shelby followed in the wake of her gardenia perfume.

Placing a box on the floor, Paige scanned Shelby from head to tennis shoes. "You're that Shelby person, ain't ya? Nice shoes."

"Thanks."

Paige flashed her sparkly red nails, then offered her hand. "Anyone that loves glitter is all right in my book."

"What can I say? I love anything pink and glittery."

"Might as well show yer sparkle. Right?" Squatting, Paige opened a box and pulled out fuzzy bears in several assorted sizes.

Shelby shoved her hands in her pockets and walked closer. "Everyone loves your bears. I was in the store the other day when a little girl found one and made a new friend. She even named him before they left."

"That so?" Paige stood, smacked her gum, and continued to fill the shelves with her bears. "Thanks for tellin' me." After letting out a long sigh, she stopped for a moment. "Good friends are hard to find…"

Shelby reached out and brushed the fur of a large black bear decorated with a fabric bow tie, waiting for Paige to continue.

"And harder when they leave." She popped a large pink bubble, then picked up a small brown bear with big brown eyes.

"When d'you start making these bears?" asked Shelby, picking at the bow.

Paige popped another bubble, then bent down and pulled a small, gray bear with a top hat from the box. "Ever since Mama made me one." She turned and looked at Shelby. "We didn't have no money growin' up, so Mama said if I did my chores, she'd make me a bear to play with." Paige placed the bear on the shelf, then moved it to the right a few inches.

"You still have that bear?"

Paige shook her head. Her cherry-red hoop earrings swished back and forth. "House caught fire—"

"I'm so sorry, Paige."

"Not yer fault." She smacked her gum and pulled a long-haired, fluffy tan bear from the box.

"Well, you're making lots of people happy with your bears."

"Uh, huh."

"Paige, I'm really sorry for your…"

She glanced back at Shelby for a moment, then turned. "Told ya, it weren't yer fault."

Shelby cleared her throat. "I meant the other day. Your friend."

Paige stopped and squared her shoulders. "Worthless piece of dog poop."

Shelby stepped back a few feet Had she gone too far?

"Made promises. Didn't keep 'em. Whoever done him in, did us all a favor." Paige moved the bear with the top hat farther to the left, then turned and glared at Shelby. "He deserved what he got."

"You have any idea who—"

Her eyes flashed. "You really want to know what I think?"

Shelby swallowed. "Sure."

"It was that good-for-nothin' wife of his. You know she smacked him around? Even broke a beer bottle over his head once. I knows it 'cause he came to me so I could stitch him up, seeing I had the needles and thread and stuff. He didn't want to go to no hospital or they'd have called the cops. And he didn't want no more trouble with the law. That woman has a temper worse than a crazed grizzly. Ain't nothin' can stop her once she put a mind to it. I say it was her. Took him out to the cemetery. Busted his head. Then left him for the coyotes to find." She turned and wiped a tear rolling down her cheek, then glared at Shelby again.

"I'll tell ya somethin' else, too. If I ever see her again, I'll give her a piece of my mind. Horrid woman, Hope. Sucked all the life outta that poor man." Paige drew in a ragged breath. "What difference did it make? She had a lover in that house. Coulda just carried on and left Buck alone." Paige kicked an empty box out of her path and stormed down the aisle toward the counter where Ella was reading a newspaper. Paige stopped and pointed a finger in Ella's face. "And you. You ain't never gave him a chance to speak his mind. Maybe if you had, it woulda never happened." Paige swept a stack of flyers off the counter and marched out the front door into the gray drizzle.

CHAPTER THIRTY-THREE

After Paige stormed out of The Bee's Knees, Ella rushed around the counter. "What was that all about?" she asked, gathering the papers scattered across the floor.

"We were talking and Paige lost it." Shelby took the flyers from Ella and placed them back on the counter. She leaned in close. "Paige told me Hope killed Buck. She was quite adamant about it too."

"Interesting. But why so upset at me?" asked Ella. "I didn't give him a chance. Chance for what?"

"I don't know," said Shelby. "She mentioned something about letting Buck speak his mind." She stopped and nodded toward an older couple coming up an aisle.

"Even to the end," Ella whispered. "Paige stuck up for him." She turned and greeted the couple.

About the same time, several other customers walked up to the counter. Shelby came around and stood by the register. "How about I wrap and bag while you ring them up?"

Ella nodded at a tall woman waking down an aisle. She poked Shelby in the side. "Was that Mac?"

"No. Thank goodness. Freaked me out too." Shelby

watched the woman, then went back to wrapping a customer's wooden spoons. "Quite a resemblance, isn't it?"

"They say we all have a twin somewhere." As Ella waited on the next person in line, a young couple in their mid-thirties walked in. The full-bearded guy wore a Padre's cap. Ella did a double-take when she noticed the gal. "Shel, look…"

Shelby stopped wrapping a ceramic bowl and gasped. "Speaking of twins, except for the red, curly hair, she could be mine."

The guy nudged the gal and pointed at Shelby. "You never told me you had a sister."

The woman turned and stared at Shelby. Twisting a thick curl around her finger, she smiled. "If I didn't know better, I'd agree with my boyfriend."

Shelby stepped from behind the counter. The two women stood a few feet apart, staring at each other. Both wore black leggings. Shelby a pink knit sweater. The other gal, a hot pink crepe top.

"Wow, this is a bit freaky," said Shelby.

"You aren't kidding. Though I have to say, I totally love your fashion sense. I'm Cheryl."

"I'm Shelby. You from around here?"

"No. San Diego. Darius and me are headed up to Reno. Last time we drove straight through. This time, we're taking the scenic route."

"Less butt stress," said Darius, pointing to his posterior side.

"I feel your pain," said Shelby, laughing. "I drove here all the way from Houston in two days."

"Houston?" Darius scratched his beard. "That's like in Tennessee, isn't it?"

Cheryl patted him on the arm. "Hon, I think you mean Texas." She turned to Ella and Shelby. "He had a few too many edible brownies yesterday."

Darius grinned, gave her a kiss on the cheek, then wandered off down an aisle.

"How did you find our shop?" asked Ella.

"We just ate at that Corner Café place and saw your sign," said Cheryl. "I love little boutique shops and told Darius we had to stop before hitting the road again." She walked over to Laura's booth, picked up a candle, and held it to her nose. "This smells amazing."

"Y'all didn't drive up this morning, did you?"

"No way," said Cheryl. "Got in last night and stayed at a motel across from the park."

Darius came back with a handful of scrunchies. "Look, hon. For your hair."

"Just before you walked in, my friend Ella and I were talking about twin strangers," said Shelby. "I think that's what it's called. Anyway, I still can't get over it."

"I know, right?" said Darius. After paying for the scrunchies, he scratched his beard again, deep in thought.

"You okay, hon?"

"Just wondering if I have a twin out there somewhere."

"Sweetie, there's no one like you," said Cheryl, laughing. "Lord help us if there was." She turned to Shelby. "Do you or Ella have a booth? We'd love to see what you make."

"Mine has all-occasion wreaths," said Ella. "Though now, most are fall-themed."

"I design clothes for big gals." said Shelby. "But, only have infinity scarves in my booth."

"No kidding?" Cheryl clapped her hands. "In high school, I wanted to design clothes for big gals. I'd love to see what you have."

Ella narrowed her eyes. "You sure you're not long-lost twins?"

Cheryl shrugged. "Only the Universe knows for sure."

Shelby looked at Ella. "I'm sure it's just a coincidence." She turned to Cheryl. "I'm still getting settled since I moved back. If you follow me, I'll show you my booth." They walked down an aisle followed by Darius.

A few minutes later Cheryl came back with two scarves, one red, the other plaid. She unzipped a small, fuchsia satchel purse and pulled out a credit card along with her license. "Shelby, we must keep in touch. Once you have more stock, let me know."

Shelby swiped the card, then handed it back. "I don't have any business cards, yet. How about one of our flyers? I'll write my contact info on it."

Cheryl dug into her purse again and handed Shelby a pink card with black lettering on it. "Here's mine. I'm serious. Get in touch when you have something." She turned around. "Hon, you ready for another six hours in the car?"

Darius groaned.

Ella and Shelby laughed and waved as the couple made their way out the door.

"That was bizarre," said Ella.

"No kidding. Never had a sister, but if I could pick one—"

Two customers walked up and paid for purchases. When the store was quiet again, Ella glanced at Shelby. "What were we talking about?"

Shelby held up her hand. "Can't remember. But first, what happened with you? Did Jasmine still have the green paper?"

"Yes." Ella crouched behind the counter and pulled out a manila envelope. "And so does half the town."

"What?"

Opening the envelope, Ella showed Shelby the green copy paper. She explained how Jasmine gave away the reams at the Chamber meeting.

Shelby leaned against the counter and let out a long sigh. "Twenty-five hundred sheets? Anyone could have written that note."

Ella squared her shoulders. "I also peeked at her appointment calendar."

"Look at you. Sleuthing it up." Shelby high-fived Ella. "And just how did you get access to her calendar?"

"Jasmine took a phone call during our session. When she left the room, I happened to see her laptop screen."

"Just happened…?"

"Fine. I was upset and pacing. Not my fault she left it open."

"What did you find out, Ms. Super Sleuth?"

"Half the town are her patients—" The shop door opened and a thin woman in a blue knit hat walked in holding the hand of a young boy. Ella waited until they had walked past them then turned to Shelby. "And you want to hear something weird?"

"As if this day wasn't weird enough already."

"One of her patients is Harold Madrigal."

Shelby straightened. "Why does that name seem familiar?"

"Harold was the venture capitalist who helped Doug and me open the Steamed Bean."

"Right," said Shelby. "Wasn't he a bit peeved at Buck when you closed the coffee place after Doug's death?"

Ella cleared her throat. "Harold was a lot peeved. He lost everything. He and Buck argued a lot. At one point, Harold threatened to sue, but filed bankruptcy instead."

Shelby looked at Ella with wide eyes. "When did Harold get back in town?"

"No idea," said Ella. "But it seems we need to add another suspect to the list."

CHAPTER THIRTY-FOUR

Standing near the front of The Bee's Knees, Shelby stared at Ella. "Do you think Harold could be a suspect?"

"He had as much motive as the other half-dozen people holding a grudge against Buck."

"Can we deal with this later?" asked Shelby, rubbing her eyes. "Too many names and motives to keep track in my head." She motioned to the pile of newspapers. "Did you read the article about Buck?"

"Not yet. Why?" Ella grabbed a copy and thumbed through it.

"Look at the part about the witnesses."

Ella moved her lips, then read aloud, "...someone, possibly a woman, in the area just after sunrise." Ella slammed the paper closed. "What witnesses? What woman?"

"I thought the same thing. I wondered who wrote the article, but it didn't have a byline."

"No description mentioned," said Ella. "Maybe they didn't get a good look. Can you chat with Laura? As editor, she'd know more about the story."

"Good idea," said Shelby.

Ella grimaced. "After what Alton said at the cemetery, you don't think someone's trying to set me up, do you?"

Shelby thought back to the conversation she had with Dawn during lunch. Her throat tightened. Her head throbbed. Dawn had mentioned Alton's impatience and even hinted that unless they rekindled their relationship, she wouldn't dispute Alton's charges against Ella.

"Shel. You okay?"

She shook off the memories of Dawn's threats. "Just thinking… Paige thought Hope did it. Maybe that's the woman the witness talked about."

Ella grabbed a water bottle. "I'm on edge over this whole thing."

"Don't blame you." She placed her hand on Ella's. "Not to make things worse, but you should read about the break in."

"Why? Did they blame that on a mysterious woman, too?"

The door opened and Vivian walked in carrying an umbrella and a newspaper. "Did you two read today's pap—"

Ella and Shelby looked up. "Yes," they said at the same time.

Vivian set her umbrella behind the counter. "Oh, I see you have it. Terrible news, isn't it?" She picked up the feather duster. "Better busy myself or I'm just going to stand here and fret, which won't do us any good."

Ella pulled out the clipboard with the volunteer schedule. "Viv, you're not supposed to be here today."

She turned. "I know. But I couldn't sit in my old house by myself knowing you were down here. Tried to sketch out a new painting, but my mind was full from ruminating. Once I get that way, the only cure is a good dose of chores. I cleaned my house and played a dozen games of solitaire, then figured I'd come down here. Didn't think you'd mind."

"I appreciate the support." Ella gave Vivian a quick hug.

"You're welcome any time. Even if you just want to visit or need to talk."

Vivian smiled. "You know me. Busy hands make a happy heart… Or something like that." Humming a familiar tune, she began dusting.

Ella pointed to the schedule. "Shel, I noticed you put yourself down for tomorrow morning. Don't you have a dentist's appointment?"

Shelby rolled her eyes. "Thanks for the reminder. Oh and don't forget about dinner with Gladys and Ed tomorrow night."

Ella pulled her phone from her pocket and scrolled through her calendar. "Got it."

Vivian walked up again and leaned on the counter. "What do you make of that break in at Doctor Parke's?"

Ella cleared her throat. "Didn't you come in to forget all your ruminating?"

Vivian chuckled and walked away again.

The door opened. Dawn strolled in, in full uniform. "Morning ladies."

Shelby forced a smile. "Dawn."

"In the area and thought I'd drop in to see your booth, Shel."

"It's not ready to show, yet." Shelby hesitated. "And right now, I'm busy helping Ella."

Dawn glanced around, then locked eyes with Shelby. "There appears to be a lull." She turned to Ella. "You wouldn't miss Shel for a few minutes. Would you?"

Ella tried to come up with an excuse, but couldn't think fast enough. She shook her head and mouthed, "I'm sorry," to Shelby when Dawn turned away.

Shelby gritted her teeth and glared at Dawn. "Follow me." They walked across the room and down an aisle. Shelby stopped and pointed. "That's it." She started back toward the front.

Dawn blocked the aisle. "Where do you think you're going?"

Shelby's blood pressure rose. She turned. "I told you it was practically empty. I'm sure you don't need me to stand here while you browse through a few scarves."

Dawn caught Shelby's eye and stepped closer. "No. But, might be worth your while to keep me company."

Shelby moved back and glared. "What do you mean?"

"You never gave me an answer about the lake." She picked up a scarf and glanced at the price tag. "I hoped you'd changed your mind. My brother is getting closer to an arrest."

Shelby's eyes widened. She wanted to stand up to Dawn, but the words, 'emotional blackmail,' caught in her throat. "Why are you doing this?"

Dawn tossed the scarf on the shelf. "Just updating you on the case. If you remember, I said I'd share all the details if we went out to the lake to see the fall colors." She picked up another scarf and held it up to her collar. "This color would bring out the green in my eyes, don't you think?"

"Yeah. Looks great." Shelby wanted to twist the scarf around Dawn's neck. She closed her eyes and counted to ten instead.

"If the changing colors aren't your thing, hon, there's a new little café out past Cal City. I'm sure we could find a quiet table to talk… about the case. My treat."

Shelby's head pounded. "Already got plans tonight."

Dawn winked. "Then tomorrow?"

"Ella and I have plans." Why did she just say that? Dawn didn't need to know her personal business.

Dawn caressed the scarf. "Then Wednesday it is. What time should I pick you up?"

"N… No. I'm going to be busy that night, too."

Draping the scarf around Shelby's neck, Dawn pulled her close. "Alton's itching to wrap up this case by the end of the week," she whispered. "If I were you, I'd make time for dinner." She let loose of one end and drew it back slowly until the scarf was in her hand.

Shelby's ears burned. "Wednesday. Is. Fine. Just dinner. No lake. I'm picking you up." She needed to maintain some control.

Dawn tossed the scarf on the shelf and smirked. "It's a date."

Shelby opened her mouth, but before she could reply, Dawn had turned and marched out the front door.

CHAPTER THIRTY-FIVE

Shelby stomped up to the front counter of The Bee's Knees, rubbing her temples. Putting up with Dawn's chiding was more than she could take. But, for the sake of her friend, she couldn't run away, even though everything inside wanted to bolt.

"You okay?" asked Ella.

"Terrible headache."

"Shel, go home and rest. Viv and I will handle things." She leaned in close. "Besides, it would do Viv good to stay."

"You sure?" Shelby cracked her neck. "What if you get busy again, like this morning?"

Ella scrutinized the schedule. "I've got two crafters scheduled for this afternoon. Along with Viv, we'll be fine. Go home before your head gets worse."

Shelby nodded and squeezed Ella's hand. "Thanks." Looping a scarf around her neck, Shelby waved to Vivian and left the shop. Outside, crimson leaves skittered around her feet as she walked across the half-empty parking lot. Patches of sapphire-blue sky peeked through the gray clouds. Shelby let out a long sigh. She didn't want to go with Dawn. But she didn't want Alton to arrest her friend. Hopefully, meeting for dinner would save Ella.

Car idling, Shelby waited for a slow-walking gray-haired man with a golden retriever before pulling out into the street. She wanted to head home but her stomach growled as she passed the Café. Shelby wondered if it would be prudent to stop after Paige's outburst. Last thing she wanted to do was rile her up at work. Plus, with a pounding head, she didn't need more drama. Shelby looked around for another choice to satisfy her hunger.

Waiting to turn left onto Juneberry, she had a few moments to decide between "Burgers and More" or "Ye Olde Sandwich Shoppe." Only a few cars in the drive-through at the burger place. Simple decision. Once she ordered, paid, and picked up her lunch, Shelby headed back to Ella's. Thank goodness she had ordered the large fries. By the time she pulled into the driveway, half were gone, though she didn't recall eating them.

Oatmeal danced and barked as he greeted Shelby. "Yes. I missed you, too." Mr. Butterfingers sniffed the air, jumped off the couch, and followed her into the kitchen. Dropping the bags of food on the table, she headed to the back door with Oatmeal. "After he goes out, everyone will get treats."

When Oatmeal and Shelby came back in, Mr. Butterfingers was on the table nosing around the lunch bags. "Hey. You know better than that." The cat jumped down and sat in the middle of the floor, swishing his tail. Shelby patted his head, then retrieved the promised treats for each pet. Once they were fed, she filled a glass with water and sat at the table to finish her meal. A double cheeseburger with lettuce, grilled onions and roasted red peppers, slathered with a specialty sauce that tasted a lot like herbed mayo, plus the rest of her thick-cut steak fries.

As Oatmeal pawed at Shelby's leg, the cat looked up and meowed. "Sorry, guys. The burger has onions. Not good for either of you. She pinched off pieces of a fry and offered it. Oatmeal gulped his and waited for more. Mr. Butterfingers gave her "the look" which Shelby imagined was equivalent to a cat's eye-roll. "I'll give you extra treats when I'm done, okay?" Mr. Butterfingers seemed to understand and sprawled out under her chair. Oatmeal pawed at her thigh again. She slipped him another tiny piece of fry and leaned over. "Don't tell Ella." After she rubbed his ears and showed empty hands, the dog settled near her feet.

Tummy full, Shelby tossed the empty bags in the trash and gave the fur babies one last treat. Although her headache had almost subsided, she took some painkillers. She'd be listing suspects and motives later with Ella and didn't want to risk a relapse.

Shelby went upstairs and grabbed one of her sketchbooks and a few pens, then came back and plopped on the comfy sofa in the front room. Oatmeal jumped up and settled next to her. Mr. Butterfingers resumed his spot on the back of the sofa. As Shelby opened to a clean page, a yawn escaped. She glanced up. Just past one o'clock. With both animals napping, Shelby figured a human nap wouldn't hurt. The ticking clock and purring cat lulled her into a drowsy state. Soon, sounds faded into the distance.

Loud knocking, followed by sharp barking, woke everyone. Shelby sat up, trying to get her bearings. Oatmeal stood on the edge of the couch, yipping and wagging his tail. "Shush, dog." She scratched his head. "It's okay." Stumbling from the couch, she caught her reflection in the glass of a framed photo on the wall. She attempted to pat down several stray hairs to no avail.

Shelby peeked out the curtain, then opened the door. "Oatmeal, it's only Laura."

"How are you feeling?" Laura walked in; her aqua-colored blouse fluttered around her like the wings of a delicate butterfly. "When I stopped by the shop to replenish stock, Ella mentioned your headache. Just had to come by and bring you something for it."

"No need. Headache's gone," said Shelby.

Laura held out a small glass jar with a purple ribbon tied across the silver lid. "Hon, this is my super-relaxing, lavender butter. Rub it on your temples and forehead. Guaranteed to relieve stress."

Knowing it was useless to refuse Laura's help, Shelby smiled and untied the ribbon. The moment she opened the jar, the calming scent enveloped her. "This is amazing."

Laura's blue eyes brightened. "I knew you'd love it."

"Where are my manners?" said Shelby. "Please have a seat. Can I get you something? Tea? Coffee?"

Laura sat on the sofa, but caught Shelby's arm. "You sit. I'm only here for a quick visit to make sure you're okay."

Shelby settled in the wingback chair, inhaling the lavender butter. "Might need another nap if I keep sniffing this stuff. It's wonderful." Oatmeal jumped up and snuggled against her leg.

Mr. Butterfingers hopped up on the cushion and settled in next to Laura. She rubbed his back and soon he was purring. "The lavender butter will help calm these critters, too. Like when Mother Nature acts up. Or…" she winked. "…the pet-parents are stressed." Her calm voice and demeanor soothed Shelby.

"It has been a bit stressful around here."

Laura smiled. "Hon, it's just part of life. Ebb and flow. We just need to let it flow through us so it doesn't make us sick… or cause headaches."

"I agree," said Shelby. "Sometimes, though, I get caught up in it all."

"You're an empath." Laura moved her hands in front of Shelby's body. "You not only feel others' emotions, but you absorb them. It's what makes you exceptional. But it can also be your downfall if you don't learn to release others' feelings stuck inside you."

Shelby thought for a moment, taking in another draw from the lavender butter. "That makes sense. Thank you."

Laura reached out and squeezed Shelby's hand, then stood. "Anytime, hon. Well, lots to do. I better get going."

Shelby headed to the door, but didn't open it. "Before you go. Mind if I ask you a question?"

"Of course not." Laura's eyes sparkled. "Ask away."

"I was wondering about that article in the paper…"

"Which one?"

"The one about Buck. It talked about witnesses seeing a woman at the cemetery. I checked the byline, but there wasn't one."

"Don't use a byline for my own articles."

"*You* interviewed the person who saw a woman?"

Laura placed her hands near, but not touching Shelby. Circling them over Shelby's head and in front of her chest, Laura closed her eyes for a moment then opened them. "I sense many emotions… Fear. Anger… No, rage. And love. You desire to protect someone close to you, but something is standing in the way."

"How do you know?"

"I'm also an empath. I feel and absorb your emotions."

"Then you must know this information is important to me. I need to know about that woman. If there was a description." Mr. Butterfingers rubbed against Shelby's leg and meowed. Maybe he sensed feelings, too.

Laura smiled. "The person I interviewed didn't give a description. They just knew it was a woman."

"Can you at least tell me who you interviewed?"

"Of course, hon. It was Sergeant Nolan."

Shelby's eyes widened. "Dawn?" Thinking back to the morning she and Ella found Buck, Dawn was nowhere near them. She even appeared to be in shock when they told her about the body. Or, Shelby wondered, was she just pretending? She clenched her jaw, then unclenched it, remembering Laura would "absorb" her frustration. Right now, she needed to hide her feelings, if that was possible. Shelby opened the door. "Thanks. For the lavender butter and the information. Both have been most helpful."

"Make sure you remember what I said about us empaths." Laura unlatched the screen and stepped out onto the porch. "And use as much butter as needed. I have more."

"Don't worry, I will." Shelby closed the door and went back into the house. She plopped down on the sofa and picked up her sketch pad. Staring at the open jar on the coffee table, she patted Oatmeal. "We might just need an entire case of that stuff before this is over."

CHAPTER THIRTY-SIX

Massaging her lower back, Ella glanced at the antique clock on the wall of The Bee's Knees. Almost five. Despite the break in the weather, the afternoon had been quiet. She never understood why people came out in droves during stormy weather, but trickled in when it cleared. Either way, she didn't mind. Business was good for the vendors.

While waiting for the last customer to finish his shopping, Ella texted Shelby. "Hope you are feeling better. What do you want me to bring home for dinner?" Though most friends used cryptic text-language, she couldn't bring herself to abbreviate words and still wrote in full sentences, including punctuation. Shelby always gave Ella a tough time and texted back using as few characters as possible.

Ella's phone chimed, signaling a response. "feel gr8 gt dnnr cvrd cu" First, she cringed at the lack of grammar, punctuation, and vowels. Then she smiled, happy to see Shelby feeling better. Ella looked up from her phone as a pleasant-looking African American gentleman with salt and pepper hair stepped up to the counter. He took a half dozen jars of the Purcell's apple butter from his basket. As he came closer, the deep scent of cedar and sandalwood caught Ella's nose. A fond memory of Doug's favorite cologne.

Pointing to the jars on the counter, he smiled and pulled out his wallet. "The wife just loves this stuff. We drive up from the Valley to get it."

"I agree. It's the best apple butter anywhere around." Ella rang up his purchase and wrapped each jar in tissue paper. Placing them in one of the store bags, she added a flyer. "Safe travels back down the hill."

The man nodded. "Hopefully, this will last through spring. Last year, they closed the freeway up here because of the snow and we had to use…" He looked around then continued, "… store bought. Worst mistake ever."

Ella chuckled. "We can always ship if you're desperate."

The man's eye's brightened. "Good to know. Happy holidays."

"And to you, too." Ella locked the door behind him, then turned the sign to "CLOSED." Vivian came from the back of the store, followed by two other vendors. She gathered her umbrella and purse and took out her keys.

"Thanks for your help today," said Ella.

Vivian embraced Ella in a tight hug. "Thank you for letting me help."

Ella arranged a scarf around her neck and grabbed a few things, along with a copy of the newspaper. The others signed out and walked over to the door, chatting about Thanksgiving recipes. As they waited under the shop's outside light, Ella locked up. Given it was dark, and with Parke's burglary still heavy on their minds, the women walked out to the parking lot together.

After the long day, Ella pulled up into her driveway. Stepping out of the car, leaves swirled around her shoes. Rustling in the pine trees caused her to look up, though all she could see were the murky outlines of treetops and something flitting between the trees. Bats, maybe? Something scampered across the drive and disappeared into the darkness. She shivered. Most likely rats. She rushed up to the porch, heart pounding. Oatmeal's barks, whines, and scratches came from behind the door. Opening it, the dog jumped and danced around her. She bent to pet him as Mr. Butterfingers padded up to offer his own welcome-home meows. Shelby came down the stairs, notebook in hand, and stood next to her cat.

Ella laughed. "Love the way you all greet me when I come home. Makes one feel special."

Shelby leaned in and embraced Ella. "You are special."

Ella lingered for a few moments, feeling the tension dissipate from her body. She stepped back and squeezed Shelby's hand. "Glad you're feeling better." Turning toward the kitchen, Ella caught the scent of garlic and onions. "You've been busy."

Shelby gestured to the animals. "We've been busy."

"Good to see everyone's been pitching in." Ella walked through the kitchen and looked around. A foil-covered baking dish sat on the table. After hanging up her scarf and sweater in the mudroom, she came back in the kitchen and found Shelby standing by the oven, a thick blue potholder on each hand.

"Almost ready, we'll eat as soon as—" A ding came from the oven timer. "It's done." Shelby turned off the oven, opened the door, and pulled out a foil-wrapped tube. "Garlic French bread to go with the lasagna."

Ella raised an eyebrow. "When did you go to the store and make everything?"

Shelby grinned. "It was Laura. After she dropped off the lavender butter, she came back to tell me she'd bring dinner."

"Can't believe Laura went through all this trouble," said Ella, lifting the foil off the main course. She scooped a hearty square dripping with cheesy goo onto Shelby's plate, then one on her own.

Shelby sat, then jumped up. "Oops. Almost forgot the salad." She opened the refrigerator, grabbed a glass bowl and two large forks. "Here ya go."

Serving herself salad, Ella rounded out the meal with a thick slice of bread covered in garlic butter and parmesan cheese. "This is fantastic."

Shelby pointed to the lasagna with her fork. "Laura said she was making dinner for Hope and doubled the recipe."

Ella took a bite of the lasagna. "Much better than the frozen ones I get from the store. Is there anything that woman can't do?"

"Wait until you try her lavender butter," said Shelby.

Ella looked at her plate and frowned. "On my bread?"

"No, silly." Shelby laughed. "On your forehead. I'll show you after dinner."

"What else did you all accomplish today?" asked Ella.

"Naps. We all took a nap. And new sketches. Of course, I did the sketches, they watched." Shelby gave Ella a toothy grin.

"Oh, Shel. That's great. I'd love to see them… when you're ready to share."

Shelby nodded. "They're rough. But soon, I promise. I also made a list of suspects. I'm curious to see what you think… after dinner, of course." She bit into a thick slice of buttery bread.

Ella sopped up sauce with the last piece of her bread. "Sounds good. You got a lot done. And to think I just stood around all day and worked."

Shelby touched Ella's hand. "I feel terrible about leaving. But, on the positive side, I got info from Laura about that article. And you'll never believe what she said."

"Please, tell." Ella took a drink of water and wiped her mouth with a napkin.

"Well…" Shelby recounted how Laura was the one who interviewed Dawn.

"Wait." said Ella. "Dawn wasn't around. How would she know who was at the cemetery?"

"That's what I thought as well. And get this, when Laura came back later with dinner, she remembered another detail not included in the article because of space constraints."

"What did she say?"

"Laura said, not only did Dawn tell her she saw a woman. But also that the woman was walking a dog in the cemetery just before they found the body."

Ella slapped her hand on the table. Oatmeal jumped up and barked. "Sorry, sweetie. It's okay." She stroked his ear and attempted to control her voice. "Dawn wasn't even in the area until someone else called in about a barking dog. We both know the woman in the cemetery was me with Oatmeal." Ella rubbed her eyes, then glared at Shelby. "Why are Dawn and Alton setting me up as their prime suspect?"

CHAPTER THIRTY-SEVEN

Sitting at the kitchen table, Ella sipped her morning coffee and nodded to her friend. "Something on your mind?"

"Oh, you know…" Shelby poked at the scrambled eggs on her plate and watched them steam. "Me and dentist appointments."

"Shel, you can do this. Look how brave you were last week."

She held out a trembling hand. "This is not brave. And, I don't even have to be there for a few hours."

Ella smiled. "Maybe you should use Laura's lavender butter. That cream took away my stress last night."

Shelby thought back to the previous evening. After going over the list of suspects (and drinking too many cups of coffee) neither one could sleep. She remembered the jar of lavender butter and showed it to Ella, who fell asleep right away. While the lavender butter helped, Shelby laid awake most of the night concerned about Dawn's advances.

"Hey, Shel." Ella's voice brought Shelby out of her thoughts. "You're far away again."

"Too much on my mind, I guess." She finished her coffee

and watched Ella carry a stack of dishes to the sink. Though Shelby looked forward to dinner with the Purcells', she just wanted the next two days to pass, then she and Ella could talk about their future.

Ella glanced out the kitchen window as she rinsed off the dishes. "Those clouds are getting darker. And closer. Looks like rain. Or maybe snow."

Shelby went to the window and peered outside. "I'll drive into town. Then I won't have to walk to the dentist's office."

"How about you get ready while I finish these up," said Ella. "Maybe we can beat the storm if we leave early."

DRIVING INTO TOWN, Shelby tried to focus on the road and Ella's conversation, but her anxious brain was the worst. No matter how hard she tried, she couldn't shake the image of big, ugly needles. She pulled up to the curb in front of The Bee's Knees. "Wish you would come with me. I'm feeling extra nervous."

Ella squeezed Shelby's hand. "I'll be here when you get back. Don't forget, the doctor has nitrous."

Shelby closed her eyes for a moment hoping he'd restocked since the break in. She steeled herself for the inevitable and headed to the appointment. After parking out front, Shelby walked into an empty waiting room infused with the smell of cinnamon and vanilla. Several ladies behind a divider bustled around pulling charts, chatting, and answering phone calls.

"Morning, Shelby," said Kelly, a perky receptionist who sounded like she'd overdosed on caffeine. "Please have a seat. Someone will be with you in a few minutes."

Before she could respond, Kelly rushed over to a stack of file folders. To have that much energy, so early in the morning. Shelby walked over to a row of empty chairs, sat in the middle one, and pulled out her phone. Though she tried to concentrate on a word game, her hands trembled. Not being able to pass a level after several attempts, she gave up and rested her head against the wall.

A few minutes later, a middle-aged Hispanic man wearing jeans and a rain-sprinkled jogging suit top walked in. After Kelly greeted him, he found a seat in a different row and plopped down. He sighed as Shelby let out her own sigh. Waiting was the worst.

A petite woman holding a chart near the divider called out. "Shelby?"

Adrenaline shot through her body. Shelby jumped up and walked toward her.

The woman's glossy, plum-colored, blunt-cut hair bobbed as she talked. "I'm Emma. Please follow me." When they arrived at an exam room, Emma pointed to a chair and studied the chart. "You're here for fillings, correct?"

Though she wanted to say, "No," Shelby nodded instead.

"How are you feeling today?" asked Emma. "Any pain?"

While Shelby's brain screamed, Why the heck am I putting myself through this torture? her voice said, "I'm fine. No pain at all." She tried to laugh, but made a weird throaty sound. Stupid nerves.

"Good to hear. Just sit tight and Doctor Parke will be in soon." After attaching a paper bib around Shelby's neck with metal clips, Emma walked out.

Shelby scanned the room. The obligatory teeth model sat on the counter along with latex gloves, cotton balls, and swabs. Though a nearby tray was covered, she knew what lurked beneath. Syringes, along with red and blue vials. She shuddered and closed her eyes.

A moment later, Shelby felt a powerful urge to relieve her nervous bladder. She climbed out of the chair and peeked around the corner. Dr. Parke leaned against a wall at the end of the hall, talking on his phone. She looked the other way and spotted coffee-loving Kelly dashing to another exam room. Shelby waved at Kelly. "Hey, can you show me where the restroom…?"

Kelly stopped for a millisecond and pointed to a door just past where Dr. Parke stood. "Over there, to your left."

Shelby walked down the hall, trying to avoid the dentist's gaze. She tried the door. Locked. As much as she tried not to listen, Shelby caught most of his side of the conversation while she waited.

"I have patients to see… After lunch would be better. My car? It's at home. Flat tire, had to get a ride into town… Emergency? What about Doctor Montgomery… His wife's in labor? Well, then… Give me a sec." Dr. Parke looked around and motioned to one of his hygienists. "Hayden, I need to borrow your car to get up to the prison. Shouldn't take but a few hours."

She reached in her pocket, and handed him a key. "You know how to drive a stick, right?"

Dr. Parke shrugged. "Actually, no."

Hayden stepped back. "I suppose I can take you up there. Or…" she pointed to another woman filing paperwork. "Jayleen? Doctor needs a car to get up to the prison."

Jayleen nodded and motioned to the dentist. "You can use mine."

He resumed his phone call. "Let them know I'll be up in a little while." After ending the call, he dropped the phone in his jacket pocket and nodded at Jayleen. "Thanks."

Finally, the other person walked out of the restroom. After Shelby relieved herself, she scurried back down the hall, mulling over Dr. Parke's conversation. She walked into the exam room, but Emma stopped her before she sat in the chair.

"Change of plans," said Emma. "Patient emergency. Doctor had to run up to the prison."

Shelby's shoulders relaxed. "I get to go home?"

"The doc suggested you get your teeth cleaned and reschedule the fillings." Emma motioned for Shelby to follow.

"Does he go up to the prison often?" asked Shelby.

"Several times a month for the last five years," said Emma. "Plus on-call each Tuesday, for emergencies like today."

Shelby said nothing, but found it thought-provoking since it was a Tuesday. Why didn't he bring his car?

Emma pointed to a thin woman wearing green scrubs with pink polka dots, her silver hair wrapped in a neat bun. "Shelby, this is Marjorie, one of our hygienists."

"Nice to meet you." Marjorie's eyes crinkled as she welcomed Shelby and showed her where to sit. Pulling a surgical mask over her mouth and nose, Marjorie donned a pair of safety glasses and gloves, then reclined the chair and started cleaning Shelby's teeth. "Tell me a little about yourself…"

Shelby never understood why dentists and hygienists asked questions when she couldn't respond. She mumbled something, then closed her eyes and listened to the country music coming through the ceiling speaker. After Marjorie finished picking and polishing, she sat the chair back up and handed her a bag of goodies. Toothpaste, toothbrush, and minty floss (Shelby's favorite).

Marjorie pulled down her surgical mask, revealing a hidden smile. "See you back in six months, dear."

"Yes. Thanks." Shelby turned and headed to what she thought was the front, but soon was turned around. The hallway went in both directions. There was a fifty/fifty chance of getting lost. And lost she was.

Shelby looked both ways and didn't see Marjorie or Kelly. In fact, for the first time since she'd arrived, there was no one in the hall with her. She proceeded about ten feet and turned into the first doorway, hoping it was Marjorie's room. Instead,

Shelby walked right into a large office. She knew at once it was Dr. Parke's since his name was emblazoned on a gold nameplate atop a large oak desk.

With no one in the hall, did she dare sleuth? As Shelby's heart thumped, she glanced around. Her eyes landed on a stack of green copy paper. Not surprising. Then, She spotted several pictures on the wall with the doctor, a guy, and a gal. In each picture, one of them was holding a trophy. Bowling league? Must be with the matching shirts and Parke's Pin Heads embroidered across the front. Interesting name, thought Shelby. Wait, who were those other people in the photo with him? She strained forward for a closer look.

A high-pitched voice scolded from behind. "What are you doing in Doctor Parke's office?"

Shelby froze, then turned.

Kelly stood in the doorway, hands on hips.

"I'm sorry," said Shelby. "I got lost and walked in here by accident. There was no one around…"

Kelly stepped back into the hall and pointed. "That way."

As Shelby rushed out of the room, Kelly closed the door without another word.

Hurrying through the waiting room and out the front door, Shelby later realized she'd forgotten to make a return appointment. Her mind was spinning. Why were Parke, Buck, and Jasmine all on the same bowling team?

CHAPTER THIRTY-EIGHT

Ella busied herself behind the counter of The Bee's Knees while Laura rearranged a row of jars on the bottom shelf of her display. "That lavender butter is amazing," said Ella.

"Thanks, hon. One of my most popular items." She stood, wiped her hands on her denim skirt, then stepped back. "Looks okay, don't you think?"

"Yes," said Ella. "Very festive."

Laura pointed to the display. "With all the cultural holidays coming up, I went with a neutral theme of lavender and silver. These two months are stressful for many harried souls. The gift of calming helps. Just hope I don't run out." She walked up to Ella, then held her hands above Ella's head and along the sides of her body. "You're feeling better, aren't you?"

Ella nodded. "Thanks to your butter."

Laura took Ella's hand in her warm grasp. "And another thing… A heart at peace. One that has been longing for a while."

Ella face flushed. She had told no one about her feelings for Shelby. In fact, she and Shelby hadn't talked about them either.

"Ella, my heart absorbs your energy. I feel positive forces glowing from your soul."

Uncomfortable with Laura's premonitions, Ella stepped back. "Before I forget, dinner last night was amazing and thoughtful. Thanks so much."

"My pleasure." Laura pulled on a pair of dark gloves and adjusted her wide-brimmed, dark blue bolero hat, then picked up the last of the empty boxes. "Anytime." As she headed out into the deluge, Shelby walked in, brushing rain off her sweater. She and Laura greeted each other, then Shelby turned and rushed over to Ella.

"You're in a much better mood," said Ella. "Told you it would be okay."

"I never got the fillings."

"I don't understand."

"Just a cleaning. Doctor Parke had to leave. And… you'll never guess what I discovered."

"The store's quiet, follow me and we can talk."

They walked to the sitting area. Shelby sat on the edge of her chair and leaned in. "Once I got there…" She explained why she got a cleaning instead of fillings. "Then, I had to use the bathroom and got lost."

"Doctor Parke went up to the prison?"

"Apparently he's been doing that for quite a while." Shelby moved closer to Ella. "And wait till you hear—"

The front door opened and Jasmine walked in carrying several small boxes stacked one on top of the other.

"Hold that thought." Ella hurried to Jasmine. "Need any help?"

Dressed in black pants and a long, red cardigan cinched around the waist, she nodded. "If you could just take that top box before it falls."

Ella reached for the teetering box, then followed Jasmine to her booth. "Didn't think you were coming in until Thursday."

Jasmine glanced past Ella, then crouched as she placed the other boxes on the carpet. Standing again, she smiled. "I had a few last-minute cancellations and thought I'd stop in. You don't mind, do—?" The front door opened. Her smile faded. Her body became rigid.

"Of course not." Ella followed her gaze. "Everything okay?"

"Yes. Fine." She reached into a box. "I'll let you get back to your customers."

Taking the hint she wanted to be alone, Ella walked to the front and greeted an older couple walking in. Shelby stood behind the counter ringing up another customer's purchases. Once the front area was clear, Ella caught Shelby's attention. "We can finish that conversation."

Shelby shook her head. "Later."

The hairs on the back of Ella's neck prickled. Maybe Laura's energy-reading stuff had rubbed off. Before she had a chance to think about it, the older couple came up to the counter with a basketful of items.

"Good morning," said Ella.

The woman patted down her wet hair. "I suppose, if you enjoy the rain."

The man gave a gapped-tooth grin. "I love a good downpour. The wife, on the other hand, wants sun all day."

The woman rolled her eyes and paid for their purchases. She watched Ella wrap each item and place it into her cloth bag. As they walked away, the woman didn't hesitate to remind the man why she preferred a dryer climate. He opened the door, and they walked back into the rain.

Out of the corner of her eye, Ella noticed Jasmine standing at the end of an aisle studying her phone. She straightened when the door opened and two young women walked in. Then she focused back on her phone. A moment later, Jasmine dropped her phone in her sweater pocket and rushed to the door. She watched the street for a few minutes, then bolted outside and stood in the rain. As Ella and Shelby watched, a large man in jeans and a dark-hooded sweatshirt walked up to her.

Ella nudged Shelby. "What's up with that?"

"No idea."

The man pulled back the hood and stepped closer to Jasmine. He pointed and gestured at something beyond their view. Jasmine stepped back. The man matched her movements.

Shelby reached for her phone. "Should we call the police?"

"Wait," said Ella. "That looks like Ben."

Jasmine glanced right, then left. She pulled a long, white envelope from her sweater and shoved it at Ben. After he took it, Jasmine hurried to her car and left. Ben rifled through the envelope and stuck something deep inside his jacket. Crumpling the envelope, he tossed it on the ground and pulled the hoodie over his head. Ben bolted around the corner and out of sight.

"What was that all about?" asked Shelby.

"Don't know," said Ella. "But now Jasmine's behavior makes more sense."

"Why do you say that?"

"Just a feeling, I guess." Ella drummed her fingers on the countertop. "I'm getting a headache. Not sure if it's from overthinking or hunger. We should get lunch and deal with this later."

Shelby grabbed her scarf. "How about I go? What sounds good?"

Ella thought for a moment. "I'm sure Gladys has been cooking up a storm today. Something light."

Shelby laughed. "You're right. Be back soon." She ventured outside in the heavy drizzle and sprinted to her vehicle. The temperature had dropped since returning from the dentist. She rubbed her hands on her thighs, hoping the friction would help until the heater kicked in. As the wipers thumped a steady rhythm, she pulled away from the curb and headed over to the Corner Café.

Once inside, Shelby ordered two Lunch Specials: Chicken soup with a choice of a half sandwich. Ham and cheese for her. A club for Ella. And a mini blueberry cobbler for a treat. Waiting, she glanced around the busy restaurant. She didn't see Paige, although several other servers bustled around. Shelby did a double-take when she noticed a familiar-looking man wearing a hoodie sitting at the counter. Ben. He forked food in his mouth with one hand while gesturing to a nearby server with the other. Shelby was too far away to catch any of the conversation, but he was more animated than the elusive shadow lurking in Hope's front room when she and Laura had visited. At one point, Ben even twisted around on his stool and patted a passing server on the backside. The woman stopped, pointed a finger in his face, and rushed off again. What a jerk.

"Two lunch specials and a blueberry cobbler to go."

Shelby signaled to the cashier it was her order and walked toward the register. Before she got there, Ben trudged past and cut in line. A stale body odor followed him. She stepped back and coughed while Ben pulled a wad of cash from inside his jacket. He flipped through the bills and dropped a fifty on the counter. Eyeing the toothpicks, he picked through them with thick, grubby fingers, placed one between his teeth, then grinned at the cashier. "Keep the change, Doll." He turned and sauntered over to the double doors, bumped one side with his hip, and left the café.

Once the young cashier handed the bill to Shelby, she paid and left with their lunches and dessert. Outside, she glanced around. Ben wasn't anywhere. Though, his stench hung frozen in the air.

CHAPTER THIRTY-NINE

The last splinters of sunlight dissolved behind the charcoal-gray clouds hovering just above the mountaintops. After locking the shop, Ella climbed into the passenger side of Shelby's idling jeep and let out a deep sigh. She rested her head on the padded headrest. "Long day. Glad to be off my feet."

"No kidding." Shelby turned on the headlights and pulled out onto the street. "Other than being at the dentist's, the only time I had a chance to sit was during lunch. I just hope dinner is calmer. Especially, after the weird encounter with Ben."

Ella turned. "You never finished the story about Ben or the dentist. What happened?"

"Gosh," said Shelby. "Too much bizarre stuff. Did you know Buck, Jasmine, and Doctor Parke are on the same bowling team?"

"No," said Ella. "But something tells me you do."

Shelby waited at the stop sign, then turned left. "I've been trying to tell you all day. I accidentally stumbled into Doctor Parke's personal office—"

"Stumbled?"

"I got lost. Anyhow, I saw a bunch of pictures on his walls with the three of them wearing team shirts and holding trophies."

Ella was quiet for a moment, then snapped her fingers. "You know, I remember a bowling tournament a few years ago. They invited all the downtown business owners. It was right after Doug's death. I wasn't up to taking part."

"The trophies I saw were from this year," said Shelby. "It seems they're still a team. Or were..."

Ella rubbed her forehead. "Wonder what brought them together? And kept them together all these years?"

"No idea." Shelby pulled into the gravel driveway and parked.

The women walked into the house, greeted by two lonely, starving pets. "You poor babies." Ella reached down and gave each pet a scratch behind their ears. "Come on, Oatmeal. Let's go potty."

Shelby headed upstairs. "Give me a few minutes to change."

Ella fed the animals, then turned on a lamp in the living room and grabbed the small package with the scented candle from the coffee table. Moments later, Shelby came downstairs wearing a buttercream sweater with pink sequins and black leggings.

"Looking festive," said Ella. They bid goodbye to the animals. Whines and meows from behind the door let them know their quick exit wasn't appreciated.

Ella held up her keys. "I don't mind driving over to the Purcells' if you'll hold their gift. It's not much, but I didn't want to go over there empty-handed." She warmed up the car, then backed out of the driveway. They headed west on Pumpkinseed Road, then south on Maple, taking them through the entrance of the Purcells' property. The rain had stopped but wind-scattered leaves covered the narrow dirt road flanked by countless rows of apple trees.

Staring out the window, Shelby shuddered. "Wouldn't want to be out there alone on a night like this."

"Kinda creepy," said Ella. "The headlights make the bare branches appear like skeleton fingers beckoning us inside the dark emptiness."

Shelby let out a nervous chuckle. "Maybe the skeletons are telling us to go away."

Ella loosened her grip on the steering wheel as the groves opened, revealing a two-story farmhouse. A wooden sign swayed on a metal post. The wood-burned letters bearing the name "PURCELL" confirmed they were in the right place. Ella exited the car and pulled her jacket tight. Shelby carried the gift bag and they headed to the house.

Before they reached the top step of the porch, Gladys pushed open the screen door. "I'm so happy you came, despite this nasty weather."

Ella stepped inside the warm home. "Gladys, your house smells like Thanksgiving."

"Just dinner." Gladys laughed and closed the door. She gave both women a big hug. "Ed's made a fire. Come in and warm yourselves by the hearth." She led them into the den, a cozy room with family pictures, porcelain figurines, and jars filled with colorful trinkets.

Ella stared at a big round jar on one table and pointed.

Gladys nodded. "Just one of my many jars of buttons. Been collecting them since… I don't know… Since my mom started collecting."

"Interesting," said Shelby. "What do you do with them?"

Gladys picked up a large canning jar and unscrewed the lid. "Depends…" She picked through the jar then fished out a glassy oval-shaped button with a colorful peacock painted on the front. She handed it to Ella. "Viv and I belong to a local button club. We get together and swap and buy from each other."

Ella passed the button to Shelby. "Sounds like a lot of fun."

Gladys smiled. "Gives me something to do after jam-making season and when Ed's playing with his radios." She handed Ella an ornate square silver button. "We even go to button conventions. If you're interested, I'll let you know when the next one comes up."

Shelby turned the peacock button over. "I didn't know buttons were popular." She looked up and noticed Ed standing next to a well-used leather chair.

A tall, wiry man in his seventies, he watched the women chat about the buttons. "Evening, ladies." Dressed in a red and black flannel shirt, high-waisted denim pants, and red suspenders, he reached out a warm hand and gave them both a firm handshake. "Welcome." A man of few words, Ed motioned to the couch, then sat down in his chair.

"Good to see you too, Ed," said Ella.

"Nice to see you, Mr. Purcell," said Shelby, handing the button to Ella.

Gladys dropped the buttons back in the jar and sniffed the air. "Supper's 'bout ready."

Ella and Shelby followed Gladys into the kitchen. Ed brought up the rear. As their guests took a seat, he took a stack of plates from a cabinet. On the harvest-themed tablecloth, he placed them next to rolled-up orange cloth napkins, secured with wooden rings in the shape of turkeys. Shelby peeked inside hers and nudged Ella. "Look. Our silverware is in the napkin. Isn't that so cute?"

Ella nodded. "Gladys, everything looks and smells wonderful."

Ed walked over to the refrigerator. "What would you ladies like to drink? We have wine, beer, pop… apple cider."

Ella's eyes widened. "How about water to start?"

"Same for me, thanks," said Shelby.

Ella nodded toward Shelby's sweater and cleared her throat.

"Oh," said Shelby. "We brought you something." She pulled out the gift bag and handed it to Gladys. "We hope you like scented candles."

Gladys gave them a shy smile. "You shouldn't have gone to all that trouble." She opened it and held it close to her husband.

Ed winked at his wife. "Reminds me of that perfume you wore when we were courting."

Gladys blushed, then patted Ed on his backside. "Oh, Ed…" She placed the candle on the counter and took several foil-covered dishes from the stove and set them on the table. As Gladys uncovered each one, their anticipation heightened. Herb-roasted whole chicken. Fluffy wild rice. Steamed green beans dotted with golden butter. Savory sausage and onion stuffing. Carrot and cheese casserole. And thick-sliced homemade bread.

When Ed reached for a serving spoon, Gladys playfully swatted at his hand. "Ed, let our guests go first. How about refilling our wine glasses." He nodded, but said nothing.

With their plates full, they feasted on the homemade meal. Conversation was brief except for occasional compliments. While they ate, Ella noticed a static-like chatter coming from the next room and inclined her head to listen.

"Oh, that's Ed's radio set-up," said Gladys. "Remember? I told you about it at the shop."

Ella turned back. "Yes. I do."

Ed cleared his throat. "After dinner, I'll show you my shack." He took a bite of bread and was silent again.

Shelby wiped her mouth and took a sip of water. "From what Gladys mentioned, it sounds interesting."

Ed smiled, gave a quick nod, then went back to eating.

They continued to eat, listening to the crackling fireplace and occasional static from the radios in the next room. Ella was tempted to eat another slice of bread, but decided to a save room for the pie bubbling with thick blue syrup cooling on the counter. "Gladys, the food is wonderful. Like a holiday."

"I agree." Shelby picked up her plate and stood. "Where do you want these?"

"No, no. You're our guests." Gladys wiped her hands on her apron and scrambled to her feet. "You two go listen to Ed's contraptions while I tidy up in here. Then we'll have boysenberry cobbler."

Ella dabbed her mouth with the soft cotton napkin. Knowing Gladys would take offense if they tried to stay and help, she nodded. Shelby protested, but Ella took her hand. "Come on, Shel. Looks like we have the night off."

The women waited for Ed to pour himself another glass of wine, then followed him into his "shack," which appeared to be a converted den. A desk with a computer, mouse, and two large monitors set against a short wall. An extended table with several shelves above it was nestled against a longer wall. Piles of paper, different colored pens, clipboards with scribbled writing, and charts lay on the table next to two C.B. radios. Several books, multiple electronic devices and gadgets with dials, tuning knobs, and numbered keypads covered the bottom shelf. The top shelf held two smaller monitors and two shoebox-sized speakers.

"Quite the set-up you have here, Ed," said Ella

"Except for the wine, I don't drink. Don't gamble. Don't have any vices," he chuckled. "Except ham radio. A man's got to have something to take his mind off apple harvests and powdery mildew."

"How does all this work?" asked Shelby. "I mean, can someone hear us talking right now?"

"Though ham radios allow two-way communication

anywhere in the world, you need to use that mic for them to hear us." He pointed to a small stand that held a microphone with a square button and a switch. "I've made friends all over. In fact, Hans in Germany and I have become great buddies."

"Oh, cool," said Shelby. "Can we call him now?"

Ed scratched his chin. "Naw. Need to wait another hour to bounce the short radio waves off the ionosphere. Otherwise we'll just get static and squawks. Then, I'll rotate the array… thirty degrees east of north-northeast will do it…"

"Sounds rather complicated," said Ella.

"Not after 40-plus years of experience." Ed pointed to the device. "Have an Extra Class license. The highest class. Had to study electronics and take more tests. Took me three times to pass one of 'em."

"What about the police scanners?" asked Ella. "Do you need a license for those?"

He pointed to a contraption with an antenna and small, digital screen and numeric keypad. "Didn't have to take a test. Those are receive-only. Anyone can listen."

Shelby stepped closer. "Interesting."

As Ed shared details of the unique pieces of equipment, the speakers on the top shelf crackled. Voices talked in codes mixed with static and long pauses.

"CHP. Out on the westbound 58," said Ed. He inclined his head toward the desk. "10-24. Disabled vehicle."

Ella leaned in. "I suppose, after a while, it's easier to understand what they're saying."

Ed nodded and pulled up a chair. He motioned for the women to join him. "Used to listen to the dispatcher and officers or paramedics all the time. When they changed to digital gear, I switched to a computer app. Now, I listen to first responders pretty much all over the world."

Shelby and Ella took a seat, one on each side of Ed. He listened again, then spoke. "That's dispatch, Pheasant Valley

PD. Hold on…" His chair squeaked as he moved. "And that was the sheriff… There's some emergency."

Shelby sat up straight. "What happened?"

"Sounds like Bart. He's on duty Tuesday nights…" More static, then voices. "10-23. That means to stand by."

Gladys came up behind them and placed her hands on Ella's shoulders. "Ed listens to that contraption twenty-four/seven. Invested half the family fortune on this equipment. You should see the antennas outside."

Ed winked at his wife, then turned around and faced the speakers. "Hmmm, something's going on."

Ella strained to listen, but with the static she could only decipher a few words.

"Code-three."

Shelby turned to Ed. "What's that?"

He picked up his clipboard and wrote the numbers, then waited. "Code three. They're rolling with emergency lights and sirens."

"Is that normal?" asked Ella.

He shook his head.

Shelby moved closer. "Did I hear them mention Lupine Road?"

Ed swiveled his chair around and brought up a map on the computer. The dispatcher's voice said a few undecipherable words, then another voice repeated, "10-79."

Shelby jumped up. "Deertrail Circle. I heard that…"

"Ed, what's going on?" asked Ella.

He wrote a few more codes and flipped through a notebook. "A fatality. Just checking since some agencies use different ten-codes."

"Near Deertrail Circle?" asked Ella. "Isn't that over by the golf course?"

Ed pointed to the computer screen. "Yup. It's in that gated

community. A fatality, for sure. They don't know if it's a homicide or suicide…"

The four of them listened as the chatter continued.

"17051 Deertrail Circle. 10-79."

Ed looked at the women. "Bart just asked for a coroner."

Ella stood. "I know that street." She drummed her fingers on the back of her chair.

Shelby looked at Ella. "Who lives there?"

She paused for a moment to think. "We had a Chamber meeting out there a few years ago. Doug and I went…" She stared at her shoes. "I hope I'm wrong, but if not… That sounds a lot like Harland Parke's address."

CHAPTER FORTY

Ed, Gladys, Shelby, and Ella stood in the Purcells' den listening to the endless chatter from the speakers. It was like they were part of a bizarre television crime show. After some time, Ed excused himself and left the room. Later, he came back and stood in front of them.

"Law enforcement buddy of mine just confirmed it was Doctor Parke. Of course, no one else knows. Said a neighbor called in saying she heard his car running in the garage and became concerned."

Ella gasped.

"Poor guy," said Ed. "Carbon monoxide poisoning."

"Did your friend say how it happened?" asked Ella. "I mean, did he just fall asleep or something?"

Ed shook his head. "According to my buddy, apparent suicide. Said the doc left a note."

Shelby glanced at Ella's sheet-white face. "You okay?"

"I've known Doctor Parke for years. He and Doug used to golf together..." Ella turned to Gladys. "I'm feeling light-headed. Shelby and I should go."

Gladys rubbed Ella's shoulders. "No need to explain, hon."

Shelby took Ella's hand. They followed Ed and Gladys through the kitchen into the front room and stood near the crackling fire.

Ella offered Shelby the keys. "Maybe you should drive."

"You ladies take care of yourselves." Gladys gave them both tight hug. "I'll check in on you tomorrow."

They said their goodbyes and headed to Ella's car. "Thought I was going to pass out for a minute," said Ella. "It was so warm. Just had to get out…"

"Though the air out here is smoky from the fireplace, it's cooler. All that radio chatter got to me, too. Like we were invading their privacy." Shelby started the car and clenched the steering wheel as they drove away from the house and down the narrow dirt road between the dark groves.

Ella stayed quiet until they turned onto Maple Road. "Why would Doctor Parke commit suicide?"

"Maybe he fell asleep after he came back from the prison?" While Shelby didn't believe what she'd said, she had no other theories.

Ella sighed. "Ed said there was a note. Do you think Parke had planned to… you know… for a while?"

"I wonder how Jasmine will take it?"

Ella looked at Shelby. "Why would you say that?"

"First Buck. Then Doctor Parke. They were on the same bowling team. They had to be friends. Or enemies."

"I'm sure it was just coincidence," said Ella.

Shelby pulled up into their gravel driveway and winced. "Maybe not." A Pheasant Valley PD unit sat parked in front of Ella's house. A sheriff's unit in Hope's driveway. "Wonder what that's all about?"

Ella looked over at Shelby and got out of the car. They walked up to the house, but before reaching the porch, they heard heavy footsteps in the gravel behind them. Ella turned and saw the silhouette of a large man.

Shelby shrieked.

Alton Nolan stepped into the light dressed in his police uniform. “Evening, ladies,” he said. “Sorry to bother you at this hour, but I need to ask more questions.”

CHAPTER FORTY-ONE

Ella jumped when she heard Alton's voice. "Why are you here at this time of night?"

"I'm sorry for the intrusion, but I must talk to you." He held up a piece of paper. "We found another note. There might be implications."

"What implications?" asked Ella, rubbing her hands together as the wind whipped around them. Her breath floated past Alton. "I don't understand."

Ella and Shelby continued up the steps. Whines and scratches came from inside the house. Shelby opened the door and went inside.

Alton stood close to Ella. "May I come inside and ask you some questions?"

Ella stood firm in front of the screen door. "Hold on, Alton. We need to let the dog out. Be back in a moment." The women went in and Ella closed the door. After they walked into the kitchen, she grabbed Shelby's arm. "What is he talking about?"

Shelby shrugged. "I don't know. But he sure scared the heck out of me."

Ella nodded glanced at the front door. "Why don't you let him in. No matter how insensitive, it's impolite to make him stand outside in that bitter wind." Shelby walked back into the living room while Ella let Oatmeal out. When they came back in, Ella gave the animals their nighttime treats. Oatmeal growled when he heard Alton's deep voice. "It's okay, boy," said Ella, bending down to rub the dog's head.

With a chance to settle her thoughts, Ella walked back into the front room. Shelby stood beside Alton, hands on her hips. Mr. Butterfingers sprawled out on the rug cleaning his paw.

"Would you like coffee or something?" asked Ella.

Alton glanced at her and unzipped his uniform jacket. "If you could just answer a few questions, I'll be on my way."

Ella motioned to the sofa. "Please have a seat."

Shelby stood at the other end of the sofa while Ella sat in the wingback chair. Oatmeal jumped in her lap. Though he snuggled on Ella's lap, he kept an eye on Alton and growled each time he moved.

"You mentioned a piece of paper," said Ella. "Are you referring to that one?"

Alton moved to the edge of the sofa and held up a crumpled sheet of paper. "Yes. Of course this is a copy. The actual one is evidence."

"My head's pounding." Ella rubbed her temples. "Tonight's been… stressful."

Alton leaned over and handed her the paper. Ella read it to herself first then out loud. "It's not what you think. He was never the one." She dropped the note on the coffee table. "Where did you get this?"

Alton studied his hands, then looked at Ella. "We found it on…"

"Doctor Parke's body?" Shelby blurted out.

Alton twisted around and stared at Shelby.

Oatmeal let out a low growl. "It's okay, boy." Ella rubbed his head to calm him.

"How do you know about Parke's death?" asked Alton.

Shelby crossed her arms. "We, um… We heard all about it at… the Purcells'."

Alton turned and faced Ella. "Two identical notes. Two dead bodies. I just can't piece together how you're involved, Ella."

"Alton, you're wrong. I had nothing to do with Buck's death… and you know it. And as for Doctor Parke's… I was, we were, at Gladys and Ed's having dinner. He has all those radios…"

"Darn ham operators…" he muttered.

"It was a computer app, actually…" Shelby uncrossed her arms. "Why do you still think Ella's involved?"

Alton ran his hand through his short brown hair. "This note is an exact copy of the one found in Buck's truck."

"Not exactly." Ella clenched her fists. "It's on different paper."

Alton stood. "It's a copy. The actual one was typed on green copy paper. Just like the other one." He rested his beefy hand on his wide, leather belt. "Ella, I really think you need to come down to the station with—"

Ella jumped up, dumping Oatmeal on the floor. "Are you saying I'm under arrest?"

"No." Alton also stood. "I need you to come with me so I can take a statement. Plus, I have questions—"

"Unless I'm under arrest, ask me here. I think you're trying to intimidate me and, well, I won't put up with it. Ask your questions. Or leave."

Alton cleared his throat and sat. He took out a small notebook and pen. "You don't want to get on my bad side, Ella."

She glared down at him. "And you don't want to get on

mine. I just lost a friend tonight and you have the gall to think I had anything to do with it. Shame on you, Alton Nolan."

He cleared his throat again. "Might I have something to drink?"

Ella looked at Shelby. "Please get Officer Nolan some water."

Shelby marched into the kitchen and took several deep breaths to calm herself. The conversation with Dawn came to mind. Ella was in trouble. She knew Dawn could help. But would they have enough time? Tears stung her eyes. She brushed them away with the back of her hand. One last deep inhale and exhale, then she returned with a water bottle. Fortunately for Alton, she handed it to him instead of throwing it.

Alton removed the cap and drank about half, then he looked at Ella. "Look. I apologize for being curt. But a man has died. And he left what was supposed to look like a suicide note. But, since it matched the note found in the other victim's truck, I'm investigating the death as a suspicious death. Between us, I'm trying to get to the bottom of this before my sister hauls you in as a prime suspect."

"Wait a minute," said Shelby. "I thought you were the one who suspected Ella. You even said so at the cemetery."

Alton shook his head. "My competitive nature led me to misspeak. I apologize for that. Dawn is the one craving a conviction. I'm only here to clear Ella's name."

Shelby looked at Ella and raised an eyebrow. What game was Dawn playing with her if Alton believed Ella innocent? Her head throbbed.

Alton squared his shoulders and opened his notebook. "Ella, where were you today? Start from right now and work backwards to lunchtime."

Ella straightened. "You scared the heck out of me and Shelby. We went to the Purcells' for dinner. We came home from work and fed the animals." She focused her gaze behind Alton to think. "The rest of the afternoon, I was at the shop. Shelby was there, too."

Alton made a few notes. "When you were at the shop, was anyone else there, other than Shelby?"

Distracted by shadows of dancing branches outside, Ella glanced at the window, then refocused. "Customers. I have receipts at the shop if you need to see them."

"And tonight?" asked Alton. "You were both at the Purcell's the whole time? And they can vouch for you?"

"Yes. Of course."

He jotted a few more notes, then looked at Ella. "And what about this morning… before lunch?"

"I was at the shop."

"With Shelby?" he asked.

Shelby came around the back of the chair and stood next to Ella. "No. I went to the dentist. In fact, I saw Doctor Parke talking on the phone, just before he left for the prison."

Alton sighed and looked at the women. "Other than that, did either one of you notice anything out of the ordinary today?"

Ella looked up at Shelby, then to Alton. "Not that I recall."

The wind howled outside. Alton paused and glanced at Shelby.

She hesitated. "No, not really. Not with Doctor Parke."

Alton turned his attention to Ella. "Do you have anything else to add? Something we might have overlooked?" He held his pen over the notebook and waited.

"Nothing that immediately comes to mind."

He made a few more notes, then tucked the pen and notebook in his pocket. After finishing the water, Alton took a business card from his pocket and laid it on the coffee table. "If you think of anything else, here's my contact info." He stood, then walked over to the door. "Thank you for your time." He zipped up his jacket and let himself out into the cold, dark night.

Ella stood. She glanced at Shelby while holding a finger to her lips. Once they heard a car door slam and engine start up, Ella exhaled. "Thought you'd mention seeing Ben at the café."

Shelby tucked a strand of hair behind her ear. "I thought you'd tell him about Ben's transaction with Jasmine."

"Are we withholding evidence?"

Shelby shrugged. "Before we mention anything, it might be prudent to do more sleuthing."

CHAPTER FORTY-TWO

Shelby poured two cups of steaming coffee and set them on the kitchen table. "Let's start with that note. Where are the other ones?"

Ella rushed down the short hall into her room. She came back with the sheet of green copy paper. "Here's the one we found in my car. The one from Buck's truck is on my phone. Dawn didn't leave a copy."

Shelby held Ella's green paper next to Alton's white paper copy. "They're identical. Perfect down to that smudge in the left corner."

"You think Parke wrote them?" asked Ella. "And the last one was a suicide note?"

Shelby tapped the paper. "We could consider that theory. If so… what did the message mean? Who was never 'the one'? Buck? Or Doctor Parke?"

"It's not what you think… Such a baffling message. Was it a suicide? A homicide?"

"Maybe it refers to something else." said Shelby.

Ella got up and went into the living room. She brought back a yellow legal pad and several pens. "Let's brainstorm."

She drew three circles. Inside each, she wrote one name: Buck, Parke, and Jasmine. "They had something in common… on the same bowling team." She drew a line from each name to the others.

"Was it only bowling that connected them?"

Ella pointed to the paper. "Who knows? Now two are dead." She added Ben's name to the page and drew a line from his name to Jasmine's. "We know something was going on between these two that involved money."

"Was it only a onetime payment?" asked Shelby.

"We don't know. Maybe Ben knew something and Jasmine paid him to keep it to himself… Or Jasmine had Ben kill…"

Shelby furrowed her brow. "I can't imagine Jasmine killing or paying someone to kill for her. Maybe Ben did repairs, and she paid for his services."

"I don't know." Ella was quiet for a moment. "My gut tells me they were trying to be discreet. Could be because he was one of her patients."

Shelby thought back to the conversation with Emma at the dentist's office. "Maybe we should brainstorm about Doctor Parke. We know he went up to the prison."

"Wait a minute," said Ella. "How long did she say he'd been going there?"

"About five years. Why?"

"Don't you see?" asked Ella. "Parke could have met Ben in prison. Maybe they had a secret that tied them together."

Shelby snorted. "And you thought I was jumping to conclusions? That's taking it to the extreme." She paused, then snapped her fingers. "Maybe, Ben offed Buck so he and Hope could, well, you know…"

"Offed?" asked Ella. "What crime shows have you been watching?"

"Shush, I'm on a roll. Then Parke found out about it

somehow and Ben didn't want to go back to prison, so Ben offed Parke."

Ella rolled her eyes. "That still doesn't explain why Jasmine would give Ben money. Your theory makes about as much sense as mine."

"At least I came up with something."

Ella nodded. "We know something connected them. The others were or are, Jasmine's patients. Betcha Ben's involved in something."

"We can get nosy," said Shelby. "You know, ask questions. Do some sleuthing."

"Wait," said Ella. "Aren't you and Dawn supposed to have dinner or something?"

"Yes, tomorrow night." Shelby cringed. Dawn wanted something, but it wasn't dinner.

"You never mentioned you'd set a time," said Ella.

"I was trying to forget. But, considering tonight's situation, it'll give me a chance to ask more questions." Shelby's chest tightened. The thought of going anywhere with Dawn made her anxious. Standing up to Dawn would take more than just courage. Shelby just hoped she wouldn't have to compromise herself to get answers.

CHAPTER FORTY-THREE

The next afternoon Dawn texted Shelby her address. Close to Ella's, it wouldn't take long. She headed east on Cardamom, then south on Poppy Street, and pulled up in front of Dawn's townhouse at six o'clock. A quiet, older neighborhood lined with leafless maple trees near Valley High School, each townhouse, though similar in style, displayed distinctive light fixtures or shutter styles to set them apart.

Moments after she arrived, Dawn stepped outside and waved. She locked her door and strolled down the sidewalk to the idling vehicle. It had been quite a while since Shelby had seen her in civilian clothes with her hair down. Sliding into the seat, it was clear Dawn had dressed to impress Shelby. Her silky blouse and skin-tight black jeans left little to the imagination.

Shelby swallowed and gripped the steering wheel. "Nice to see you."

"And you, too, Shel."

Dawn's smooth voice and sweet cologne teased up memories of their clandestine encounter. Memories Shelby had tried to forget. Especially now that she was in a different place in her life.

Dawn clicked her seatbelt into place. "You know the way?"

"Yes, it's in my phone." Thank goodness the navigation voice would provide another sound during the thirty-plus-mile trip. Something to focus on, other than Dawn. Shelby's mind raced to make idle conversation. "Enjoying the chilly weather?"

"Really? You want to talk about the weather?" Dawn shifted her hand, brushing it against Shelby's thigh.

Shelby flinched.

"Relax," said Dawn, laughing. "We're just having dinner. Dessert… that's up to you."

Shelby didn't respond. Feeling hopeless and trapped, it was all she could do to concentrate on the two-lane mountain road.

"Recalculating." The female GPS voice from the phone cut through the road noise.

"You missed your turn," said Dawn. "Do you want me to drive?"

"I'm fine. Just haven't been out this way in a while." Forty minutes later, Shelby pulled up in front of Casita de Pollo, a tiny Mexican restaurant at the end of a dark street. The only light on the block emanated from a neon sign flickering overhead.

"Are they even open?" asked Shelby.

Dawn nodded, then stepped out of the jeep and pulled on a suede jacket. "That's why I picked this place. The food is great, and it's always quiet on a Wednesday.

When Dawn slipped her arm in Shelby's, she cringed, but didn't pull away. Shelby's only reason for being there was to get information. She had to play along. After all, Dawn had promised to share if they had dinner.

They walked inside the dimly-lit restaurant. Two couples sat at the bar, drinking and laughing as a three-piece mariachi band played. Maria, a smiling woman dressed in a colorful skirt and solid green blouse, greeted them from the sign-in desk. "Table for two?" she asked in a heavy accent.

"Yes," said Dawn. "I made reservations."

With only four other people in the place, Shelby wondered why Dawn bothered. But if she were paying for dinner, she wouldn't question it. At least not out loud.

Maria picked up two menus and took them to a corner booth near the back. After the women sat, Maria handed them menus and took out an order pad. "Anything to drink? Cocktails? Wine?"

Shelby shook her head. "Water is fine. Thanks."

"Since I'm not driving…" Dawn scanned the drink menu on the table. "How about an Old Fashioned?" After Maria left, Dawn scooted closer to Shelby and winked. "I'm anything but old-fashioned, if you get my drift."

Shelby opened her menu, hoping the darkened room would hide her disgust. Her mind raced as she tried to concentrate on the dinner choices. How would she ever get through this and stay calm?

Maria brought their drinks along with a bowl of warm chips and chunky red salsa. She turned to Shelby. "Ready?"

Shelby pointed to an image on the menu. "I'll have the two chicken soft tacos with beans and rice, please."

Maria looked at Dawn. "And you?"

Dawn picked up a chip and dipped it in the salsa. "Same for me, but make it beef tacos on flour tortillas. And no onions."

Maria nodded as she wrote, then took the menus and left.

Shelby felt Dawn watching as she scooped salsa with a chip. Holding it over a napkin, she returned the look. "What are you willing to share about the case?"

"Hold on, sweetie. We haven't even gotten our food yet." Dawn knocked back her drink. "Plus, that was only my first round."

Shelby cleared her throat. Coming here was a mistake, but after Alton said Dawn was out to prove Ella guilty, she had to find out what Dawn knew.

Dawn looked around the small room. "Nice place they have here. Out of the way. You know, there's a little motel around the corner… if you're not in a hurry to head back." Her knee brushed up against Shelby's leg.

Shelby's heart pounded in her ears. Trying not to overreact, she moved her leg, hoping Dawn would get the message.

After a long, uncomfortable silence, Maria walked over carrying plates of steaming food. She set one in front of Shelby, another in front of Dawn. "Anything else?"

Shelby shook her head.

Dawn pointed to her empty drink glass. "Another."

Maria nodded and left.

Shelby picked up her fork and ate, eager for Dawn to copy. Maybe the food would counteract the alcohol and she'd be less flirty. At least that's what she hoped would happen. When Maria brought a second drink, Dawn picked up a taco. Thank goodness. They ate listening to the mariachi band.

Shelby finished her meal much too quickly. Her nerves on edge, she didn't even taste it. She grazed on the last of the chips and salsa while taking in the restaurant's atmosphere. Colorful tapestries depicting children playing and families eating together hung on walls painted in turquoise, red, yellow, or cream. Tiny twinkling white lights strung out across a low-set, sloped ceiling. Clay pots filled with bright red poinsettias sat atop wide wooden borders between tables and booths.

Dawn finished her tacos and drink. She signaled Maria for another round, then leaned back and eyed Shelby. Pulling out a notebook, she laid it on the table, tapping the cover with her thin fingers. "What do you want to know?"

Shelby squared her shoulders. "What do you want to tell me?"

"You get five questions. If I know the answer, I'll tell you. If not, your loss. When you run out of questions…" She winked. "We'll discuss ways to add more."

Shelby's stomach tightened at the thought of Dawn's mind games. If this were for anyone else but Ella, she would have walked out. Then again, she would have never agreed to go. Gathering what little courage she had, Shelby knew she needed to get the most information without wasting questions. "How did Buck die… was it homicide?"

"That's two questions," said Dawn.

Shelby rubbed her aching forehead and sighed.

"Blunt force trauma—"

"Wait." Shelby held up her hand. "I want to re-ask my second question."

"Just this one time. Go ahead."

Shelby paused. "Was Buck killed at the cemetery?"

"No." Dawn smiled. "You have three questions remaining."

"Okay, give me a minute."

Dawn brushed her hand over Shelby's. "No hurry, hon. We have all night."

Ella sat up in bed and checked her phone. Eleven o'clock. They should have been back by now. She closed her eyes but couldn't relax. Oatmeal yawned and rolled onto his side. Ella crawled out of bed, slipped on a bathrobe, and walked into the dim kitchen. After scanning the counter, she decided on a banana, hoping it would help her fall asleep.

Mr. Butterfingers padded up and meowed. She reached down to scratch his ear. He pawed at her snack. "I don't think you'll like it." Offering him the last bite, he sniffed the peel, then sulked away. "Your loss," said Ella.

She stared out the kitchen window. Branches on a nearby pine trembled in the wind as raindrops splattered against the glass. Ella squinted at the wall clock. Eleven-fifteen. A tinge of anxiety shot through her. Maybe it was taking longer to drive back because of the weather.

She walked into the bedroom and pulled the chain on a wooden lamp on the nightstand. Just enough light to read. Ella thumbed through a stack of books. A romantic suspense, not an appropriate choice right now. Julia Child's autobiography. It didn't pique her interest either. A short story collection. Self-improvement. Container gardening. Hopefully, Shel was gathering a lot of useful information.

Oatmeal stretched and stared at Ella. "Sorry, boy. I just can't sleep." She adjusted the shade to keep the light from hitting his eyes, then reclined on a pile of pillows.

Ella soon realized her thoughts betrayed her emotions. Was she jealous? She trusted Shelby to be faithful. To what, though? They'd never finished that conversation. They'd never verbalized their feelings. She pounded her fist into a pillow.

Oatmeal stirred and sat up.

Ella looked at him. "What if I blew it? What if Dawn…?" She bounded out of bed and paced. Her mind spiraled. Needing to calm down, she knew she wasn't helping anyone by freaking out. Mr. Butterfingers came in and jumped up on a pile of blankets. He kneaded them, then settled next to Oatmeal.

Ella stopped pacing. When Shelby came home, she would share her feelings. She wanted them to be partners… in life and in business. It was time to commit. Ella only hoped it wasn't too late.

Oatmeal stood in the middle of the bed and cocked his head.

"What is it, boy?" A few seconds later, the front door opened, then closed. Oatmeal jumped off, followed by Mr. Butterfingers. Ella heard Shelby greet the animals and drop her keys on the kitchen table. She tapped on the bedroom door and stuck her head inside. "El, you still up?"

"Yeah. Couldn't fall asleep." Ella motioned for her to come in.

Shelby sat on the corner of the bed. Oatmeal pawed at her leg, wagging his tail. Then he jumped up and settled next to her.

"How did it go?"

"It was interesting." As Shelby pulled a thick rubber band from her ponytail, her hair fell across her shoulders. Her eyes sparkled and met Ella's. "She let me ask five questions. Afterwards, we left the restaurant, and I took her home." Shelby sighed and massaged the back of her neck. "According to Dawn, someone killed Buck and dumped him at the cemetery."

"Did you ask about suspects?"

"I did. She hinted it was a familiar person."

"Did she give you a name?"

Shelby shook her head. "I asked about Doctor Parke's death. Dawn didn't think anything connected it, but didn't rule out homicide."

"Interesting. Anything else?"

"No."

"No mention me being a prime suspect, like Alton said?"

"I don't know who to believe." Shelby stroked Oatmeal's silky ear. "I think they're pushing our buttons, hoping to get a reaction."

Ella tried to catch her gaze. "Any way to get more information?"

Shelby picked at the quilt, then hesitated. "Dawn offered to share all of her information, if I'd…" Tears welled in her eyes.

Ella reached out. "If you what?"

"Dawn said she would tell me everything. If… I'd slept with her."

Ella's throat tightened. She grabbed a bottle of water and took a drink.

Shelby placed her hand on Ella's leg. "I refused." While she didn't have the courage to call Dawn out for emotional blackmail, she had, for the first time, found the courage to speak up for herself. "I said no information was worth losing the trust of a person I cared about."

Ella blinked back tears. "What happened next?"

"Once Dawn figured I wouldn't give in, she threw a fit and demanded we leave the restaurant. Never said a word all the way back to her place. Not even goodnight, which was fine with me." Shelby took Ella's hand and pulled her into a hug.

Ella buried her face in Shelby's shoulder. They hugged and rocked each other for several minutes, then Ella pulled back. "Thank you."

Shelby scooted next to Ella, resting her head on her shoulder. "For what?"

"For coming back."

Shelby nestled closer. "You're worth coming back for."

Ella swallowed. "What would you say if I asked you to be my partner?"

Shelby sat up and gazed at her. "Would you clarify that?"

"For one, I want you to be my business partner at The Bee's Knees. And two—" A loud knock at the front door interrupted them. Oatmeal barked, jumped down, and ran out of the bedroom. Ella looked at her phone. "It's almost midnight. Who could that be?"

Shelby shrugged and left the bedroom.

Ella put on her slippers and a robe, then followed Shelby

and Oatmeal down the hall and through the kitchen. She walked into the front room and found Shelby gazing out the front window.

She turned and stared at Ella wide-eyed. "It's Dawn. In her sheriff's uniform."

"Who died this time?"

Shelby opened the door a crack. "What are you doing here?"

An icy chill filled the room. Dawn's voice lowered. "I need to speak to Ella. Official business."

Shelby moved aside.

Goosebumps appeared on Ella's legs as she neared the open door. Thinking back to her robe choice, she wished she'd chosen something heavier. "Do you want to come in?"

Dawn glared at Ella through the screen. "Ella, please step outside."

"What's this about?"

Dawn's voice grew louder. "Please step outside."

Ella looked at Shelby, then opened the screen and stepped out on the frigid porch. Her teeth chattered. She rubbed her arms against the bitter cold.

"Ella Denton, I'm taking you in for questioning regarding the murder of Buck Wilson."

Ella gasped. "There must be some mistake—"

Shelby pushed against the screen door.

Dawn jerked around and blocked the screen with her body. She sneered at Shelby. "You should have opted for dessert." Facing Ella, Dawn grabbed her arm and marched them off the porch. She opened the door of her sheriff's unit and shoved Ella in the back seat. She hopped in the front, started the vehicle, then pulled away.

Wrapping her fingers around the cold, metal bars blocking the window, Ella watched her house fade into the dark night while Dawn drove them away from everyone she loved.

CHAPTER FORTY-FOUR

Shelby slammed the front door and pounded the front room wall with her fist. How could Dawn take Ella? Rubbing her aching hand, she watched rain pelt the front windows. A flash lit up the front room. The lights flickered as thunder rumbled overhead. Where was that flashlight?

Clenching her fists, Shelby paced across the room and into the kitchen. All because she wouldn't give in to Dawn… She marched into the kitchen, mind racing. The lights flickered again as another crash rolled over the house. Oatmeal pawed her leg and whined. "I'm sorry, boy. I miss her too." Shelby hated thunderstorms. She hated being alone during thunderstorms. But mostly, she hated herself for not standing up for Ella when Dawn took her away.

Grabbing a banana and a bag of chocolate chip cookies from the counter, Shelby stomped into the front room. Before reaching the stairs, she spotted the flashlight on the coffee table. Alton's card lay under it. Shelby shoved the card in her back pocket, tucked the flashlight under her arm, and headed upstairs. Oatmeal's tags jingled as he bounded ahead. She found him waiting on the bed when she turned on the nightstand light.

Shelby plopped on the bed and tore open the cookies. Between bites, she pulled Alton's card out of her pocket and stared at it. Not only was his work number on the card, but also his cell. Did she dare call now? She ate a few more cookies and leaned back. Oatmeal walked across the bed and rested his head on her tummy. His soft snores calmed Shelby along with the rhythmic sounds of rain on the roof. Soon the storm subsided, along with her anger.

SHELBY WOKE up in a tangle of blankets. Cookie crumbs and chocolate stuck to her clothes and exposed areas of her skin. She blinked several times as her eyes adjusted to the light. Seven o'clock. At least she'd slept, though her head ached. Oatmeal opened his eyes, stretched his back, and licked her face. "Give me a minute and I'll take you out." She sat up and regained her bearings. As they went downstairs, Shelby hoped last night's events were a nightmare. But the quiet, empty house brought her back to reality.

Pulling a sweater over her shirt and jeans, she took Oatmeal out. Back inside, Shelby fed the animals and made coffee. After a quick shower and a change of clothes, she came downstairs with Alton's card and a new determination to rectify Ella's situation.

DARK CLOUDS BLOTTED out the sun as Shelby rushed outside. Wind chimes played in the breeze. Pines swayed. Leaves swirled. Another storm would arrive soon. After buckling her seatbelt, Shelby adjusted her headset and punched in Alton's cell number. She started the engine and let it warm up, waiting for him to answer.

"Hello, Alton. This is Shelby... Sorry to call early, but I need to talk to... Did you hear...? Dawn took Ella... Last night, about midnight... I'm on my way into town. Can we meet at the shop...? Half-hour? Yes. Thank you. See you in a little while." She ended the call and backed out of the driveway.

SHELBY ARRIVED at The Bee's Knees thirty minutes before it opened. Checking the schedule, she expected Laura and Paige that morning, Jasmine in the afternoon. Though her thoughts kept drifting back to Ella, she had to keep going. Ella would count on her and Shelby wanted to make up for what had happened last night, though nothing seemed worthy enough to relieve the pain Dawn had caused.

Keys tapping on the front door brought Shelby out of her reverie. Alton, thank goodness. She walked over and let him in.

"Thank you for coming," said Shelby, leading him to the sitting area.

"Tell me what happened."

She shared the details of the evening before.

"I don't understand." He rubbed the back of his neck. "What would provoke Dawn to do that?"

Shelby chewed her lip, debating whether she should share more.

"Is there something else?" asked Alton. "Something you're not telling me?"

Shelby bounced a knee and nodded. "I made her mad." She described the previous night's details while Alton listened without interrupting.

"She has a flair for revenge," he said.

Shelby wiped a tear running down her cheek. "I feel so helpless."

"Let me make a few calls." Pulling out his phone, Alton stood and walked to another part of the shop.

A few minutes later, Laura knocked on the front door. Shelby realized it was after nine and hurried over to open it. Laura, along with two customers, walked in.

"Good morning. Welcome." The women smiled and walked toward a display of hand-painted bookshelves.

"Morning," said Laura. "Everything okay?"

Shelby forced a smile. "Yes, why?"

Laura picked up the clipboard and signed in. "Seeing the police car outside concerned me." She took off her thick sweater and placed it behind the counter, then looked around. "I feel tension in the air."

"Oh, you know. Never a dull moment."

Laura came closer. "Sweetie, tell me what—"

Paige walked in. Shrugging off her coat, she balled it up and tossed it behind the counter. "How're you ladies this mornin'?" She clicked her long, red nails on the clipboard and glanced at Shelby. "Ella in?"

Shelby shook her head.

"Usually has a list for me to do." She popped a big pink bubble. "Shame 'bout the doc, ain't it?"

Alton strolled up an aisle and stood near Paige. He cleared his throat. "Pardon me, ladies. Shelby, when you have a moment."

Shelby nodded to Alton and turned to Paige. "Why don't you… straighten the shelves along the display window? Laura, would you stay up front and help customers? I'll be right back."

"I heard you have a booth," said Alton.

Shelby hesitated, then pointed to the middle aisle. "Follow

me." They walked to the end and Shelby stopped. "Not much to show. I need to restock."

"Don't worry about it." He shifted on his feet. "Just preferred to talk in private."

"You find out anything?"

"She's okay." He moved closer and picked up a plaid scarf. "Dawn kept her waiting most of the night. Only started the questioning this morning. Ella should be home in the next few hours."

Shelby's lip quivered. "Thanks, Alton."

"I'll let you know if I hear anything else. I need to get down to the station."

Shelby held up her hand. "I shouldn't ask, but… I'm curious. Why are you being helpful? I mean, after the cemetery. We didn't get off on the right foot…"

Alton stared at his shoes. "Not proud of my behavior. And I'm ashamed of Dawn's. We get competitive. Too competitive. But last night she crossed a line. I want to make it right."

"Thanks." Shelby checked the aisle and around the corner, then looked at him, lowering her voice. "Say I came across some information. Would you be interested? I mean, it's the least I can do."

His eyes brightened. "Like what kind of information?"

"I've got a hunch about something, but I'm still working on it. Can we talk later?"

He nodded. "Why a sudden urge to get involved?"

Shelby stuck her hands in her pockets. "For some unknown reason, I trust you. And after what happened last night, I want you get the credit in this investigation."

"I know I can be a horse's arse but I won't tolerate a vengeful cop. Even if it's my sister. From now on, I'll do whatever I can to help you clear Ella's name."

Shelby extended her hand. "That means a lot. Thank you."

"Thank you," he said, shaking it. "Maybe with your

information, we can make this right. Call me later." He handed Shelby the scarf and left the shop.

She wandered up to the front. With Paige there and Jasmine coming in later, Shelby had a lot of sleuthing before she and Alton could meet and discuss the case.

CHAPTER FORTY-FIVE

After Alton left The Bee's Knees, Shelby searched the shop for Paige. She found her randomly dusting a shelf while checking her phone.

"Paige. I'm so sorry I just walked away," said Shelby. "And yes, it was a shame to hear about Doctor Parke."

Paige shoved the phone in the back pocket of her jeans. "Guess he just couldn't take it no more, could he?" She blew a big, thin bubble, then sucked it through her teeth with a pop.

"Excuse me?" asked Shelby. "I don't understand."

"Oh, you know." She leaned forward, exposing her ample cleavage. "All them charges."

"Charges?"

Paige stared at Shelby with wide eyes. "Them patient complaints. Got a whole laundry list of 'em to deal with. Hearin' was comin' up next week."

"What are you talking about, Paige?"

She held her thumb and pointer finger so close, her sparkly nails were within a hair-width apart. "Doc was that close to losin' his license. If ya don't believe me, look him up. It's all there on that dentist registry site." She covered her mouth and sneezed a tiny little "a-choo," then sniffed, making her lip curl up. She turned and sneezed again. Pulling a wadded tissue from her bra, she gave a quick blow into it, then shoved it back inside. "Need to get back to my chores… 'less you gots more questions."

Shelby shook her head. Every question she'd planned to ask vanished after Paige's information. Her mind raced. Why would Parke be in danger of losing his dental license? She wanted to excuse herself and search the internet for answers but knew it wouldn't be practical. Shelby needed to focus on the shop. Maybe, she'd have time during lunch, which according to clock was another two hours.

A steady flow of customers helped keep Shelby's mind occupied. Each time the door opened, she stopped and glanced up, hoping it was Ella. So far, no word from her. She figured once Ella left the sheriff's office she'd want to go home, take a shower, and eat something. And take a nap after not sleeping all night.

"How much for the game board?" A woman about Shelby's height held out the wooden piece. Her raven-black hair was clipped to the side in a red barrette.

"It should be on the back," said Shelby.

"Already checked." The woman brushed a loose strand of hair from her cheek and waited.

Shelby inspected the board. "Come with me and I'll have someone look at the inventory sheet."

They walked up to the front. Shelby handed Laura the colorful, painted wooden board. "Would you see if you can find the price for this item?" She turned to the woman. "Laura should be able to help you."

The woman nodded and leaned against the counter.

Shelby's heart pounded when the front door opened again. Jasmine entered, dressed in forest-green slacks and a thick, cream-colored sweater. She carried a cardboard box in her gloved hands.

"Morning, Jasmine," said Shelby. "You're early."

"I wanted to set up the last of my display, then grab lunch before my shift."

Shelby followed her to the half-filled space. "This is looking great."

"Thank you." Jasmine placed the box on the rug, then slipped off her gloves. Opening the box, she dropped them in, then pulled out two tangled necklaces. Once untangled, she hung them on a metal holder. Reaching back into the box, she handed Shelby a sheet of green copy paper with a typed list. "Inventory. Ella asked me to bring it in today."

"Yes, thanks. I'll make sure she gets it." Shelby folded the paper and tucked it in her pocket. So many questions raced through her mind. She didn't want to just blurt one out, but had to say something.

Jasmine arranged beaded jewelry on the top shelf, then draped a few more items on a small wooden turkey. She stood back and tapped her lips with a long, thin finger. "What do you think? Keep the turkey? Lose the turkey?"

Shelby stood next to her. "Well, it is almost Thanksgiving."

"Do people think of gift-giving at Thanksgiving?"

Shelby scratched her nose. "I don't."

Jasmine bent over and pulled a small, white iridescent Christmas tree from the box. After fluffing the branches, she tossed the turkey back in. She placed the tree on the shelf and hung several colorful stone necklaces on the branches. "How's that?"

Shelby nodded. Her mind reeled. Ask her something. But what? She rocked on her heels and smiled. "So, Jasmine. Mind if I ask a question?"

"Much better." She continued to arrange the necklaces on the branches. She stopped and leaned back for a moment, then went back to her display. "Question? Sure, go right ahead. Is it where I get my stones because I found this wonderful place online—"

"It's something else." Shelby cleared her throat. "I saw a picture of you, Buck and Doctor Parke in his office the other day."

Jasmine turned and faced Shelby. Her eyes wide.

"I didn't know y'all bowled."

Jasmine swallowed.

"I used to bowl got a two-twenty once which was one hundred pins over my average ended up getting a trophy for best over-average that year and I just thought I'd ask and all what's your average?" She stopped, took a breath, and stared at Jasmine.

"One ninety-five."

"That's great." Trails of perspiration rolled down Shelby's back. "You ever get a turkey you know three strikes in a row because I—"

Jasmine held up her hand. Her eyes teared up. "If you don't mind, I'd rather not talk about bowling. With Buck and Harland gone, I won't be taking part any longer."

"I'm so sorry." Now what?

Jasmine gazed at a necklace in her hands. "It's okay. We were a wonderful team."

Shelby stepped back a few feet. "If you don't mind me asking, how long?"

"Six years. Went through a lot together." She separated two other necklaces and hung them on separate branches. Jasmine rubbed her thumb over tiny beads strung on a jade bracelet. "In the beginning, a chronic disease brought us together."

"I'm sorry," said Shelby.

Jasmine hung the bracelet on the tree. "And in the end, that disease tore us apart. Fortunately, they no longer have to struggle."

"And you?" Shelby whispered.

"I'll struggle until I die." After pulling on her gloves, Jasmine picked up the box. "I'll be back after lunch." She turned and walked away.

Shelby opened her mouth to say something, but stopped when she heard an alert for a missed call. She swiped the screen and gasped. The call had been from Ella.

CHAPTER FORTY-SIX

Relieved to be back home, Ella took in the familiar scent of hours-old coffee and called Shelby while Oatmeal pawed at her legs. When the call went to voicemail, she left a brief message and crouched down, receiving multiple doggie kisses. "Yes, I'm home. Let's go outside." Before they reached the back door, Ella's phone signaled an incoming call. "Shelby. Yes, I'm home… I'm okay… Tired and hungry… What's that? No, go help the customer, I need to take Oatmeal out." She held the phone between her chin and shoulder, then opened the back door.

Stepping onto the damp wooden porch, Ella shivered. "Come on. You don't have to sniff every single bush." Her breath appeared, then vanished with the wind. "Finally, you weird dog." She held the door as Oatmeal rushed back into the warm kitchen. "Yes, Shelby… still here. Sounds like it's busy down there…" Ella gave both animals treats then looked for something to eat. "What was that? It's hard to hear you..." She turned up the volume and pressed it against her ear. "Jasmine… and Paige… said what?"

She opened a can of tomato soup and poured it into a pot

to warm on the stove. While listening, Ella took the makings for a grilled cheese sandwich from the refrigerator and prepared lunch. "You're sure about Paige's information? I'll do an online search after I eat… By the way, have you eaten lunch? Why don't you call Viv? I'm sure she'd love to come down and help. Can almost run the shop by herself… Okay, call me back after you talk to her." Ella ended the call and placed her phone on the table. Back at the stove she flipped the sizzling sandwich and poured a mugful of steaming soup. Ella held the mug in both hands and took a sip. The creamy, thick liquid warmed her from the inside. She let out a long sigh, turned off the stove, and plated the grilled cheese sandwich.

Halfway through the meal, Ella's phone rang. "What did Viv say? All afternoon… that's great. I'll have lunch ready when you get here. See you in ten." Ella smiled, knowing Shelby was on her way. She lifted her arm and sniffed. Her nose crinkled. She smelled like a sweaty holding cell. Popping the last bit of toasted, cheesy bread in her mouth, she rushed to the bathroom for a quick shower.

After toweling off, Ella put on a pair of soft denim pants and a navy-blue cowl neck sweater. A spritz of mousse in her hair, thank goodness it was short. A swipe of deodorant under each arm. And fuzzy, blue and yellow-striped socks. Warm and clean, Ella went back into the kitchen to make Shelby's sandwich. As she turned on the stove, Oatmeal jumped up and barked, then trotted into the front room with Mr. Butterfingers close behind.

Shelby closed the door behind her. She wanted to rush into the kitchen, but forced herself to stay calm. "Ella?"

"In the kitchen."

When Shelby walked in, Ella's eyes teared up seeing her friend's face.

"You look pretty good for spending the night in the big house," said Shelby.

Ella did a mock curtsey. "Well, I gussied up at bit before you got here."

Walking over, Shelby enveloped Ella in a warm embrace. "I'm just glad you're home…" She cleared her throat, choking back tears. "… and okay."

"Don't you bawl or you'll get me started." Ella focused on the stove. The butter sizzled as she flipped the sandwich. She watched cheese ooze out of the sides. Moments later, Ella slid the sandwich on a plate and handed it to Shelby along with a steaming mug of soup.

"This looks amazing, El. Thank you."

Ella smiled, grabbed an apple from the fruit bowl, and sat.

Shelby's eyes met Ella's. "I'm just so happy to see you."

She nodded. Her feelings had deepened for her friend while Dawn had kept her at the sheriff's office. During the long night, her heart knew it was more than just a chance feeling. Ella's mind raced. Her heart rate increased. She ached to tell Shelby how she felt but the fear of rejection stopped her again. Ella picked up a pen and pad of paper from the table. "Let's go over what you know."

Between bites, Shelby shared Paige's information about Doctor Parke's upcoming hearing. Ella listened and made notes. After hearing Jasmine's comments about the bowling team, Ella tapped the paper with her pen. "We can check the internet for info on Parke. Regarding that team… six years, you say? I can ask Will at the bowling alley for the league rosters. All great info. Anything else?"

Shelby finished her soup and swallowed. "I never even had the chance to tell you about Alton…" She shared their conversation. "He was so upset with Dawn's behavior he wants to help. Can you imagine that?"

Ella scowled. "I couldn't call anyone until this morning. She kept me in that holding room all night. No food. No water. No bathroom break."

"All to get back at me." Shelby shuddered. "I still can't believe it."

"No matter what she tried I said nothing. When I got my call, I called Harold—"

"Isn't that the guy that helped you and Doug get the coffee shop up and running?"

"Yes. Harold has deep pockets and lots of connections. He promised to be in touch in the next day or so, after I rested and was up to talking."

"Speaking of resting." Shelby stood. "You should take a nap. I'll clean up in here, then go online and search for that information Paige talked about. I'll need it before I talk to Alton."

Ella nodded and covered a yawn. "Guess I'll save the apple for later and try to rest."

Shelby hugged Ella again, rubbing her back with warm hands.

After a few moments, Ella stepped back. "Come on, Oatmeal. I need a snuggle buddy."

"You know, I might just take a quick nap on the couch," said Shelby, yawning. "It'll help me think better."

Ella rolled her eyes and glanced at the sink. "Anything to get out of doing the dishes."

CHAPTER FORTY-SEVEN

After Ella and Oatmeal left the kitchen to take a nap, Shelby laid on the couch. Mr. Butterfingers jumped up, purring, and curled on her tummy. Trying to relax, she finally gave up as her mind went over the latest information. When she sat up, Mr. Butterfingers jumped off the couch and twitched his tail. As she opened her laptop, he nudged her arm and purred. Shelby looked at him. "And what do you want?" He meowed, jumped up on the couch, then flopped down next to her. Once Shelby scratched behind his ears, he settled down and fell asleep.

Shelby explored the internet and found the Department of Consumer Affairs, which brought up the dental license search page. She typed in Harland Parke and waited. Two records came up. One for Harry Park and another for Harland Parke. She rubbed Mr. Butterfingers' head and clicked on Parke's license number. Along with his name, it listed his office address and the date he was first licensed. She also found clickable links for Disciplinary Actions, Public Record Actions, and Public Record Documents with Accusations. Not good.

Oatmeal jumped on the couch and sniffed the cat. Shelby

looked down at the dog. "What are you doing in here?" A noise from the kitchen caused her to turn. "Ella? I thought you were taking a nap."

Ella came in and sat next to Oatmeal. "Turns out, I don't sleep well during the day, especially after our conversation." She stared at the laptop. "Find anything?"

Shelby pointed to the screen. "Looks like Parke was facing a lot of accusations. Listen to this: First cause of discipline, On or about, April 18, four years ago, respondent was convicted on a plea of nolo contendere…" She looked at Ella. "Maybe we should skip the legalese…" Continuing to scroll, Shelby read, "…a misdemeanor… theft of property. Second, unprofessional conduct, gross negligence in the dental treatment… failing to provide post-treatment follow-up…" She looked over at Ella. "This is crazy."

Ella nodded. "There's a lot more…"

"Um, let's see… Third cause, while working on the Medical Staff of the Pheasant Valley State Prison… failed to protect a 45-year-old, male patient… failed to use proper sterilization procedures prior to a tooth extraction… when patient stated the area had not become numb he screamed in pain…"

Ella gasped. "How could Parke be so cruel?"

"Sounds barbaric to me," said Shelby

"When was that?" asked Ella.

"January, two… no, three years ago." Shelby scrolled down. "Fourth cause… arrested for public intoxication. Dental tools and needles confiscated from his vehicle. Fifth cause… respondent committed acts that would have warranted the denial of a license… see paragraph 12…"

"Oh my goodness…" Ella rubbed her eyes. "This is shocking."

"And that's only the first document." Shelby looked at her. "Shall I read more?"

"Yes," said Ella. "But first, let me note those dates and accusations. That one about the public intoxication, in January… that was three months after Doug's death."

Shelby thought for a moment. "And what about the issue at the prison with the patient inmate? Do you think Parke's death had anything to do with it? I mean, he'd just been to that same prison in the afternoon, then found dead that night."

"The incident was years ago." Ella looked at Shelby. "I wonder, who was the patient? He'd be about forty-eight now."

Shelby looked at the screen and clicked on another link. "This document has eight causes of discipline."

"You can't be serious," said Ella. She moved Oatmeal to her other side and scooted closer to Shelby. "What does this one say?"

Shelby clicked the mouse. "Oh, geez. A DUI. Pled guilty, sentenced to five-years' probation, required to comply with the DUI-Multiple Conviction Program, pay a fine, and serve thirty days in jail."

Ella picked up the pad and pen. "When was that?"

"Um, let's see. About three years ago."

Ella leaned over and pointed. "And look. Possession of a controlled substance." She read from the screen. "… initially respondent had filed a police report saying he was robbed at gunpoint and kidnapped, then forced to withdraw money from his ATM…' And get this…" Ella gasped. "…write illegal prescriptions."

"Kidnapped *and* robbed?" Shelby rolled her eyes.

"Yes," said Ella. "The two men he named later told the authorities Parke had partied with them and then traded prescriptions for meth."

"Even though I'm reading with you, I can't believe it."

Ella tapped the pen on the pad. "It makes me question that break-in at his office the night of Buck's death. Parke gave the police almost the same story. Well, except for the gunpoint and kidnapping…"

Shelby stared at Ella, wide-eyed. "What if there wasn't a break-in? What if he traded the nitrous for illegal drugs?"

Ella leaned back. "Do you think he staged the break-in just to get drugs?"

"I don't know. But, at this point I wouldn't put anything past him. Lying, fraud, deceit, subterfuge." Shelby pointed to the screen. "There's more…"

"No need to go on," said Ella. "I've heard enough."

Shelby continued to read, then held up her hand. "Wait, there's one more thing… This first document said his license was suspended three years ago, but they stayed it and placed him on probation. The next document showed that since he broke his probationary rules, the next hearing would revoke it permanently. That must have been what Paige was referring to."

"I can see why the man would have had reason to commit suicide," said Ella.

"On the other hand," said Shelby. "Whoever he was trading drugs with could have killed him to avoid being implicated."

Sighing, Ella ran her fingers through her hair. "Sounds like Parke had quite a few enemies."

CHAPTER FORTY-EIGHT

After completing the internet search on Dr. Parke, Ella went back over her notes with Shelby. "Not only was Parke an alcoholic," said Ella. "But he was involved with illegal drugs and stolen property. Enough trouble for anyone, much less a well-respected dentist."

"Well-respected? That guy had serious addiction problems." Shelby leaned back against the couch cushion. "I'm curious about the relationship between Buck, Jasmine, and Parke. When do you think you'll be able to get ahold of your friend at the bowling alley?"

"I'll call now," said Ella. "Let me get my phone." She went into the kitchen and yelled back to Shelby. "You want anything?"

"Something sweet sounds good, thanks."

Ella came back with a package of cookies and an apple. She placed them on the coffee table. Oatmeal sniffed at the bag before Ella shooed him away. "Chocolate's not good for doggies." She sat and scrolled through her contacts. "I don't see Will's name. Would you mind looking up The Blue Oak Bowling Alley?"

Shelby clicked and scrolled, then pointed to a number. "Is that it?"

Ella nodded and put it in her phone. When she called, a woman answered.

"Hello," said Ella. "Is Will available?… Not until six?... No, no message. I'll call back. Thank you." She turned to Shelby. "I'm sure you got the gist of that."

Shelby picked up a cookie and waved it at the screen. "What would you say about eating at the bowling alley tonight? Their pizzas are amazing."

Ella smiled. "And those nachos."

"What better way to chat with Will than to do it in person? Besides, it might give us a chance to discover something new."

"Sounds like a plan," said Ella. "By the way, when are you supposed to meet with Alton?"

"I'll call him when we get back from the bowling alley. Hopefully, we'll have more information to share by then." Shelby popped another cookie in her mouth, then closed the bag. "Better save room for dinner."

Shelby and Ella walked from the frigid air outside into the warm bowling alley. Music thumped from loudspeakers. Thrown balls dropped and rolled on the wooden lanes, then crashed into the scuffed pins. Cheers went up among four people in matching red shirts. They high-fived each other and clapped. Ella nodded to the young attendant behind the check-in counter as they took their place in line behind a family of four.

"Need shoes?" asked a thin, blue-eyed young man.

"No, thank you," said Ella. "Is Will around?"

He checked his watch. "Should be in any time. There a problem?"

Ella shook her head. "Will's an old friend. Just wanted to say hi. We'll wait for him in the restaurant."

"May I tell him who's waiting?" asked the man.

"Let him know Ella came by to chat."

"Sure thing, ma'am." He sprayed a pair of worn shoes with deodorizer and placed them in a cubby filled with other bowling shoes.

The women made their way over to the restaurant. Built years ago, it still reflected the avocado green and bright orange décor. Thick glass shielded the inside from the alley noises. A middle-aged, blonde woman with Marnie written in black marker on a name tag met them at the entrance. "Just two tonight?"

"Yes," said Ella. They followed her to a booth and slid in.

Marnie came back with two waters and stood with a pen and order pad. "Ready?"

"We'll have a pizza..." Ella looked at Shelby. "Pepperoni and olive..."

"And mushrooms."

"Anything else?" Marnie scribbled on the pad. "Cocktails, perhaps?"

Shelby shook her head. "But we'll have nachos."

Marnie nodded and looked at Ella. "Small or large?"

"Large. Just water for both of us."

A few minutes later Marnie returned with an enormous plate of chips covered in thick cheese. She placed it between Ella and Shelby with a stack of napkins and left.

Ella picked up a cheesy chip and held it over her napkin. "Better wait til it cools. That ooze will take the top layer of skin off your tongue."

Shelby grabbed a chip and laughed. "I remember putting one of these in my mouth and regretting it for a long time." She looked around the restaurant, then pointed. "All the team pictures. I wonder..." She placed the chip on a napkin, slid from the booth, and walked around the small room, stopping every few feet. When she came to one grouping, she turned and motioned for Ella to join her.

Ella's eyes widened as she got closer to the image. It was a picture of Buck, Jasmine, and Dr. Parke side-by-side holding a trophy. "Look at that date."

"Here's another one," Shelby pointed to the next picture. "All in costumes."

Ella stared at the framed image. Buck was dressed in overalls and a silly pumpkin hat. Dr. Parke wore pants and a black shirt painted with a huge, grinning Jack-o'-lantern. Jasmine, a black jumpsuit and dangly pumpkin-shaped crystal earrings. "Very festive," said Ella.

Placing a steaming pizza on their table, Marnie caught Shelby's attention. She left a stack of paper plates and napkins then walked to another table.

Shelby nodded and elbowed Ella. "Dinner's ready." They walked to the booth and scooted in. Ella served herself a thick wedge and listened to the couple behind them laugh and clink glasses. She looked at Shelby. "According to the plaque under the first photo, they won that trophy on October twenty-seventh. Doug was killed the following Wednesday, the thirty-first."

Shelby took a bite of pizza and was quiet for a moment. "Is that significant?"

"Not sure," said Ella. "But now I have more questions for Will."

Shelby stared at Ella, but kept eating.

Halfway through their meal, a short, ruddy-faced, balding man rushed up. "Ella? Ella Denning? Well, I'll be a monkey's uncle."

Ella scooted out and gave him a big hug. "Great to see you again, Will. It's been way too long."

He placed his warm hand in the small of her back and turned. "And who is this beautiful young lady?"

"Will, this is my close friend, Shelby." Ella scooted back into the booth.

"Well, any friend of Ella's is a friend of mine." He chuckled. "Can I buy you two a drink?"

"Nothing for me," said Ella. "But, we'd love to have you join us and visit for a bit."

He let out a belly laugh and squeezed in next to Ella. "Sure thing, hon." He raised a finger and Marnie walked over. "A beer, please." After she left, he turned to Ella. "You're just as beautiful as the last time I saw you. What was it, three years ago at the memorial service?"

"Yes. And you're still the same sweet-talker, aren't you?"

Marnie set Will's beer on the table and left. He took a long swig from the bottle, then laughed. "My three ex-wives think so."

Ella rolled her eyes. "You haven't changed a bit, have you?"

He grinned. "Would you want it any other way?" He took another drink, then looked at Ella. "What brings you in after all these years?"

She straightened. "I need to ask you a few questions…"

He placed the bottle on the table and leaned toward her. "If one of my ex's is accusing me of something, I didn't do it." He laughed and leaned back. "Tell me what's on your mind, hon."

"Nothing about your wives, I promise. It's about one of the bowling leagues. I noticed a few friends of mine played here a while back. In fact, I think they still did, well until lately. Can you tell me something about them?"

"Sure." He took a drink. "Which league? We have quite a few."

Ella looked at Shelby and nodded. "My friend knows more and will ask you."

Shelby cleared her throat and pointed. "It's the group on the wall over there. They won a trophy a few years ago."

Will squinted to see where Shelby was pointing. "Who was on the team?"

Shelby straightened. "It was Buck Wilson, Jasmine Green, and—"

"The Pin Heads." Will lowered his head. "Shame we just lost two of them. They were a wonderful team."

Ella patted Will's hand. "We were all in shock to hear about their deaths." She pinched off a piece of the doughy, thick crust. "What night did they play?"

"They were part of the Mixed Triplets. You know, three on a team, men and women." He finished his beer and pointed to the picture with the bottle. "Mixed Triplets play Wednesday nights, mid-February through end of October."

Ella tapped her finger on the table. "That picture showed them with a trophy on a Saturday. But, you said they bowled on Wednesdays."

"Hmmm." He mumbled, then took out his phone and scrolled. "Looks like we had awards early that year because Halloween was on Wednesday. I remember, the teams voted to end the week before, with awards on Saturday. Then a costume bowling party on that last Wednesday. Everyone dressed up and none of the games counted for leagues."

Ella picked up a piece of pizza. "Is that what the other picture with them in costume was about?"

"Oh, yes. It was such fun. Until… You know…"

Ella looked at him. "What?"

Will lowered his eyes. "That was the night Doug was killed in that tragic accident."

Ella coughed. "What did Doug's death have to do with bowling? This bowling alley's a half-mile from where he was killed."

"I thought you knew, Ella." Will traced his finger on the

bottle. "They'd been here. In costumes, bowling. Though, they left hours before the accident."

"Will, what are you saying?" Ella sat up and caught his eye. "I'd never read any of this in the police reports."

He sniffed, then cracked his thick neck. "Look, Ella. This is just my gut talking, not in the reports… After the Neon Bowl, those three left together. 'Round eight o'clock." He leaned in close. "If you'd asked me, I think they all knew something 'bout that accident."

Ella's heart rate increased. "Why would you say that?"

"Call it an old man's ruminating. But they saw what happened that night." He frowned at Ella. "Doug's death went down much differently from what was in the reports.

CHAPTER FORTY-NINE

Confused after Will's comments, Shelby and Ella left The Blue Oak Bowling Alley. Tiny snowflakes swirled about, landing on their shoulders and in their hair. Pulling her sweater tighter around her waist, Shelby buried her hands deep into the pockets. "You sure you're up to driving?"

Ella opened the car door, placed the pizza box with the leftovers on the back seat, then leaned over to unlock the other side. "I'm okay, just puzzled." She started the car and dialed the heater to the highest setting. "I read that police report a half-dozen times, at least. It never mentioned Jasmine or Doctor Parke being witnesses."

Shelby rubbed her hands in front of the vent. "Do you have a copy handy? I'd like to read it when we get home."

Ella nodded. "I'll need to dig through my files." She pulled out of the parking lot and into the northbound lane of Blue Oak Street.

Shelby looked behind them. "I thought we were headed home."

"I want to go by the accident site first." Ella turned right on the corner of Blue Oak and Main and headed east. "One, two… five, six blocks." She pulled to the curb and stopped. "It's been a while, but I needed to see it to get a picture in my head." She pointed to the street behind a bar. "Doug was killed walking over there."

"Seems kind of dark."

"City officials said they'd fix that light, but you know how that goes. If Buck, Jasmine, and Parke had been celebrating, they might have driven down this street and parked by the bar."

"Or…" Shelby pointed. "The taco stand next door might have stayed open for the extra business on Halloween night."

Ella tapped the steering wheel. "According to the police report, the streetlight was out. Buck hit Doug as he walked across the street. Buck was the only one in the truck. His blood alcohol was over the limit." She sighed. "You know, Buck always maintained he never saw Doug. In fact, never remembered hitting him."

"I've heard that's typical after drinking."

"But, after what Will just told us…" She pulled away from the curb and waited to turn left onto Thornapple. "I wonder…" she paused when the light turned.

"Ella, what are you thinking?"

As they waited for the light on East Pheasant Valley Boulevard, Ella turned to Shelby. "What did that paper say?"

She looked at Ella and frowned. "What paper?"

"That green paper. The one we found in my car and Dawn found in Buck's truck." The light changed, and she turned left. She drove for a while, then asked, "What if Buck was too drunk and Parke took them home?"

"Do you think that's what the message meant?" Multiple scenarios rushed through Shelby's mind. "Oh no…"

"What?" asked Ella.

"I just had the most horrible thought. What if Buck didn't

kill Doug, but Doctor Parke did? But, because of all his DUI's he pinned it on Buck?"

Ella pulled into the driveway and parked. "You don't think he'd stoop that low, do you?" She grabbed the pizza box and got out.

Shelby closed her car door. "He lied about being kidnapped and robbed just to get illegal drugs. If lying about the accident that killed Doug would save his arse, I wouldn't put it past him." Their shoes crunched on the gravel. Snowflakes drifted down around them. An owl hooted as a small critter skittered along the bushes. Walking up the front porch stairs, Oatmeal's whines and scratches came from behind the door.

Ella placed her key in the lock and looked at Shelby. "If your theory is correct, then how does Jasmine fit into all of this?" She opened the door, greeted by two excited pets.

"I don't know." Shelby followed Ella through the front room and into the kitchen. "But, if Jasmine knew something and now the other two are dead, she could be in terrible danger."

CHAPTER FIFTY

Ella went into the kitchen and opened the treat container. "Do you really feel like Jasmine's in danger?" She offered Oatmeal a biscuit. "If they were in it together, there's no one left to cause a threat."

"You don't think she had anything to do with their deaths. Do you?" asked Shelby.

Ella leaned against the counter. "I think your imagination's got the best of you."

Shelby laughed. "Guess all those mysteries I read made me extra suspicious. Though, after what Will said, I'm curious to know where Doctor Parke and Jasmine were when the accident happened."

Fitting the pizza box in the refrigerator, Ella stepped back. "Guess we'll never know."

"You could ask Jasmine…" Shelby gave her a toothy grin.

"Oh sure," said Ella. "I'll just bring it up at my next therapy session. I'm sure she'd love that. How about you ask her? After all, you're the sleuth."

Shelby pulled out a chair and sat at the table. She

drummed her fingers on the placemat. "We still don't know why she gave Ben all that money."

Ella joined her and rested her chin on her hands. "Most likely, he did handyman work, and she paid him cash under the table. You know, so he wouldn't have to report it and mess up his state checks."

"You sure she didn't pay Ben to off Doctor Parke?" asked Shelby.

Ella rolled her eyes. "No. I don't. After reading Parke's accusations, I bet he couldn't face losing his license and all the ramifications that went with it."

"Maybe you're right." Shelby glanced at her phone. "It's almost eight. I should call Alton to see if he still wants to meet."

Ella caught her eye. "You think you could postpone?"

"What are you thinking?"

"I want to make a therapy appointment with Jasmine," said Ella. "While I'm there, I'll ask if she knows someone to do work around the house. It could confirm my theory about Ben."

"And then what?"

Ella gave Shelby a look. "I can't just come out and ask her where she was at the time of the accident. I'll try to bring Buck into it somehow. In the meantime, can you talk to Paige again? She seems to respond better to you."

"Why Paige?"

"Because we all know she and Buck had something going on. Paige would know if he bowled that night and what happened afterward. Remember how she always stood up for him and wanted me to forgive him? Maybe there was more to it than I thought."

Shelby nodded and pulled her phone from her pocket. She swiped the call icon. "Alton… Yes, this is Shelby… Good. And you? I know I promised to meet you tonight, but is there any way we can wait a few days? Ella and I came across more information and wanted to verify it first. Yes… we think it's significant. What?… Thanks for sharing. In the meantime, can you get us another copy of the accident report? From the night of Doug's murder… Doug Denning… That's great, thanks. Okay, when we know something, I promise to call. Thanks for the heads-up. Bye."

Ella leaned forward. "What was that all about?"

"A break in Buck's murder case. Apparently the missing nitrous cylinder was located."

"The one stolen from Parke's office?"

"Yes," said Shelby. "Alton said the forensic specialists are testing it now to see if the matter they found on it is human blood…"

"And if it is?" asked Ella.

"If it is, and it matches Buck's blood type..."

Ella straightened. "Oh, Harland. How could you?"

CHAPTER FIFTY-ONE

After breakfast the next morning, Shelby rinsed her coffee cup and placed it in the drying rack on the counter. She turned to her friend. "Okay El, we both have our missions. Then we'll meet at the shop for lunch, right?"

Ella wiped off the stovetop and hung the dishtowel on the refrigerator handle. "Yes. I've got an appointment with Jasmine and you're going over to Paige's to pick out material for a special-made Teddy bear. I hope our strategy works." She pulled on her sweater and draped a pale-blue knit scarf around her neck. "You going to be okay?"

Shelby nodded and embraced her. "Hopefully, this will be over soon and we'll all know the truth."

Ella lingered a few moments then stepped back. "Good luck."

"Same to you," said Shelby. "We're both going to need it."

Gray clouds hung low in the sky disguising everything in a dismal drizzle. Sitting at the light waiting for the train, Shelby watched the windshield wipers slosh up. Then down. Then up again. She was so distracted with the mesmerizing movement she didn't notice the crossing arms raise. Thankfully, the car behind gave a quick honk. Shelby turned left and went across the railroad tracks, then east on Deergrass. Another left on North Acorn, past the auto repair shops, then right on Airport Drive until she reached Paige's small house at the end of the street. Shelby pulled up and parked.

A thin, short-haired dog bounded out of the broken gate, barked several times, then ran off when Paige came outside. She stood on the wooden porch and waved. "Come on in. He's harmless."

Shelby exited the jeep and made her way up the broken sidewalk. The wooden boards creaked as she walked up the steps.

"Careful," said Paige. "That one's broke. Keep meanin' to fix it." She held the door open then pulled it closed behind Shelby. "Can I get you somethin' to drink?"

Shelby feigned a smile as the scent of bitter coffee and burnt toast wafted from the kitchen. "Oh, no thanks. Just finished breakfast."

Paige motioned to the threadbare couch. "Have a sit. I'll get my bears so you can tell me what you want."

The couch wobbled and creaked as Shelby tried to get comfortable. Each of the three cushions poked at her backside. She sat between two of them hoping to keep her body intact. Mounds of clothes were stacked against the legs and covered the top of a rickety card table. Tabloid magazines were scattered on the floor and on the end cushions. A loud bark at the front door made Shelby jump.

"Just my pup, Georgie." Paige nodded to the pile of bears in her arms and offered them to Shelby. "You want brown, black, or cream fur?"

"I'm not sure yet." Shelby brushed her fingers along the

soft material. "I guess I need to see a few before I decide." She glanced over at the door. "You think Georgie might need to come in out of the cold?"

"Nah," said Paige. "He stays out most of the time, otherwise he pees in the house."

Shelby shivered. "That's not good."

Paige held up a large, brown bear. "What size you lookin' for?"

"Something smaller. Like the ones at the shop." Shelby's mind raced. She needed to change the conversation, but not too abruptly.

Paige pointed to a plump, tan bear with blue denim overalls. "Like that?"

Shelby nodded. "May I see it?"

She handed it to Shelby who nudged a worn ottoman next to the couch and sat.

"He's cute," said Shelby. "I love the clothes. He just needs a little cap."

"I got lots of them." Paige leaned to the side and pulled out a box. She opened it and peeked inside. "What kind you want?"

Shelby petted the bear's fuzzy head. "Do you have a baseball-type?"

Paige tapped her cheek with one of her long fingers. The glittery-red polish sparkled in the dull, overhead light from a lopsided ceiling fan. "Think so. Lemme check." She pulled out several caps along with shirts and pants. "See anything that strikes your fancy?"

Shelby picked up a few, then found a blue baseball cap under the pile. "Like this," she said, holding it up.

Taking it from Shelby, Paige placed it on the bear's head. She made some adjustments, then turned it around. "How's that?"

Shelby nodded. "Just out of curiosity… do you have

anything for the holidays? Like Thanksgiving? Or Christmas? Or Halloween?"

"Hmmm." Paige picked through the pile again. "Here's a little orange shirt to go with them overalls. No matching hat. Though, I could make him one."

Shelby held up the bear and thought back to the picture of Buck, Jasmine, and Parke at the costume party. "You know…" She paused to choose the right words. "This bear kinda reminds me of a picture I saw at the bowling alley."

Paige stopped digging and stared at Shelby. "Oh yeah? Which one?"

"It was a costume party, with Jasmine and Doctor Parke, and, um, Buck, I think."

Throwing back her head, Paige guffawed and slapped her leg. "I remember that night. They were a hoot. All dressed like punkins." She paused, stared at the bear, then lowered her voice. "Yeah, I remember that night like it was yesterday."

"Why do you say that?" asked Shelby.

Paige straightened the fur on the bear and clicked her tongue. "That's the night Buck got 'ccused of hittin' that guy, Doug."

Shelby chest tightened.

Paige dug through the box and pulled out a small, black bear and stroked its fur. "Ain't never could figure it out."

"What do you mean?"

She glared at Shelby. "I never saw Buck drink nothin' but pop that night. But then they 'ccused him of drivin' drunk."

"You sure?"

"So sure I could spit. Buck was proud of that six-month chip and told 'em he wasn't 'bout to start over."

"Chip?" Shelby scratched her head and frowned. "What are you referring to?"

Paige got up and walked over to an unfinished desk in the corner of her living room. She picked up a small wooden jewelry box and brought it back to the couch. Opening it, she pulled out a palm-sized bronze token and handed it to Shelby. "That there was his first six-month sobriety chip. He was so proud the night he received it, he came by and showed it to me. Said it was a big 'ccomplishment."

Shelby ran her finger over the number six in the middle of a raised triangle, then turned it over. The serenity prayer was on the reverse side. "You know," said Shelby, "when Buck dropped his backpack at the dentist's office, a bunch of these fell out. Though some were more like plastic or acrylic." She handed the chip back to Paige.

"Yep, them others were for years. This one was months. After that accident he had to start over again. Though, he never remembered takin' a drink. Almost gave up on trying to stay sober, but he stuck with it." She sucked in a deep breath. "Terrible disease. His daddy and mamma struggled, too. They lost. Ol' Buck. Now, he was a winner. Well, til Hope did him in at the cemetery."

Rubbing her eyes, Shelby forced herself to stay focused instead of reacting to Paige's accusation. "Wait, a minute. Are you sure Buck never drank that night at the bowling alley?

"I'd bet my life savings," said Paige.

"What about afterwards? There were a few bars in the area."

Paige fingered the chip between her thumb and fingers, then placed it back in the box. "Nope. Buck was takin' some pill. Made him sick as a dog if he drank anything. He wouldn't touch alcohol. In fact, I'd get a kick out of teasin' him. Weren't nice, but was my way of keepin' him dry. He never budged. Not even a sip."

"Then how did his blood alcohol show over the limit after the accident?" asked Shelby.

Paige glared. "I've been wonderin' that same thing for the last three years."

CHAPTER FIFTY-TWO

Ella's knee bounced as she sat in the therapists' waiting room. The pumpkin-spiced, orange-glowing candle helped calm her nerves as she stared at the twinkly lights draped on the Ficus tree.

The hall door opened. Jasmine stood in the doorway wearing black leggings, a tan blouse, and a long, honey-colored cardigan. "Ella?"

Gathering her things, Ella followed Jasmine back to her office.

"I'm sorry about the last time," she said. "I promise not to take any calls during today's session." She closed the door and Ella made her way over to the comfy chair. "Coffee?" She poured herself a cup, then waited for Ella's response.

"No, thank you." Ella took off her sweater and laid it across her lap. She stared at Jasmine's indigo diamond patterned chair. The dark, muted colors reminded her of all the time she'd spent there, making no progress.

Jasmine placed her mug on the short table between them, then sat and picked up a pad and pen. "The last time you were here, we were talking about…" She flipped back through her notes.

"If you don't mind…" Ella held up her hand. "I'd like to work on forgiveness today."

Jasmine looked up. "Forgiveness? That's a big step for you, Ella. Who would you like to forgive?"

Ella shifted in her chair. "I'd like to forgive Buck for killing Doug."

"It was an accident, you know." Jasmine made notes. "I'm glad you've been able to come to terms with that. What helped you change your perspective?"

"Several things…" said Ella. "Something you said. Plus, a photograph I saw."

"Something I said?" Jasmine smoothed a bent page in her notebook.

"Every time I mentioned Buck killing Doug, you said it was an accident. And a while back, you said you knew the secrets of half the town."

Jasmine straightened her shoulders and glanced at Ella. "It was just an expression. Several people in town are my clients, and I do pride myself on keeping their secrets. Now regarding Buck, we know he didn't intend to hit Doug. Can we agree on that?"

Ella caught her eye. "Here's the thing. Recent information has led me to believe it might not have been Buck's fault at all. Maybe someone else was driving. Maybe someone else hit Doug and blamed it on Buck, since he was already drunk."

Jasmine cleared her throat. "Whatever do you mean? You told me the police report said he was behind the wheel when they arrived on scene."

"It said that." Ella didn't break eye contact. "But I think you knew who was driving. It was one of those secrets you've kept all these years."

Jasmine took a sip of coffee and swallowed. "Ella, whatever

you read in the police report was the truth. What gave you the idea something else happened?"

Ella watched Jasmine's reaction. "I think Doctor Parke was driving."

"And why would you think that?"

"I know this might seem crazy, but hear me out. I came across information that Parke had several DUIs around the time of Doug's death. That's public knowledge, and I can prove it. It's obvious Buck had also been drinking since it showed up in his blood test after the accident. But I believe Doctor Parke was driving Buck's truck that night. He hit Doug, then made it look like Buck was driving."

Jasmine stared at Ella. "I'm not sure how to respond."

"You can tell me if I'm right. Then I can put this all to rest and forgive Buck."

She tucked a strand of coarse, tight curls behind her ear. "Ella, you know I cannot talk about anything a client and I have discussed. Patient confidentiality."

"They're both dead. So, who are you protecting? Don't you think it's time to let them all rest in peace? I mean, who's going to sue you for breaking a confidence?" Ella paused for a moment to collect her thoughts. "Buck always maintained he didn't remember hitting Doug. It made me livid. I hated that man. But now it makes sense. I need to deal with this and forgive him."

"This could get me into a lot of trouble. I'm bound to keep conversations between clients private."

"I saw the pictures at the bowling alley."

Jasmine swallowed. "Which pictures?"

"The ones with you, Buck, and Doctor Parke. With the trophy and in costumes. You were wearing the cutest pumpkin earrings."

Jasmine let out a nervous laugh. "I loved those earrings."

"You should wear them now," said Ella. "Perfect time of the year to show them off."

Jasmine fingered a small diamond stud in her earlobe. "I wish… They were one-of-a-kind. A special gift from a friend. Made me sick when I lost one."

"That's terrible. What made them one-of-a-kind?"

"Blown glass," said Jasmine. "Handmade. Only pair like them."

Ella turned. "So dreary today. I wish it would just rain. I don't like that misty fog; it makes me feel… disheartened." She continued to stare out the window while she considered what to say next.

Jasmine drank her coffee and waited. She didn't seem in a hurry either.

Ella looked back at Jasmine. "An off the wall question, but do you know of a handyman I could hire to do some work around the house? I can pay cash."

She placed her mug on the end table. "What kind of work do you need done?"

"Just a few things. Outside fence repair. Inside sheetrock work. It's too much for me with the shop."

Jasmine tapped her pen on the tablet. "I can't think of anyone off hand. But, if I do, I'll let you know."

Darn, no mention of Ben. "Okay, thanks. I'd appreciate it." Ella glanced at her phone, then at Jasmine. "I'm sorry I asked you to betray Doctor Parke's confidence. It's just… I'm ready to forgive, and knowing the truth about Doug's death would let me move on. It's been three years, Jasmine. I need to know."

She looked at Ella, then down at her notes. "I could lose my license…"

"Please…"

Jasmine pointed a slim finger at Ella. "This goes no further than this room."

Ella nodded.

"After we left the bowling alley, the guys wanted to get a drink. I had coffee. They had beer. Buck had a few too many and Harland offered to drive Buck's truck. I would have, but it was a stick. Harland said he had everything under control, so I left and went home. The next thing I know, Harland's pounding on my door. Said there'd been a terrible accident."

Jasmine looked down at her lap. "It's true. Harland was driving. He knew he'd hit something, but didn't check on what it was. Afraid of another DUI, he left Buck in the truck to take the blame. In the end, it all worked out. Buck got a few days in jail and Harland and I vowed to never speak of it again." She looked up, exhaled, and smiled. "Boy, you don't know what a relief it is to finally get that off my chest."

Ella's heart rate increased. She forced herself to stay calm as her mind raced. It all worked out. For whom? Not for Doug. He was her husband, not just some thing left for dead. Ella swallowed to compose herself. "Thank you. I appreciate knowing the truth." She stood and put on her sweater.

"We still have some time left, if you need to talk."

Ella shook her head. "After what you told me, I need to be alone and process this." She walked out and closed the door behind her. While it felt like a weight had lifted, her chest ached. Tears ran down her cheeks. How could everyone lie to her for three years? Jasmine was her therapist. Parke was her dentist. Did they have no conscience? Ella rushed to her car and started the engine. She needed to find Shelby.

CHAPTER FIFTY-THREE

After Shelby picked out a bear and clothing, she gave Paige a deposit and left. Thinking about everything Paige had mentioned regarding Doug's death, another question came to mind. If Buck couldn't have been drunk, who was driving his truck? She waited for a train and considered the only two options. Dr. Parke or Jasmine. But how would she and Ella figure it out?

Shelby pulled into the lot at The Bee's Knees and parked next to Ella's car. Hopefully, she'd also have information to share. Locking her door, she turned. Ben stood across the street in the drizzle. Shelby's head tingled. Something wasn't right. Fighting to control her anxiety, she rushed across the parking lot to the shop.

Ella stood behind the counter waiting on a customer. She acknowledged Shelby as she put her sweater away and went to the sitting area. Once there, Shelby took time to steady her breathing and calm down. The relaxing scent of Laura's lavender candles helped.

A few minutes later, Ella pulled up a chair next to her frazzled friend. "Were you able to talk with Paige?"

Shelby nodded, then motioned to a tall, red-haired man walking toward them.

"Morning," said Ella. "May I help you find something?"

"Just browsing," he said. "I'll give you a holler if I need anything." He picked up a basket and placed several scented candles in it. Then went over to a handmade card display and picked through the holiday offerings.

"We should wait until lunchtime to talk," said Ella. "I've got Gladys, Vickie, and Lilibeth coming in soon."

"A talented group of ladies," said Shelby. "Apple butter and needle felting, Those Wooly Sisters always make me laugh." She shoved her trembling hands in her pants pockets. Between Paige's information and seeing Ben outside, she couldn't shake her anxiety. "I have a lot to tell you."

"And I have a lot to tell you," said Ella.

Shelby checked the time, almost noon. Waiting would be tough. She wasn't the most patient person.

Gladys bumped the front door with her hip and walked in carrying a box. She smiled at everyone and made her way to her booth, setting the box down with a grunt.

Shelby jumped up. "Need some help?"

"Yes, hon. That would be great." She handed Shelby jars tied with yellow and orange gingham ribbons. "New recipe. Apple butter with a twist."

"Sounds yummy." Shelby placed the jars on a shelf and looked sideways at Gladys. "What's the twist? Or is it a closely guarded secret?"

She leaned in close and whispered. "Extra cinnamon and vanilla, with a hint of maple syrup."

Shelby licked her lips and held up a jar. "Might need to buy one to test it."

"Keep that one. My treat." Gladys patted her arm. "Just let me know what you think."

Shelby laughed. "Have you promoted me to an official taste-tester?"

Gladys nodded. "Ed didn't complain, so you'll be my second-opinion." She winked. "You know, that's an important job. Make sure you, ahem, test it thoroughly."

Shelby gave her a quick hug, then carried the jar upfront and placed it behind the counter in the pocket of her sweater. She turned when the front door opened. The Wooly Sisters walked in laughing, each carrying cardboard boxes.

"Morning, Shelby." Lilibeth pointed to Vickie's box. "Our new holiday line."

"That's exciting," said Shelby. "What is it?"

Vickie opened her box and held up a tiny sheep with a red bow and gold bell. "These are our jingle sheep."

Reaching into hers, Lilibeth handed Shelby a snowman with a little jacket and matching hat. "And these are our Wooly persons. You know, like snow men and women, but made with wool."

"So cute. I love them all. You two are so creative." Shelby noticed Ella coming up the aisle and handed the wool creations back to Vickie. "I think Ella needs me. I'll see you later." She grabbed her sweater and headed over to Ella, leaving the Wooly Sisters to chat about texture differences in alpaca fur.

"You about ready for lunch?"

"Yes." She pulled on her sweater and held up the jar from Gladys. "Lookie. A new flavor of apple butter. I'm a taste-tester."

"Aren't you the lucky one?" Ella caught Gladys' eye and waved. "Headed to lunch. Call if you need anything."

Outside the shop, Shelby scanned the area across the street. Ben didn't seem to be around. She let out a long breath and climbed into the jeep. "I'm glad we're getting out of here for a while. I have so much to tell you."

"Instead of going out, how about we head home?" asked

Ella. "We can feed the animals and eat while we talk, then make notes to share with Alton."

SHELBY SAT at the kitchen table buttering a thick slice of bread. She laid it on her plate. "What did you find out from Jasmine?"

Ella turned to a new page in a notebook. "She confirmed Buck wasn't the one driving because he was too drunk. Instead, Doctor Parke drove. He was the one who hit Doug." Ella recounted the rest of their conversation, then pounded her fist on the table. "I can't believe they both lied to me."

Shelby straightened. "Jasmine still might be lying. That doesn't match the information Paige told me."

Ella frowned. "Why? What did she say?"

Shelby consulted her notes, then looked up. "Paige told me Buck wasn't drunk. He had just gotten his six-month's sobriety chip and was taking pills to keep from drinking. She swore he wasn't intoxicated."

"But…" said Ella. "His blood alcohol level was well over the limit. How did Paige explain that?"

"She never could figure it out," said Shelby. "She said something wasn't right, but didn't know how to prove it." She doodled on the paper, then looked at Ella. "You know the chip she showed me resembled the one on Jasmine's key chain, except hers was acrylic. I found out that meant years sober, not just months. At least that's how Paige explained it."

Ella caught Shelby's attention. "Are you saying Jasmine is a recovering alcoholic?"

Shelby tapped her finger on the table. "You know, a few days ago at the shop Jasmine mentioned a chronic illness brought them together. Do you think she was referring to alcoholism?"

Ella shrugged.

Shelby continued. “If so, any of them could’ve been behind the wheel and trying to protect the others.”

“We know Jasmine wasn’t driving Buck’s truck because it was a stick shift. So it had to be—”

Shelby slapped her hand on the table. “What did you just say?”

Ella stared at her friend. “I said, Buck wasn’t driving.”

“No, after that.”

“Buck’s truck was a stick.”

Shelby stood. “I need to call Alton. Ella, I think I know what really happened.”

CHAPTER FIFTY-FOUR

The next morning, Shelby pulled up to the curb and parked. "You know what you're going to say?"

"Yes." Ella's voice broke. "I just hate confrontation."

"You and me, both." Shelby grasped Ella's trembling hand. "Remember, I'll be right next to you the whole time."

"I know," said Ella. "But it still stinks."

They walked across the street through a light rain. Once inside, Ella signed in and sat next to Shelby. Fingering a wad of tissues in her pocket, Ella took slow breaths, practicing the calming exercises Jasmine had printed out.

"It'll be okay," said Shelby. "I promise." Though her heart was racing, Shelby knew she couldn't back down. Not this time. She had to find the courage to protect Ella. All her life she'd run away and hid. Memories of letting others down flooded back. Her brother's cries. Ella's face when Dawn took her away. Even though Shelby had no confidence in herself, it was now or never. Her feelings for Ella had grown. She needed, no, she wanted to protect the woman she loved.

Ella patted Shelby's hand. "Wish I had your confidence."

Shelby rolled her eyes. If only Ella knew. Pulling out her phone, she focused on a game to calm herself.

The hall door opened. A young woman came into the waiting room. She stopped at the desk and made a follow-up appointment, then left.

Ella nudged Shelby. "Look, a TV. That's new. Now one can watch home improvement shows while they wait…"

She tried to listen, but the negativity in her head drowned out Ella's voice. She nodded and went back to the game.

Meanwhile, Ella tried to ignore her pounding heart.

A few minutes later, Jasmine came to the doorway wearing black slacks, a burgundy blouse, and a fitted black jacket. She nodded to the two women.

They followed Jasmine down the hall to her office. Somehow the walls seemed narrower.

Closing the door, Jasmine motioned to the couch. "Have a seat, ladies. Would either of you like something to drink?"

Ella shook her head and held up a water bottle. Shelby did the same. They sat on a stiff couch and waited.

Jasmine filled her red coffee mug and set it on an end table next to her chair. She grabbed her pad and pen; a ritual Ella witnessed at each therapy appointment over the years. Jasmine's actions were meticulous, never changing. Ella imagined it was how she maintained control over her life.

"Ladies, nice to see you today. Are you ready for the Thanksgiving holiday coming up?"

"Turkey's thawing." Ella looked over at Shelby.

Shelby forced a smile. "Still need to make a shopping list."

Ella cleared her throat. She hated the pointless chit-chat at each appointment. The warming up to the inevitable question, "What's on your mind, Ella?"

"You said it was important and I don't normally see patients on Saturdays," said Jasmine. "What's on your mind today, Ella?" She held her pen over the notepad and stared.

Everything inside Ella wanted to bolt out of the room, but she gripped the edge of the couch and forced herself to stay. Shelby's warm hand covered hers. It was time to get this over with. "Yesterday, when we talked about the night of Doug's death, you asked if I needed to talk further. So, here I am."

Jasmine held up her hand. "That was an offer when we were alone. I advised you that our conversation would never leave this office."

"We're in your office," Ella said, staring at her. "And I need to talk about it."

Jasmine capped the pen and placed it on the notepad. "I'm sorry, Ella, but I will not discuss it with you any further. What about something else?"

Ella's mind raced. "This is what I came to talk about."

"Fine," said Jasmine. "As long as you understand, I have nothing further to say."

"You won't have to," said Ella. "Last night, Shelby, and I figured out what really happened the night of Doug's murder." Jasmine opened her mouth, but Ella put her hand up. "And don't remind me it was an accident because I know. You've been telling me that since I started therapy. But the only accident was the cover-up you were all involved in. Doug just got caught up in it."

Jasmine stared at Ella, then at Shelby, but didn't respond.

"Harland Parke had an addiction problem. That wasn't a secret, though he tried to keep it that way. He couldn't drink or he'd lose his dental license. So, he figured out other ways to get high."

Jasmine blinked. Her breathing increased.

"He reported three robberies, one the night of Doug's death, one the night of Buck's death, and then another one in between. I know because we checked the police records. Each time, a cylinder of nitrous went missing." Ella watched Jasmine's eyes. They showed no emotion.

"Shelby and I know the three of you shared a common chronic disease. You told Shelby the other day. Not only did it bring you together, but it also tore you apart. That night, after the costume party, you couldn't go out drinking. Someone might have noticed. You and Doctor Parke's licenses would have been in jeopardy. So the doc figured a work-around. He broke into his own office, took a cylinder of nitrous, and reported it stolen. That gave the three of you the opportunity to get high. Legally. But you didn't figure Doug would see the fake robbery. Buck was too high to drive. Parke couldn't drive a stick. You were the only one left."

"I told you, I wasn't there," said Jasmine, her voice raising in pitch.

Shelby straightened. "Doctor Parke couldn't drive a stick shift. I overheard him tell someone in his office the day he went up to the prison."

Ella pointed at Jasmine. "Doug was on foot, running to report the alleged robbery, wasn't he? Parke couldn't risk Doug getting to the police station. So, you waited until he got to the street with the broken streetlight. And you... Ran. Him. Down."

Jasmine cupped her hand over her mouth. "No. It didn't happen that way at all. It was an accident—"

"Then you and Parke decided Buck would take the blame," said Ella. "You couldn't make him drink because of the anti-alcohol pills. While he was high from the nitrous, Parke injected him with alcohol. After all, he carried needles because of his drug habit. He also had alcohol. It was an easy out, just enough in his blood to show over the limit. Since Buck was already an alcoholic, no one would question it."

Jasmine tightened her hand into a fist. "You are making this all up. You can't prove anything. I'll sue you for slander."

"It would have been fine until Buck finally figured it out." Ella glared at Jasmine. "You had to get rid of him."

Spittle flew out of Jasmine's mouth. "I had nothing to do with Buck's death. It was all Harland's idea."

"And that's when the notes started showing up," said Ella.

"What notes?" asked Jasmine.

Shelby pulled out a green piece of copy paper and read, "It's not what you think. He was never the one." She tossed it on the table in front of Jasmine. "Those notes."

Jasmine stood. "You think you're so creative. But you can't prove anything. I was never in that truck the night Doug was killed. It was all Harland." She marched over to the door and grabbed the handle. "You need to leave before I call the police and have you arrested—" She opened the door, then stepped back and gasped. "Alton. What are you doing in the hallway?"

CHAPTER FIFTY-FIVE

Alton walked into Jasmine's office, dressed in full uniform. "I'd let Ella finish if I were you."

Jasmine's eyes went wide. She scowled at Alton. "You just can't come in here during one of my sessions."

Alton held up some paperwork. "Actually, this gives me a legal right to enter and search." He nodded to Ella. "Go on, finish what you were saying."

Jasmine sat on the edge of her chair and glared at Ella. "You're lying."

Ella smiled. "I'd be careful about accusing someone of lying. I think that's called slander." She reached in her pocket and took out a wad of tissues and laid them on her lap. "You know, Jasmine, you almost got away with it. Doug and Buck were dead. Everyone thought Parke was distraught and committed suicide, or so it seemed."

Jasmine cleared her throat. "You don't know what you're talking about. I had nothing to do with any of this. I told you, Harland drove Buck's truck. He told me about the accident. It was client privilege—"

Ella wagged her finger at Jasmine. "It came down to something you said at my last session that tipped off Shelby."

"Wait," said Jasmine. "You promised our conversation wouldn't leave the office."

"It was when I told Shelby about your earrings."

Jasmine wrinkled her brow. "Excuse me?"

"You know," said Shelby. "Those hand-blown, one-of-a-kind pumpkin earrings that you wore in the picture at the bowling alley costume party. You mentioned you'd lost one."

"That's true," said Jasmine. "But what does that have to do with—" She stopped talking and stared as Ella unwrapped the wad of tissues in her lap. One-by-one, until she held a single, hand-blown glass pumpkin earring between her fingers.

Jasmine's eyes flashed. "Where did you get that?" She grabbed for the earring.

Alton stepped forward and took the earring from Ella. "I found it."

"Where in heaven's name?"

"After Shelby called me," he said. "I got a search warrant for Buck Wilson's pickup truck. Last night, I found it hanging from the fabric wedged behind the seat. We dusted it for prints and guess who's came up on our database. A nice one of your thumb made identification easy."

Jasmine gasped, then buried her face in her hands. "No. No. No…"

Alton held out his hand. "Jasmine, you need to come with me. You're under—"

"You don't need to say it." She looked up at him. "Do you have to use handcuffs?"

Alton's voice was firm, but calm. "No. We can just walk out together. I'll wait and cuff you by the unit."

Drawing in a ragged breath, Jasmine stood. Avoiding Ella's gaze, she lowered her head and said nothing.

As Alton walked her out of the office, he turned back and nodded. Shelby and Ella followed several steps behind. They went through the pumpkin-scented waiting room. Past the muted TV. Past the twinkling Ficus tree. Once outside, they rushed across the street, through the rain, and got into Shelby's jeep. Sitting there together, they watched the scene unfold. A sheriff's cruiser pulled up and parked behind Alton's. Dawn got out and waited as Alton helped Jasmine into the back seat of his patrol car. Afterwards, he sauntered over to Dawn and they exchanged words. She turned and glared at Ella and Shelby for a few moments, then returned to her vehicle and left.

"Such a shame about Jasmine," said Shelby. "Though, I'm glad we could help Alton." She started the engine and pulled away from the curb.

While it relieved Ella to know the truth, her heart ached from the pain she'd endured from those who had betrayed her trust over the years. Jasmine lied. Dawn used her to get to Shelby. And Parke, a sorry excuse for a human being. She shuddered, thinking about the hatred she'd directed toward Buck. As they headed home, Ella wept, wiping her eyes with the last of the tissues from her pocket.

CHAPTER FIFTY-SIX

When the front door opened, Shelby looked up and placed her sketchbook on the coffee table. A biting wind passed through the front room as Ella walked in. Oatmeal jumped up from his spot near Shelby's feet and wagged his tail.

"How are you doing?" asked Shelby.

Ella glanced at her and smiled. "Better than yesterday, I guess. The cemetery was quiet. I sat on the cement bench under the tree next to Doug's grave and listened to the rain on my umbrella. We had a good chat." She hung up her sweater in the mudroom, then came back and sat next to her friend.

Mr. Butterfingers leapt up on Shelby's lap and meowed. She stroked his fur until he settled down.

"Of course," said Ella, "I did all the talking, like always. I told him how sorry I was that it took so long to figure out what really happened." Oatmeal jumped on the couch and licked her face. "I also told him I would have never known if it wasn't for you."

"Just a lot of lucky guesses," said Shelby.

Ella shook her head. "It was more than that. Ever since I've known you, you've had a knack for noticing small details. You meant something in my life then and you do now. Being here again means more than you know."

Shelby felt a blush rise in her neck. "You helped figure it out, too. I'm just glad Alton got full credit for solving the case. I bet the look on Dawn's face was priceless."

"Last I heard she was putting in for a transfer," said Ella. "Guess she finally realized they wouldn't tolerate her unethical tactics any longer."

"She lost a lot of credibility after word got out of how she treated you."

Ella nodded. "You know, the only thing I never figured out was Ben's connection with Jasmine. How do we know he wasn't involved?"

Mr. Butterfingers purred as Shelby scratched his ears. "I asked Alton about that. He said after he interviewed Ben, the only thing that connected them was Jasmine's under-the-table payments for maintenance work. That's why he'd hang around looking for her, hoping for another job."

"She never said anything to anyone about it?" asked Ella.

"Funny how she was more interested in keeping Ben's secrets than her own. With all the hints she dropped, I think her conscience was getting to her. Especially after Parke died."

Ella looked at Shelby. "Do you think he took his own life?"

"Alton said the evidence was inconclusive." Shelby shrugged. "Guess we'll never know. Though he did confirm Parke left the three notes. Knowing he was about to lose his license, Parke wanted someone to know the truth. It's just too bad he didn't have the courage to come forth earlier. Apparently, he wouldn't betray Jasmine." She leaned her head back on the cushion. "I'm glad it's over and we can get on with our lives."

"No kidding." Ella ran her fingers through Oatmeal's silky fur, then caught Shelby's eye. "When I went to see Doug, I told him about us."

Shelby gasped. "Us?"

"You know," said Ella. "We never had that conversation."

"We were distracted solving a couple of murders… "

Ella leaned over and rested her head on Shelby's shoulder. "So… you still want to be my partner?"

Shelby blinked. "In business?" Her heart rate quickened. "Or, in life?"

Ella turned and kissed her cheek. "Both."

"You sure?"

Ella snuggled up against Shelby. "You do know I love you, right?"

A soft rain pattered against the windows. The cat snored on Shelby's lap. She closed her eyes and smiled. Ella loved her. Turning, Shelby whispered. "I love you, too."

INTERESTING IN LEARNING MORE about Pheasant Valley? Go to joanraymondwriting.com/cozy-mysteries to download free PDF maps. You'll also be the first to know when, *Crafty Motives*, book two in The Bee's Knees series will be released!

ACKNOWLEDGMENTS

I am fortunate to have had so many people support me while I authored this book.

First, to my husband, David. Thank you for your encouragement and countless hours of help while I researched, listened to podcasts, and wrote and re-rewrote plot twists and re-worked characters.

Many thanks to my adult children, Michelle, Brian, and Matt. I appreciate your support and input when I contemplated murder weapons and motives. I'm sure you think your mother is a bit weird, but at least you don't hold it against me.

While we're talking about family... Thanks to my fur babies, Madison, Jackie, Molly and Stormie for providing the inspiration for the fur-baby characters in the book.

Thanks to my critique partners Donnee, Jenny, Larry, and Tabi, and my VIP Readers, Annis, Cyn, Jenny, Natalia, Patsy, and Sandy who read the final version of my book and gave constructive feedback. Through complete rewrites to changes in point of view, your comments and suggestions made me a better writer. Your encouragement kept me going and reminded me why I write.

Thanks to Brent Gill for his help with the CB and Ham radio information and lingo. I learned so much during our chats about everything from bouncing waves off the ionosphere to the differences between digital and analog signals. I appreciate you sharing your knowledge and expertise.

A heartfelt thanks to those who helped with the specialized stuff. For the information about police procedure and terminology I appreciate B. Adam Richardson of the Writer's Detective Bureau Podcast and Facebook Group for offering help and responding so quickly to my questions. I also appreciate the Trauma Fiction Facebook Group for answering my death-related questions in wonderfully accurate detail.

Thank you to Cathy Walker of Cathy's Covers for the amazing cover design. You created the perfect cozy cover that I'd envisioned from the beginning.

And special thanks to an AA member who wishes to remain anonymous. I appreciate your insight on what it means to be a recovering alcoholic. Your candor and willingness to share experiences from your own life mean more than you know.

To my readers, thank you so much for reading *Crafty Alibis*. Your support and comments mean so much. Because of you, I write and create my stories and quirky characters.

ABOUT THE AUTHOR

Joan's earliest memories of writing go back to the fourth grade. An avid reader of The Happy Hollister's Mystery series, she penned her first two short stories, "The Mystery of the Missing Bread" and "The Snake That Had Legs." Not best-sellers by any means, but her teacher loved them, as did her classmates, which sparked her interest in writing.

Joan lives in Bakersfield, California, with her family and four rescue pets: Two energetic Australian Shepherd mixes (Madison and Jackie), a claustrophobic Maine Coon mix (Molly), and an independent tuxedo cat (Stormie).

Joan welcomes contact from her readers. Find her at joanraymondwriting.com where you can sign up for her newsletter (and keep up with her and new releases), read her blog, and find her on social media.

ALSO BY JOAN RAYMOND

For Adults

The Bee's Knees Mystery Series

Crafty Alibis (Book One) 2021

Crafty Motives (Book Two) - coming in 2022

Women's Fiction

Guardian of the Gifts 2019

For Children

Metamorphosis Series

Fly on the Wall (Book One) 2020

Spaghetti and Meatball (Book Two) - coming in 2022

www.ingramcontent.com/pod-product-compliance
Ingram Content Group UK Ltd.
Pitfield, Milton Keynes, MK11 3LW, UK
UKHW042004190726
13854UKWH00005B/2161

9 781733 791540